Make Death Love Me

Make Death Love Me

RUTH RENDELL

PUBLISHED BY

DOUBLEDAY & COMPANY, INC.

GARDEN CITY, NEW YORK

1979

All of the characters in this book
are fictitious, and any resemblance
to actual persons, living or dead,
is purely coincidental.

ISBN 0-385-15184-5
Library of Congress Catalog Card Number 78-22621
Copyright © 1979 by Kingsmarkham Enterprises Ltd.
All Rights Reserved
Printed in the United States of America
First Edition

To David Blass with love

In writing this novel, I needed help on some aspects of banking and on firearms. By a lucky chance for me, John Ashard was able to advise me on both. I am very grateful to him.

THE AUTHOR

Make Death Love Me

1

Three thousand pounds lay on the desk in front of him. It was in thirty wads, mostly of fivers. He had taken it out of the safe when Joyce went off for lunch and spread it out to look at it, as he had been doing most days lately. He never took out more than three thousand, though there was twice that in the safe, because he had calculated that three thousand would be just the right sum to buy him one year's freedom.

With the kind of breathless excitement many people feel about sex—or so he supposed, he never had himself—he looked at the money and turned it over and handled it. Gently he handled it, and then roughly as if it belonged to him and he had lots more. He put two wads into each of his trouser pockets and walked up and down the little office. He got out his wallet with his own two pounds in it, and put in forty and folded it again and appreciated its new thickness. After that he counted out thirty-five pounds into an imaginary hand and mouthed, thirty-three, thirty-four, thirty-five, into an imaginary face, and knew he had gone too far in fantasy with that one as he felt himself blush.

For he didn't intend to steal the money. If three thousand pounds goes missing from a subbranch in which there is only the clerk in charge (by courtesy, the manager) and a girl cashier, and the girl is there and the clerk isn't, the Anglian-Victoria Bank will not have far to look for the culprit. Loyalty to the bank didn't stop him taking it, but fear of being found out did. Anyway, he wasn't going to get away or be free, he knew that. He might be only thirty-eight, but his thirty-eight was somehow much older than other people's thirty-eights. It was too old for running away.

He always stopped the fantasy when he blushed. The rush of shame told him he had overstepped the bounds, and this always happened when he had got himself playing a part in some dumb show or even actually said aloud things like, That was the deposit, I'll send you the balance of five thousand, nine hundred in the morning. He stopped and thought what a state he had got himself into and how, with this absurd indulgence, he was even now breaking one of the bank's sacred rules. For he shouldn't be able to open the safe on his own, he shouldn't know Joyce's combination and she shouldn't know his. He felt guilty most of the time in Joyce's presence because she was as honest as the day, and had only told him the B List combination (he was on the A) when he glibly told her the rule was made to be broken and no one ever thought twice about breaking it.

He heard her let herself in by the back way, and he put the money in a drawer. Joyce wouldn't go to the safe because there was five hundred pounds in her till and few customers came into the Anglian-Victoria at Childon on a Wednesday afternoon. All twelve shops closed at one and didn't open again till nine-thirty in the morning.

Joyce called him Mr. Groombridge instead of Alan. She did this because she was twenty and he was thirty-eight. The intention was not to show respect, which would never have occurred to her, but to make plain the enormous gulf of years which yawned between them. She was one of those people who see a positive achievement in being young, as if youth were a plum job which they have got hold of on their own initiative. But she was kind to her elders, in a tolerant way.

"It's lovely out, Mr. Groombridge. It's like spring."

"It is spring," said Alan.

"You know what I mean." Joyce always said that if any-one attempted to point out that she spoke in clichés. "Shall I make you a coffee?"

"No thanks, Joyce. Better open the doors. It's just on two."

The branch closed for lunch. There wasn't enough custom to warrant its staying open. Joyce unlocked the heavy oak outer door and the inner glass door, turned the sign which said *Till Closed* to the other side which said *Miss J. M. Culver,* and went back to Alan. From his office, with the door ajar, you could see anyone who came in. Joyce had very long legs and a very large bust, but otherwise was nothing special to look at. She perched on the edge of the desk and began telling Alan about the lunch she had just had with her boy friend in the Childon Arms, and what the boy friend had said and about not having enough money to get married on.

"We should have to go in with Mum, and it's not right, is it, two women in a kitchen? Their ways aren't our ways. You can't get away from the generation gap. How old were you when you got married, Mr. Groombridge?"

He would have liked to say twenty-two or even twenty-four, but he couldn't because she knew Christopher was grown up. And, God knew, he didn't want to make himself out older than he was. He told the truth, with shame. "Eighteen."

"Now I think that's too young for a man. It's one thing for a girl but the man ought to be older. There are respon-sibilities to be faced up to in marriage. A man isn't mature at eighteen."

"Most men are never mature."

"You know what I mean," said Joyce. The outer door

opened and she left him to his thoughts and the letter from
Mrs. Marjorie Perkins, asking for a hundred pounds to be
transferred from her deposit to her current account.

Joyce knew everyone who banked with them by his or her
name. She chatted pleasantly with Mr. Butler and then with
Mrs. Surridge. Alan opened the drawer and looked at the
three thousand pounds. He could easily live for a year on
that. He could have a room of his own and make friends of
his own and buy books and records and go to theatres and
eat when he liked and stay up all night if he wanted to. For
a year. And then? When he could hear Joyce talking to Mr.
Wolford, the Childon butcher, about inflation, and how he
must notice the difference from when he was young—he was
about thirty-five—he took the money into the little room between his office and the back door where the safe was. Both
combinations, the one he ought to know and the one he
oughtn't, were in his head. He spun the dials and the door
opened and he put the money away, along with the other
three thousand, the rest being in the tills.

There came to him, as always, a sense of loss. He couldn't
have the money, of course, it would never be his, but he felt
bereft when it was once again out of his hands. He was like
a lover whose girl has gone from his arms to her own bed.
Presently Pam phoned. She always did about this time to
ask him what time he would be home—he was invariably
home at the same time—to collect the groceries or Jillian
from school. Joyce thought it was lovely, his wife phoning
him every day "after all these years."

A few more people came into the bank. Alan went out
there and turned the sign over the other till to *Mr. A. J.
Groombridge* and took a cheque from someone he vaguely
recognised called, according to the cheque, P. Richardson.

"How would you like the money?"

"Five green ones and three portraits of the Duke of Wellington," said P. Richardson, a wag.

Alan smiled as he was expected to. He would have liked to hit him over the head with the calculating machine, and now he remembered that last time P. Richardson had been in he had replied to that question by asking for Deutschemarks.

No more shopkeepers today. They had all banked their takings and gone home. Joyce closed the doors at three-thirty, and the two of them balanced their tills and put the money back in the safe, and did all the other small meticulous tasks necessary for the honour and repute of the second smallest branch of the Anglian-Victoria in the British Isles. Joyce and he hung their coats in the cupboard in his office. Joyce put hers on and he put his on and Joyce put on more mascara, the only make-up she ever wore.

"The evenings are drawing out," said Joyce.

He parked his car in a sort of courtyard, surrounded by Suffolk flint walls, at the bank's rear. It was a pretty place with winter jasmine showing in great blazes of yellow over the top of the walls, and the bank was pretty too, being housed in a slicked-up L-shaped Tudor cottage. His car was not particularly pretty since it was a G registration Morris 1100 with a broken wing mirror he couldn't afford to replace. He lived three miles away on a ten-year-old estate of houses, and the drive down country lanes took him only a few minutes.

The estate was called Fitton's Piece after a Marian Martyr who had been burnt in a field there in 1555. The Reverend Thomas Fitton would have been beatified if he had belonged to the other side, but all he got as an unremitting Protestant was fifty red boxes named after him. The houses in the four streets which composed the estate (Tudor Way,

Martyr's Mead, Fitton Close, and—the builder ran out of inspiration—Hillcrest) had pantiled roofs and large flat windows and chimneys that were for effect, not use. All their occupants had bought their trees and shrubs from the same very conservative garden centre in Stantwich and swapped cuttings and seedlings, so that everyone had Lawson's cypress and a laburnum and a kanzan, and most people a big clump of pampas grass. This gave the place a curious look of homogeneity and, because there were no boundary fences, it looked as if the houses were not private homes but dwellings for the staff of some great demesne.

Alan had bought his house at the end of not very hilly Hillcrest on a mortgage granted by the bank. The interest on this loan was low and fixed, and when he thought about his life one of the few things he considered he had to be thankful for was that he paid two and a half per cent and not eleven like other people.

His car had to remain on the drive because the garage, described as integral and taking up half the ground floor, had been converted into a bed-sit for Pam's father. Pam came out and took the groceries. She was a pretty woman of thirty-seven who had had a job for only one year of her life and had lived in a country village for the whole of it. She wore a lot of make-up on her lips and silvery-blue stuff on her eyes. Every couple of hours she would disappear to apply a fresh layer of lipstick because when she was a girl it had been the fashion always to have shiny pink lips. On a shelf in the kitchen she kept a hand mirror and lipstick and pressed powder and a pot of eyeshadow. Her hair was permed. She wore skirts which came exactly to her knees, and her engagement ring above her wedding ring, and usually a charm bracelet. She looked about forty-five.

She asked Alan if he had had a good day, and he said he had and what about her? She said, all right, and talked

about the awful cost of living while she unpacked cornflakes
and tins of soup. Pam usually talked about the cost of living
for about a quarter of an hour after he got home. He went
out into the garden to put off seeing his father-in-law for as
long as possible, and looked at the snowdrops and the little
red tulips which were exquisitely beautiful at this violet
hour, and they gave him a strange little pain in his heart. He
yearned after them, but for what? It was as if he were in
love, which he had never been. The trouble was that he had
read too many books of a romantic or poetical nature, and
often he wished he hadn't.

It got too cold to stay out there, so he went into the living
room and sat down and read the paper. He didn't want to,
but it was the sort of thing men did in the evenings. Sometimes he thought he had begotten his children because that
also was the sort of thing men did in the evenings.

After a while his father-in-law came in from his bed-sit.
His name was Wilfred Summitt, and Alan and Pam called
him Pop, and Christopher and Jillian called him Grandpop.
Alan hated him more than any human being he had ever
known and hoped he would soon die, but this was unlikely
as he was only sixty-six and very healthy.

Pop said, "Good evening to you," as if there were about
fifteen other people there he didn't know well enough to address. Alan said hallo without looking up and Pop sat down.
Presently Pop punched his fist into the back of the paper to
make Alan lower it.

"You all right then, are you?" Like the Psalmist, Wilfred
Summitt was given to parallelism, so he said the same thing
twice more, slightly rephrasing it each time. "Doing O.K.,
are you? Everything hunky-dory, is it?"

"Mmm," said Alan, going back to the Stantwich *Evening
Press*.

"That's good. That's what I like to hear. Anything in the paper, is there?"

Alan didn't say anything. Pop came very close and read the back page. Turning his fat body almost to right angles, he read the "Stop Press." His sight was magnificent. He said he saw there had been another one of those bank robberies, another cashier murdered, and there would be more, mark his words, up and down the country, all over the place, see if he wasn't right, and all because they knew they could get away with it on account of knowing they wouldn't get hanged.

"It's getting like Chicago, it's getting like in America," said Pop. "I used to think working in a bank was a safe job, Pam used to think it was, but it's a different story now, isn't it? Makes me nervous you working in a bank, gets on my nerves. Something could happen to you any day, any old time you could get yourself shot like that chap in Glasgow, and then what's going to happen to Pam? That's what I think to myself, what's going to happen to Pam?"

Alan said his branch was much too small for bank robbers to bother with.

"That's a comfort, that's my one consolation. I say to myself when I get nervy, I say to myself, good thing he never got promotion, good thing he never got on in his job. Better safe than sorry, is my motto, better a quiet life with your own folks than risking your neck for a big wage packet."

Alan would have liked a drink. He knew, mainly from books and television, that quite a lot of people come home to a couple of drinks before their evening meal. Drinks the Groombridges had. In the sideboard was a full bottle of whisky, an almost full bottle of gin, and a very large full bottle of Bristol Cream sherry which Christopher had bought duty-free on the way back from a package tour to Switzerland. These drinks, however, were for other people.

They were for those married couples whom the Groombridges invited in for an evening, one set at a time and
roughly once a fortnight. He wondered what Pam and Pop
would say if he got up and poured himself a huge whisky,
which was what he would have liked to do. Wondering was
pretty well as far as he ever got about anything.

Pam came in and said supper was ready. They sat down
to eat it in a corner of the kitchen that was called the dining
recess. They had liver and bacon and reconstituted potato
and brussels sprouts and queen of puddings. Christopher
came in when they were halfway through. He worked for an
estate agent who paid him as much as the Anglian-Victoria
paid his father, and he gave his mother five pounds a week
for his board and lodging. Alan thought this was ridiculous
because Christopher was always rolling in money, but when
he protested to Pam she got hysterical and said it was
wicked taking anything at all from one's children. Christopher had beautiful trendy suits for work and well-cut
trendy denim for the weekends, and several nights a week
he took the girl he said was his fiancée to a drinking club in
Stantwich called the Agape, which its patrons pronounced
Agayp.

Jillian didn't come in. Pam explained that she had stayed
at school for the dramatic society and had gone back with
Sharon for tea. This, Alan was certain, was not so. She was
somewhere with a boy. He was an observant person and
Pam was not, and from various things he had heard and noticed he knew that, though only fifteen, Jillian was not a vir-
gin and hadn't been for some time. Of course he also knew
that as a responsible parent he ought to discuss this with
Pam and try to stop Jillian or just get her on the pill. He was
sure she was promiscuous and that the whole thing ought
not just to be ignored, but he couldn't discuss anything with
Pam. She and Pop and Jillian had only two moods, apathy

and anger. Pam would fly into a rage if he told her, and if he insisted, which he couldn't imagine doing, she would scream at Jillian and take her to a doctor to be examined for an intact hymen or pregnancy or venereal disease, or the lot for all he knew.

In spite of Christopher's arrant selfishness and bad manners, Alan liked him much better than he liked Jillian. Christopher was good-looking and successful and, besides that, he was his ally against Wilfred Summitt. If anyone could make Pop leave it would be Christopher. Having helped himself to liver, he started in on his grandfather with that savage and, in fact, indefensible teasing which he did defend on the grounds that it was "all done in fun."

"Been living it up today, have you, Grandpop? Been taking Mrs. Rogers round the boozer? You'll get yourself talked about, you will. You know what they're like round here, yak-yak-yak all day long." Pop was a teetotaller, and his acquaintance with Mrs. Rogers extended to no more than having once chatted with her in the street about the political situation, an encounter witnessed by his grandson. "She's got a husband, you know, and a copper at that," said Christopher, all smiles. "What are you going to say when he finds out you've been feeling her up behind the village hall? Officer, I had drink taken and the woman tempted me."

"You want to wash your filthy mouth out with soap," Pop shouted.

Christopher said sorrowfully, smiling no more, that it was a pity some people couldn't take a joke and he hoped he wouldn't lose his sense of humour no matter how old he got.

"Are you going to let your son insult me, Pamela?"

"I think that's quite enough, Chris," said Pam.

Pam washed the dishes and Alan dried them. It was for some reason understood that neither Christopher nor Pop should ever wash or dry dishes. They were in the living room, watching a girl rock singer on television. The volume was turned up to its fullest extent because Wilfred Summitt was slightly deaf. He hated rock and indeed all music except Vera Lynn and ballads like "Blue Room" and "Tip-toe Through the Tulips," and he said the girl was an indecent trollop who wanted her behind smacked, but when the television was on he wanted to hear it just the same. He had a large colour set of his own, brand-new, in his own room, but it was plain that tonight he intended to sit with them and watch theirs.

"The next programme's unsuitable for children, it says here," said Christopher. "Unsuitable for people in their first or second childhoods. You'd better go off beddy-byes, Grandpop."

"I'm not demeaning myself to reply to you, Pig. I'm not lowering myself."

"Only my fun," said Christopher.

When the film had begun Alan quietly opened his book. The only chance he got to read was while they were watching television because Pam and Pop said it was unsociable to read in company. The television was on every evening all the evening, so he got plenty of chances. The book was Yeats, *The Winding Stair and Other Poems*.

2

Jillian Groombridge hung around for nearly two hours outside an amusement arcade in Clacton, waiting for John Purford to turn up. When it got to eight and he hadn't come, she had to get the train back to Stantwich and then the Stoke Mill bus. John, who had a souped-up aged Singer, would have driven her home, and she was more annoyed at having to spend her pocket money on fares than at being stood up.

They had met only once before and that had been on the previous Sunday. Jillian had picked him up by a fruit machine. She got him starting to drive her back at nine because she had to be in by half-past ten, and this made him think there wouldn't be anything doing. He was wrong. Jillian being Jillian, there was plenty doing, the whole thing in fact on the back seat of the Singer down a quiet pitch-dark country lane. Afterwards he had been quite surprised and not a little discomfited to hear from her that she was the daughter of a bank manager and lived at Fitton's Piece. He said, for he was the son of a farm labourer, that she was a cut above him, and she said it was only a tin-pot little bank subbranch, the Anglian-Victoria in Childon. They kept no more than seven thousand in the safe, and there was only her dad there and a girl, and they even closed for lunch, which would show him how tin-pot it was.

John had dropped her off at Stoke Mill at the point where Tudor Way debouched from the village street, and said maybe they could see each other again and how about Wednesday? But when he had left her and was on his way back to his parents' home outside Colchester, he began having second thoughts. She was pretty enough, but she was a bit too easy for his taste, and he doubted whether she was the seventeen she said she was. Very likely she was under the age of consent. That amused him, that term, because if anyone had done any consenting it was he. So when Tuesday came and his mother said, if he hadn't got anything planned for the next evening she and his father would like to go round to his Aunt Elsie's if he'd sit in with his little brother, aged eight, he said yes and saw it as a let-out.

On the morning of the day he was supposed to have his date with Jillian he drove a truckload of bookcases and record-player tables up to London, and he was having a cup of tea and a sandwich in a cafe off the North Circular Road when Marty Foster came in. John hadn't seen Marty Foster since nine years ago when they had both left their Colchester primary school, and he wouldn't have known him under all that beard and fuzzy hair. But Marty knew him. He sat down at his table, and with him was a tall fair-haired guy Marty said was called Nigel.

"What's with you then," said Marty, "after all these years?"

John said how he had this friend who was a cabinetmaker and they had gone into business together and were doing nicely, thank you, mustn't grumble, better than they'd hoped, as a matter of fact. Hard work, though, it was all go, and he'd be glad of a break next week. This motoring mag he took was running a trip, chartering a plane and all, to Daytona Beach for the International Motorcycle Racing, with a sight-seeing tour to follow. Three weeks in sunny Florida wouldn't do him any harm, he reckoned, though it was a bit pricey.

"I should be so lucky," said Marty, and it turned out he hadn't had a job for six months, and he and Nigel were living on the Social Security. "If you can call it living," said Marty, and Nigel said, "There's no point in working, anyway. They take it all off you in tax and whatever. I guess those guys who did the bank in Glasgow got the right idea."

"Right," said Marty.

"No tax on that sort of bread," said Nigel. "No goddamned superann. and N.H.I."

John shrugged. "It wouldn't be worth going inside for," he said. "Those Glasgow blokes, they only got away with twenty thousand and there were four of them. Take that branch of the Anglian-Victoria in Childon—you know Childon, Marty—they don't keep any more than seven thou. in the safe there. If a couple of villains broke in there, they'd only get three and a half apiece *and* they'd have to deal with the manager and the girl."

"You seem to know a lot about it."

He had impressed them he knew, with his job and his comparative affluence. Now he couldn't resist impressing them further. "I know the manager's daughter, we're pretty close, as a matter of fact. Jillian Groombridge, she's called, lives in one of those modern houses at Stoke Mill."

Marty did look impressed, though Nigel didn't. Marty said, "Pity banks don't close for lunch. You take a branch like that one, and Groombridge or the girl went off to eat, well, you'd be laughing then, it'd be in the bag."

"Be your age," said Nigel. "If they left the doors open and the safe unlocked, you'd be laughing. If they said, Come in and welcome, your need is greater than ours, you'd be laughing. The point is, banks don't close for lunch."

John couldn't help laughing himself. "The Childon one does," he said, and then he thought all this had gone far enough. Speculating about what might be, and if only, and if this happened and that and the other, was a sort of disease that kept people like Marty and Nigel where they were, while not doing it had got him where he was. Better find honest work, he thought, though he didn't, of course, say this aloud. Instead he got on to asking Marty about this one and that one they had been at school with, and told Marty what news he had of their old schoolfellows, until his second cup of tea was drunk up and it was time to start the drive back.

The hypothetical couple of villains John had referred to had been facing him across the table.

Marty Foster also was the son of an agricultural labourer. For a year after he left school he worked in a paintbrush factory. Then his mother left his father and went off with a lorry driver. Things got so uncomfortable at home that Marty too moved out and got a room in Stantwich. He got a job driving a van for a cut-price electrical-goods shop and then a job trundling trolleys full of peat and pot plants about in a garden centre. It was the same one that supplied Fitton's Piece with its pampas grass. When he was sacked from that for telling a customer who complained because the garden centre wouldn't deliver horse manure, that if he wanted his shit he could fetch it himself, he moved up to London and into a squat in Kilburn Park. While employed in packing up parcels for an Oxford Street store, he met Nigel Thaxby. By then he was renting a room with a kitchen in a back street in Cricklewood, his aim being to stop working and go on the Social Security.

Nigel Thaxby, like Marty, was twenty-one. He was the son and only child of a doctor who was in general practice in Elstree. Nigel had been to a very minor public school because his father wanted him brought up as a gentleman but didn't want to pay high fees. The staff had third-class honours or pass degrees and generally no teachers' training certificates, and the classroom furniture was blackened and broken and, in fact, straight Dotheboys Hall. In spite of living from term to term on scrag end stew and rotten potatoes and mushed peas and white bread, Nigel grew up tall and handsome. By the time excessive cramming and his father's threats and his mother's tears had squeezed him into the University of Kent, he was over six feet tall with blond hair and blue eyes and the features of Michelangelo's *David*. At Canterbury something snapped in Nigel. He did no work. He got it into his head that if he did do any work and eventually got a degree, the chances were he wouldn't get a job. And if he did get one all that would come out of it was a house like his parents' and a marriage like his parents' and a new car every four years and maybe a child to cram full of useless knowledge and pointless aspirations. So he walked out of the university before the authorities could ask his father to take him away.

Nigel came to London and lived in a sort of commune. The house had some years before been allocated by the Royal Borough of Kensington and Chelsea to a quartet of young people on the grounds that it was being used as a centre for group therapy. So it had been for some time, but the young people quarrelled with each other and split up, leaving behind various hangers-on who took the padding off the walls of the therapy room and gave up the vegetarian regime, and brought in boy friends and girl friends and sometimes children they had had by previous marriages or liaisons. There was continuous coming and going, people drifted in for a week or a month and out again, contributing to the rent or not, as the case might be. Nigel got in on it because he knew someone who lived there and who was also a reject of the University of Kent.

At first he wasn't well up in the workings of the Social Security system and he thought he had to have a job. So he also packed up parcels. Marty Foster put him wise to a lot of useful things, though Nigel knew he was cleverer than Marty. One of the things Marty put him wise to was that it was foolish to pack up parcels when one could get one's rent paid and a bit left over for doing nothing. At the time they met John Purford in Neasden, Marty was living in Cricklewood and Nigel was sometimes living in Cricklewood with Marty and sometimes in the Kensington commune, and they were both vaguely and sporadically considering a life of crime.

"Like your friend said, it wouldn't be worth the hassle," said Nigel. "Not for seven grand."

"Yeah, but look at it this way, you've got to begin on a small scale," said Marty. "It'd be a sort of way of learning. All we got to do is rip off a vehicle. I can do that easy. I got keys that'll fit any Ford Escort, you know that."

Nigel thought about it.

"Can you get a shooter?" he said.

"I got one." Marty enjoyed the expression of astonishment on Nigel's face. It was seldom that he could impress him. But he was shrewd enough to put prudence before vanity, and he said carefully, "Even an expert wouldn't know the difference."

"You mean it's not for real?"

"A gun's a gun, isn't it?" And Marty added with, for him, rare philosophical insight, "It's not what it does, it's what people'll think it'll do that matters."

Slowly Nigel nodded his head. "It can't be bad. Look, if you're really into this, there's no grief in going up this Childon dump tomorrow and casing the joint."

Nigel had a curious manner of speech. It was the result of careful study in an attempt to be different. His accent was mid-Atlantic, rather like that of a commercial radio announcer. People who didn't know any better sometimes took him for an American. He had rejected, when he remembered to do so, the cultured English of his youth and adopted speech patterns which were a mixture of the slang spoken by the superannuated hippies, now hopelessly out of date, in the commune, and catch phrases picked up from old films seen on TV. Nigel wasn't at all sophisticated really, though Marty thought he was. Marty's father talked Suffolk, but his mother had been a cockney. Mostly he talked cockney himself, with the flat vowels of East Anglia creeping in, and sometimes he had the distinctive Suffolk habit of using the demonstrative pronoun "that" for "it."

Seeing that Marty was serious or "really into" an attempt on the Childon bank, Nigel went off to Elstree, making sure to choose a time when his father was in his surgery, and got a loan of twenty pounds off his mother. Mrs. Thaxby cried and said he was breaking his parents' hearts, but he persuaded her into the belief that the money was for his train fare to Newcastle where he had a job in line. An hour later—it was Thursday and the last day of February—he and Marty caught the train to Stantwich and then the bus to Childon which got them there by noon.

They began their survey by walking along the lane at the back of the Anglian-Victoria subbranch. They saw the gap in the flint walls that led to the little yard, and in the yard they saw Alan Groombridge's car. On one side of the yard was what looked like a disused barn and on the other a small apple orchard. Marty, on his own, walked round to the front. The nearest of the twelve shops was a good hundred yards away. Opposite the bank was a Methodist chapel and next to that nothing but fields. Marty went into the bank.

The girl at the till labelled Miss J. M. Culver was weighing coins into little plastic bags and chatting to the customer

about what lovely weather they were having. The other till
was opened and marked Mr. A. J. Groombridge, but though
there was no one behind it, Marty went and stood there,
looking at the little office an open door disclosed. In that
office a man was bending over the desk. Marty wondered
where the safe was. Through that office, presumably behind
that other closed door. There was no upstairs. Once there
had been, but the original ceiling had been removed and
now the inside of the steeply sloping roof could be seen,
painted white and with its beams exposed and stripped.
Marty decided he had seen as much as he was likely to and
was about to turn away, when the man in the office seemed
at last to be aware of him. He straightened up, turned
round, came out to the metal grille, and he did this without
really looking at Marty at all. Nor did he look at him when
he murmured a good morning, but kept his eyes on the
counter top. Marty had to think of something to say so he
asked for twenty five-pence pieces for a pound note, wanted
them for parking meters, he said, and Groombridge counted
them out, first pushing them across the counter in two
stacks, then thinking better of this and slipping them into a
little bag like the ones the girl had been using. Marty said
thanks and took the bag of coins and left.

He was dying for a drink and tried to get Nigel to go with
him into the Childon Arms. But Nigel wasn't having any.

"You can have a drink in Stantwich," he said. "We don't
want all the locals giving us the once-over."

So they hung about until five to one. Then Nigel went
into the bank, timing his arrival for a minute to. A middle-
aged woman came out and Nigel went in. The girl was
alone. She looked at him and spoke to him quite politely but
also indifferently, and Nigel was aware of a certain indignation, a resentment, at seeing no admiration register on her
large plain face. He said he wanted to open an account, and

the girl said the manager was just going out to lunch and would he call back at two?

She followed him to the door and locked it behind him. In the lanc at the back he met Marty, who was quite excited because he had seen Alan Groombridge come out of the back door of the bank and drive away in his car.

"I reckon they go out alternate days. That means the bird'll go out tomorrow and he'll go out Monday. We'll do the job on Monday."

Nigel nodded, thinking of that girl all alone, of how easy it would be. There seemed nothing more to do. They caught the bus back to Stantwich, where Marty spent the twenty five-pences on whisky and then set about wheedling some of Mrs. Thaxby's loan out of Nigel.

3

Fiction had taught Alan Groombridge that there is such a thing as being in love. Some say that this, indirectly, is how everyone gets to know about it. Alan had read that it had been invented in the Middle Ages by someone called Chrétien de Troyes, and that this constituted a change in human nature.

He had never experienced it himself. And when he considered it, he didn't know anyone else who had either. Not any of those couples, the Heyshams and the Kitsons and the Maynards, who came in to drink the duty-free Bristol Cream. Not Wilfred Summitt or Constable Rogers or Mrs. Surridge or P. Richardson. He knew that because he was sure that if it was a change in human nature their natures would have been changed by it. And they had not been. They were as dull as he and as unredeemed.

With Pam there had never been any question of being in love. She was the girl he took to a couple of dances in Stantwich, and one evening took more irrevocably in a field on the way home. It was the first time for both of them. It had been quite enjoyable, though nothing special, and he hadn't intended to repeat it. In that field Christopher was conceived. Everyone took it for granted he and Pam would marry before she began to "show," and he had never thought to protest. He accepted it as his lot in life to marry Pam and have a child and keep at a steady job. Pam wanted an engagement ring, though they were never really engaged, so he bought her one with twenty-five pounds borrowed from his father.

Christopher was born, and four years later Pam said they ought to "go in for" another baby. At that time Alan had not yet begun to notice words and what they mean and how they should be used and how badly most people use them, so he had not thought that phrase funny. When he was older and had read a lot, he looked back on that time and wondered what it would be like to be married to someone who knew it was funny too and to whom he could say it as a tender ribaldry; to whom he could say as he began to make love with that purpose in view, that now he was going in for a baby. If he had said it to Pam in those circumstances she would have slapped his face.

When they had two children they never went out in the evenings. They couldn't have afforded to even if they had known anyone who would baby-sit for nothing. Wilfred Summitt's wife was alive then, but both Mr. and Mrs. Summitt believed, like Joyce, that young married people should face up to their responsibilities, which meant never enjoying themselves and never leaving their children in the care of anyone else. Alan began to read. He had never read much before he was married because his father had said it was a waste of time in someone who was going to work with figures. In his mid-twenties he joined the public library in Stantwich and read every thriller and detective story and adventure book he could lay his hands on. In this way he lived vicariously quite happily. But around his thirtieth birthday something rather peculiar happened.

He read a thriller in which a piece of poetry was quoted. Until then he had despised poetry as above his head and something which people wrote and read to "show off." But he liked this poem, which was Shakespeare's sonnet about fortune and men's eyes, and lines from it kept going round and round in his head. The next time he went to the library he got Shakespeare's *Sonnets* out and he liked them, which made him read more poetry and, gradually, the greater novels that people call (for some unapparent reason) classics, and plays and more verse, and books that critics had written about books—and he was a lost man. For his wits were sharpened, his powers of perception heightened, and he became discontented with his lot. In this world there were other things apart from Pam and the children and the bank and the Heyshams and the Kitsons, and shopping on Saturdays and watching television and taking a caravan in the Isle of Wight for the summer holidays. Unless all these authors were liars, there was an inner life and an outer experience, an infinite number of things to be seen and done, and there was passion.

He had come late in life to the heady intoxication of literature and it had poisoned him for what he had.

It was adolescent to want to be in love, but he wanted to be. He wanted to live on his own too, and go and look at things and explore and discover and understand. All these things were equally impracticable for a married man with children and a father-in-law and a job in the Anglian-Victoria Bank. And to fall in love would be immoral, especially if he did anything about it. Besides, there was no one to fall in love with.

He imagined going round to the Heyshams one Saturday morning and finding Wendy alone, and suddenly, although, like the people in the Somerset Maugham story, they had known and not much liked each other for years, they fell violently in love. They were stricken with love as Lancelot and Guinevere were for each other, or Tristan and Isolde. He had even considered Joyce for this role. How if she were to come into his office after they had closed, and he were to

take her in his arms and . . . He knew he couldn't. Mostly
he just imagined a girl, slender with long black hair, who
made an appointment to see him about an overdraft. They
exchanged one glance and immediately they both knew
they were irrevocably bound to each other.

It would never happen to him. It didn't seem to happen to
anyone much any more. Those magazines Pam read were
full of articles telling women how to have orgasms and men
how to make them have them, but never was there one telling people how to find and be in love.

Sometimes he felt that the possession of the three thousand pounds would enable him, among other things, to be in
love. He took it out and handled it again on Thursday, resolving that that would be the last time. He would be firm
about his obsession and about that other one too. After this
week there would be no more reading of Yeats and Forster
and Conrad, those seducers of a man's mind, but memoirs
and biography as suitable to a practical working bank manager.

Alan Groombridge wondered about and thought and fantasised about a lot of odd and unexpected things. But, apart
from playing with bank notes which didn't belong to him,
he only did one thing that was unconventional.

The Anglian-Victoria had no objection to its Childon staff
leaving the branch at lunchtime, providing all the money
was in the safe and the doors locked. But, in fact, they were
never both absent at the same time. Joyce stayed in on Mon-
days and Thursdays when her Stephen wasn't working in
Childon and there was no one with whom to go to the Childon Arms. On those days she took sandwiches to the bank
with her. Alan took sandwiches with him every day because
he couldn't afford to eat out. But on Monday and Thursday
lunchtimes he did leave the bank, though only Joyce knew

of this and even she didn't know where he went. He drove off, and in winter ate his sandwiches in the car in a lay-by, in the spring and summer in a field. He did this to secure for himself two hours a week of peace and total solitude.

That Friday, 1 March, Joyce went as usual to the Childon Arms with Stephen for a Ploughman's Lunch and a half of lager, and Alan stuck to his resolve of not taking the three thousand pounds out of the safe. Friday was their busiest day and that helped to keep temptation at bay.

The weekend began with shopping in Stantwich. He went into the library, where he got out the memoirs of a playwright (ease it off gradually) and a history book. Pam didn't bother to look at these. Years ago she had told him he was a real bookworm, and it couldn't be good for his eyes, which he needed to keep in good condition in a job like his. They had sausages and tinned peaches for lunch, just the two of them and Wilfred Summitt. Christopher never came in for lunch on Saturdays. He got up at ten, polished his car, perquisite of the estate agents, and took the seventeen-year-old trainee hairdresser he called his fiancée to London, where he spent a lot of money on gin and tonics, prawn cocktails and steak, circle seats in cinemas, long-playing records, and odds and ends like *Playboy* magazine and bottles of wine and after-shave and cassettes. Jillian sometimes came in when she had nothing better to do. This Saturday she had something better to do, though what it was she hadn't bothered to inform her parents.

In the afternoon Alan pulled weeds out of the garden, Pam turned up the hem of an evening skirt and Wilfred Summitt took a nap. The nap freshened him up, and while they were having tea, which was sardines and lettuce and bread and butter and madeira cake, he said he had seen a news flash on television and the Glasgow bank robbers had been caught.

"What we want here is the electric chair."

"Something like that," said Pam.

"What we want is the army to take over this country. See a bit of discipline then, we would. The army to take over, under the Queen of course, under Her Majesty, and some general at the head of it. Some big pot who means business. The Forces, that's the thing. We knew what discipline was when I was in the Forces." Pop always spoke of his time at Catterick Camp in the 1940s as "being in the Forces" as if he had been in the navy and air force and marines as well. "Flog 'em, is what I say. Give 'em something to remember across their backsides." He paused and swigged tea. "What's wrong with the cat?" he said, so that anyone coming in at that moment, Alan thought, would have supposed him to be enquiring after the health of the family pet.

Alan went back into the garden. Passing the window of Pop's bed-sit, he noticed that the gas fire was full on. Pop kept his gas fire on all day and, no doubt, half the night from September till May whether he was in his room or not. Pam had told him about it very politely, but he only said his circulation was bad because he had hardening of the arteries. He contributed nothing to the gas bill or the electricity bill either, and Pam said it wasn't fair to ask anything from an old man who only had his pension. Alan dared to say, How about the ten thousand he got from selling his own house? That, said Pam, was for a rainy day.

Back in the house, having put the garden tools away, he found his daughter. His reading had taught him that the young got on better with the old than with the middle-aged, but that didn't seem to be so in the case of his children and Pop. Here, as perhaps in other respects, the authors had been wrong.

Jillian ignored Pop, never speaking to him at all, and Pam, though sometimes flaring and raving at her while Jillian

flared and raved back, was generally too frightened of her to
reprove her when reproof was called for. On the face of it,
mother and daughter had a good relationship, always chatting to each other about clothes and things they had read in
magazines, and when they went shopping together they always linked arms. But there was no real communication.
Jillian was a subtle little hypocrite, Alan thought, who ingra-
tiated herself with Pam by presenting her with the kind of
image Pam would think a fifteen-year-old girl ought to have.
He was sure that most of the extra-domestic activities she
told her mother she went in for were pure invention, but
they were all of the right kind: dramatic society, dressmak-
ing class, evenings spent with Sharon, whose mother was a
teacher and who was alleged to be helping Jillian with her
French homework. Jillian always got home by ten-thirty because she knew her mother thought sexual intercourse invariably took place after ten-thirty. She said she came home
on the last bus, which sometimes she did, though not alone,
and Alan had once seen her get off the pillion of a boy's mo-
torbike at the end of Martyr's Mead. He wondered why she
bothered with deception, for if she had confessed to what she
really did Pam could have done little about it. She would
only have screamed threats while Jillian screamed threats
back. They were afraid of each other, and Alan thought their
relationship so sick as to be sinister. Among the things he
wondered about was when Jillian would get married and
how much she would expect him to fork out for her wedding.
Probably it would be within the next couple of years, as she
would very likely get pregnant quite soon, but she would
want a big white wedding with all her friends there and a
dance afterwards in a discotheque.

Pop had given up speaking to her. He knew he wouldn't
get an answer. He was trying to watch television, but she
had got between him and the set and was sitting on the floor

drying her hair with a very noisy hair dryer. Alan could bring himself to feel sorry for Pop while Jillian was in the house. Fortunately she often wasn't, for when she was she ruled them all, a selfish bad-tempered little tyrant.

"You haven't forgotten we're going to the Heyshams' for the evening, have you?" said Pam.

Alan had, but the question really meant he was to dress up. They were not invited to a meal. No one at Fitton's Piece gave dinner parties, and "for the evening" meant two glasses of sherry or whisky and water each, followed by coffee. But etiquette, presumably formulated by the women, demanded a change of costume. Dick Heysham, who was quite a nice man, wouldn't have cared at all if Alan had turned up in old trousers and a sweater and would have liked to dress that way himself, but Pam said a sports jacket must be worn and when his old one got too shabby she made him buy a new one. To make this possible, she had for weeks denied herself small luxuries, her fortnightly hairdo, her fortnightly trip to Stantwich to have lunch in a cafe with her sister, the cigarettes of which she smoked five a day, until the twenty-six pounds had been garnered. It was all horrible and stupid, an insane way to live. He resigned himself to it, as he did to most things, for the sake of peace. Yet he knew that what he got was not peace.

Jillian, unasked, said that she was going with Sharon to play Scrabble at the house of a girl called Bridget. Alan thought it very handy for her that Bridget lived in a cottage in Stoke Mill which had no phone.

"Be back by ten-thirty, won't you, dear?" said Pam.

"Of course I will. I always am."

Jillian smiled so sweetly through her hair that Pam dared to suggest she move away out of Pop's line of vision.

"Why can't he go and watch his own TV?" said Jillian.

No one answered her. Pam went off to have a bath and

came back with the long skirt on and a frilly blouse and lacquer on her hair and her lips pink and shiny. Then Alan
shaved and got into a clean shirt and the sports jacket. They
both looked much younger dressed like that, and smart and
happy. The Heyshams lived in Tudor Way so they walked
there. Something inside him cried aloud to tell her that he
was sorry, that he pitied her from his soul, poor pathetic
woman who had lived her whole life cycle by the age at
which many only just begin to think of settling down. He
couldn't do it, they had no common language. Besides, was
he not as poor and pathetic himself? What would she have
replied if he had said what he would have liked to say?
Look at us, what are we doing, dressed up like this, visiting
people we don't even care for, to talk about nothing, to tell
face-saving lies? For what, for what?

At the Heyshams' the hosts and guests divided themselves
into two groups. The men talked to each other and the
women to each other. The men talked about work, their
cars, the political situation, and the cost of living. The
women talked about their children, their houses, and the cost
of living. After they had been there about an hour Pam went
to the bathroom and came back with more lipstick on.

By ten-fifteen they were all bored stiff. But Alan and Pam
had to stay for another three quarters of an hour or the
Heyshams would think they had been bored or had quarrelled before they came out or were worried about one of
their children. At exactly two minutes to eleven Pam said:

"Whatever time is it?"

She said "whatever" because that implied it must be very
late, while a simple "What time is it?" might indicate that
for her the time was passing slowly.

"Just on eleven," said Alan.

"Good heavens, I'd no idea it was as late as that. We *must*
go."

The Cinderella Complex, its deadline shifted an hour back, operated all over Fitton's Piece. Evenings ended at eleven. Yet there was no reason why they should go home at eleven, no reason why they shouldn't stay out all night, for no one would miss them or, probably, even notice they were not there, and without harming a soul, they could have stayed in bed the following day till noon. But they left at eleven and got home at five past. Pop had gone to his bed-sit, Jillian was in the bath. Where Christopher was was any-body's guess. It was unlikely he would come in before one or two. That didn't worry Pam.

"It's different with boys," he had heard her say to Gwen Maynard. "You don't have to bother about boys in the same way. I insist on my daughter being in by half-past ten and she always is."

Jillian had left a ring of dirty soap round the bath and wet towels on the floor. She was playing punk rock in her bed-room, and Alan longed for the courage to switch the elec-tricity off at the main. They lay in bed, the room bright with moonlight, both pretending they couldn't hear the throb-bing and the thumps. At last the noise stopped because, presumably, the second side of the second LP had come to an end and Jillian had fallen asleep.

A deep silence. There came into his head, he didn't know why, a memory of that episode in Malory when Lancelot is in bed with the queen and he hears the fourteen knights come to the door.

"Madam, is there any armour in your chamber that I might cover my poor body withal?"

Would he ever have such panache? Such proud courage? Would it ever be called for? Pam's eyes were wide open. She was staring at the moonlight patterns on the ceiling. He de-cided he had better make love to her. He hadn't done so for a fortnight, and it was Saturday night. Down in Stoke Mill the church clock struck one. To make sure it would work, Alan fantasised hard about the black-haired girl coming into the bank to order *lire* for a holiday in Portofino. What Pam fantasised about he didn't know, but he was sure she fantasised. It gave him a funny feeling to think about that, though he didn't dare think of it now, the idea of the fantasy people in the bed, so that it wasn't really he making love with Pam but the black-haired girl making love with the man who came to read the meter. The front door banged as Christopher let himself in. His feet thumped up the stairs. Madam, is there any armour in your chamber . . . ?

His poor body finished its work and Pam sighed. It was the last time he was ever to make love to her, and had he known it he would probably have taken greater pains.

4

Marty Foster's room in Cricklewood was at the top of the house, three floors up. It was quite big, as such rooms go, with a kitchen opening out of it, two sash windows looking out onto the street, and a third window in the kitchen. Marty hadn't been able to open any of these windows since he had been there, but he hadn't tried very hard. He slept on a double mattress on the floor. There was also a couch in the room and a gate-leg table marked with white rings and cigarette burns, and a couple of rickety Edwardian dining chairs, and a carpet with pink roses and coffee stains on it, and brown cotton curtains at the windows. When you drew these curtains clouds of dust blew out of them like smoke. In the kitchen was a gas stove and a sink and another gate-leg table and a bookcase used as a food store. Nobody had cleaned the place for several years.

The house was semidetached, end of a terrace. An Irish girl had one of the rooms next to Marty's, the one that overlooked the side entrance, and the other had for years been occupied by a deaf old man named Green. There was a lavatory between the Irish girl's room and the head of the stairs. Half a dozen steps led down to a bathroom which the top-floor tenants shared, and then the main flight went on down to the first floor where a red-haired girl and the man she called her "fella" had a flat, and the ground floor that was inhabited by an out-all-day couple that no one ever saw. Outside the bathroom door was a pay phone.

On Saturday Marty went down to this phone and got onto a car-hire place in South London called Relyacar Rentals, the idea of stealing a vehicle having been abandoned. Could they let him have a small van, say a Mini-van, at nine on Monday morning? They could. They must have his name, please, and would he bring his driving licence with him? Marty gave the name on the licence he was holding in his hand. It had been issued to one Graham Francis Coleman of Wallington in Surrey, was valid until the year 2020, and Marty had helped himself to it out of the pocket of a jacket its owner had left on the rear seat of an Allegro in a cinema car park. Marty had known it would come in useful one day. Next he phoned the Kensington commune and asked Nigel about money. Nigel had only about six pounds of his mother's loan left and their Social Security *Giro*'s weren't due till Wednesday, but he'd do his best.

Nigel had learnt the sense of always telling everyone the same lie, so he announced to his indifferent listeners that he was going off to Newcastle for a couple of weeks. No one said, Have a good time, or Send us a card, or anything like that. That wasn't their way. One of the girls said, In that case he wouldn't mind if her Samantha had his room, would he? Nigel saw his opportunity and said she'd pay the rent then, wouldn't she? A listless argument ensued, the upshot of which was that no one was violently opposed to his taking ten pounds out of the tin where they kept the rent and light and heat money so long as he put it back by the end of the month.

With sixteen pounds in his pocket, Nigel packed most of his possessions into a rucksack he borrowed from Samantha's mother and a suitcase he had long ago borrowed from his own, and set off by bus for Cricklewood. The house where Marty lived was in a street between Chichele Road and Cricklewood Broadway, and it had an air of slightly

down-at-heel respectability. In the summer the big spread-
ing trees, limes and planes and chestnuts, made the place
damp and shady and even rather mysterious, but now they
were just naked trees that looked as if they had never been
in leaf and never would be. There was a church opposite
that Nigel had never seen anyone attend, and on the street
corner a launderette, a paper shop, and a grocery and delicatessen store. He rang Marty's bell, which was the top one,
and Marty came down to let him in.

Marty smelt of the cheap wine he had been drinking, the
dregs of which with their inky sediment were in a cup on
the kitchen table. Wine, or whisky when he could afford it,
was his habitual daily beverage. He drank it to quench his
thirst as other people drink tea or water. One of the reasons
he wanted money was for the unlimited indulgence of this
craving of his. Marty hated having to drink sparingly, knowing there wasn't another bottle in the kitchen waiting for
him to open as soon as this one was finished.

He swallowed what remained in the cup and then
brought out from under a pile of clothes on the mattress an
object which he put into Nigel's hands. It was a small
though heavy pistol, the barrel about six inches long. Nigel
put his finger to the trigger and tried to squeeze it. The trigger moved but not much.

"Do me a favour," said Marty, "and don't point that
weapon at me. Suppose it was loaded?"

"You'd have to be a right cretin, wouldn't you?" Nigel
turned the gun over and looked at it. "There's German writing on the side. *Carl Walther, Modell P.P.K. Cal. 9 mm.
kurz.* Then it says *Made in W. Germany.*" The temptation to
hold forth was too much for him. "You can buy these things
in cycle shops, I've seen them. They're called nonfiring replica guns and they use them in movies. Cost a bomb too.
Where'd you get the bread for a shooter like this?"

Marty wasn't going to tell him about the insurance policy his mother had taken out for him years ago and which had matured. He said only, "Give it here," took the gun back, and looked at the pair of black stockings Nigel was holding out for his inspection.

These Nigel had found in a pile of dirty washing on the floor of the commune bathroom. They were the property of a girl called Sarah who sometimes wore them for sexy effect. "Timing," said Nigel, "is of the essence. We get to the bank just before one. We leave the van in the lane at the back. When the polone comes to lock up, Groombridge'll be due to split. We put the stockings over our faces and rush the polone and lock the doors after us."

"Call her a girl, can't you? You're not a poove."

Nigel went red. The shot had gone home. He wasn't homosexual—he wasn't yet sure if he was sexual at all and he was unhappy about it—but the real point was that Marty had caught him out using a bit of slang which he hadn't known was queers' cant. He said sullenly, "We get her to open the safe and then we tie her up so she can't call the fuzz." A thought struck him. "Did you get the gloves?"

Marty had forgotten and Nigel let him have it for that, glad to be once more in the ascendant. "Christ," he said, "and that finger of yours is more of a giveaway than any goddamned prints."

Neither affronted nor hurt, Marty glanced at his right hand and admitted with a shrug that Nigel was right. The forefinger wasn't exactly repulsive to look at or grotesque but it wasn't a pretty sight either. And it was uniquely Marty's. He had sliced the top off it on an electric mower at the garden centre—a fraction nearer and he'd have lost half his hand, as the manager had never tired of pointing out. The finger was now about a quarter of an inch shorter than the one on the other hand, and the nail, when it grew again, was warped and puckered to the shape of a walnut kernel.

"Get two pairs of gloves Monday morning when you get the van," snapped Nigel, "and when you've got them go and have your hair and your beard cut off."

Marty made a fuss about that, but the fuss was really to cover his fear. The idea of making changes in his appearance brought home to him the reality of what they were about to do. He was considerably afraid and beginning to get cold feet. It didn't occur to him that Nigel might be just as afraid, and they blustered and brazened it out to each other that evening and the next day. Both were secretly aware that they had insufficiently "cased" the Childon subbranch of the Anglian-Victoria, that their only experience of robbery came from books and films, and that they knew very little about the bank's security system. But nothing would have made either of them admit it. The trouble was, they didn't like each other. Marty had befriended Nigel because he was flattered that a doctor's son who had been to college wanted to know him, and Nigel had linked up with Marty because he needed someone even weaker than himself to bully and impress. But among these thieves there was no honour. Each might have said of the other, He's my best friend and I hate him.

That weekend the thought uppermost in Nigel's mind was that he must take charge and run the show as befitted a member of the elite and a descendant of generations of army officers and medical personages, though he affected to despise those forbears of his, and show this peasant what leadership was. The thought uppermost in Marty's, apart from his growing fear, was that with his practical know-how he must astound this upper-class creep. He got a pound out of Nigel on Sunday to buy himself a bottle of Sicilian wine,

and wished he had the self-control to save half for Monday
morning when he would need Dutch courage.

On Sunday night Joyce Culver steamed and pressed the
evening dress she intended to wear on the following evening. Alan Groombridge broke his resolution and reread *The
Playboy of the Western World* while his family, with the ex-
ception of Jillian, watched a television documentary about
wildlife in the Galapagos Islands. Jillian was in the cinema
in Stantwich with a thirty-five-year-old cosmetics salesman
who had promised to get her home by ten-thirty and who
doubted, not yet knowing Jillian, that there would be anything doing on the way.

John Purford, with fifty other car and motorcycle fanat-
ics, was taking off from Gatwick in a charter aircraft bound
for New York and thence for Daytona Beach, Florida.

5

The fine weather broke during the night, and on Monday morning, 4 March, instead of frost silvering the lawns of Fitton's Piece, heavy rain was falling. It was so dark in the dining recess that at breakfast the Groombridges had to have the unearthly, morgue-style, lymph-blue strip light on. Wilfred Summitt elaborated on his idea of an army takeover with a reintroduction of capital punishment, an end to Social Security benefits, and an enforced exodus of all immigrants. Christopher, who didn't have to be at work till ten, had lit a cigarette between courses (cereal and eggs and bacon) and was sniping back at him with the constitution of his own Utopia, euthanasia for all over sixty, and a sexual free-for-all for everyone under thirty. Jillian was combing her hair over a plate of cornflakes while she and Pam argued as to whether it was possible to put blond streaks in one's hair at home, Pam averring that this was a job for a professional. They all made a lot of irritable humourless noise, and Alan wondered how he would feel if the police came into the bank at ten and told him a gas main had exploded and killed all his family five minutes after he left. Probably he would be a little sorry about Pam and Christopher.

He left the sandwiches in the car because it was his day for going out. Along with her coat, Joyce had hung an evening dress in the cupboard. It was her parents' silver wedding day, and she and Stephen were going straight from work to a drinks party and dinner at the Toll House Hotel.

"You'll be having your silver wedding in a few years, Mr. Groombridge," said Joyce. "What'll you give your wife? My mother wanted a silver fox but Dad said, if you don't watch out, my girl, all you'll get is a silver*fish*, meaning one of those creepy-crawlies. We had to laugh. He's ever so funny, my dad. He gave her a lovely bracelet, one of those chased ones."

Alan couldn't imagine how one bracelet could be more chaste than another, but he didn't ask. The bank was always busy on a Monday morning. P. Richardson was the first customer. He asked for two portraits of Florence Nightingale and sneered at Alan, who didn't immediately guess he meant ten-pound notes.

Marty showed Graham Coleman's driving licence to the girl at Relyacar Rentals in Croydon and gave his age as twenty-four. She said she'd like a ten-pound deposit, please, they'd settle up tomorrow when they knew what mileage he'd done, and if he brought the van back after six would he leave it in the square and put the keys through Relyacar's letter box?

Marty handed over the money and said yes to everything. The Mini-van was white and clean and, from the registration, only a year old. He drove it a few miles, parking outside a barber's shop where he had his hair and beard cut off and his chin and upper lip closely shaved. He hadn't really seen his own face for three years and he had forgotten what a small chin he had and what hollow cheeks. Depilation didn't improve his appearance, though the barber insisted it did. At any rate, the Relyacar girl wouldn't know him again. His own mother wouldn't.

There was something else he had to do or buy, but he couldn't remember what it was, so he drove back to pick up

Nigel. He went over Battersea Bridge and up through Kensington and Kensal Rise and Willesden to Cricklewood, where Nigel was waiting for him in Chichele Road.

"Christ," said Nigel, "you look a real freak. You look like one of those Hare Krishna guys."

Marty was a good driver. He had driven for his living while Nigel's experience consisted only in taking out his father's automatic Triumph, and he had never driven a car with an ordinary manual gear shift. Nor did he know London particularly well, but that didn't stop him ordering Marty to take the North Circular Road. Marty had already decided to do so. Still, he wasn't going to be pushed around, not he, and to show off his knowledge he went by a much longer and tortuous route over Hampstead Heath and through Highgate and Tottenham and Walthamstow. Thus it was well after eleven before they were out of London and reaching Brentwood.

When they were on the Chelmsford By-pass, Nigel said, "The shooter's O.K. and you've got your stocking. We can stuff the bread in this carrier. Let's have a look at the gloves."

Marty swore. "I knew there was something."

Nigel was about to lay into him when he realised that all this time Marty had been driving the van with ungloved hands, and that he too had put his ungloved hands on the doors and the dashboard shelf and the window catches, so all he said was, "We'll have to stop in Colchester and get gloves and we'll have to wipe this vehicle over inside."

"We can't stop," said Marty. "It's half eleven now."

"We have to, you stupid bastard. It wouldn't be half eleven if you hadn't taken us all round the houses."

It is twenty-three miles from Chelmsford to Colchester, and Marty made it in twenty minutes, somewhat to the distress of the Mini-van's engine. But there is virtually no on-street parking in Colchester, whose narrow twisty streets evince its reputation as England's oldest recorded town. They had to go into a multistorey car park, up to the third level, and then hunt for Woolworth's.

When the gloves were bought, woollen ones because cash was running short, they found they had nothing with which to wipe the interior of the van. Neither of them had handkerchiefs, so Nigel took off one of his socks. The rain, of which there had been no sign in London, was lashing down.

"It's twenty past twelve," said Marty. "We'll never make it. We'd better do it Wednesday instead."

"Look, little brain," Nigel shouted, "don't give me a hard time, d'you mind? How can we do it Wednesday? What're we going to use for bread? Just drive the bugger and don't give me grief all the goddamned time."

The narrower roads to Childon did not admit of driving at seventy miles an hour, but Marty, his hands in green knitted gloves, did make it. They put the van in the lane behind the bank, up against the flint wall. Nigel got out and came cautiously to the gap in the wall, and there he was rewarded.

A middle-aged man, thin, paunchy, with greased-down hair, came out of the back door and got into the car that stood on the forecourt.

Half an hour before, Mrs. Burroughs had come into the bank with a cheque drawn on the account of a firm of solicitors for twelve thousand pounds. She didn't explain its source but her manner was more high-handed than usual. Alan supposed it was a legacy and advised her not to put it in her Deposit Account but to open a new account under the Anglian-Victoria Treasure Trove scheme which gave a higher rate of interest. Mrs. Burroughs said offendedly that she couldn't possibly do that without consulting her husband. She would phone him at his office and come back at two.

The idea of Mrs. Burroughs, who lived in a huge house outside Childon and had a Scimitar car and a mink coat, acquiring still more wealth, depressed him so much that he broke his new rule and took the three thousand out of the safe while Joyce was busy talking about the price of beef with Mr. Wolford. Strange to think, as he often did, that it was only paper, only pictures of the Queen and a dead Prime Minister and a sort of super-nurse, but that it could do so much, buy so much, buy happiness and freedom and peace and silence. He tore one of the portraits of Florence Nightingale in half just to see what it felt like to do that, and then he had to mend it with Sellotape.

He heard Mr. Wolford go. There was no one else in the bank now and it was nearly ten to one. Joyce might easily come into his office, so he put the money into a drawer and went out to the lavatory where there was a washbasin to wash the money dirt off his hands. It looked like more rain was coming, but he'd go out just the same, maybe up to Childon Fen where the first primroses would be coming out and the windflowers.

Joyce was tidying up her till.

"Mr. Groombridge, is this all right? Mr. Wolford filled in the counterfoil and did the carbon for the bank copy. I don't know why I never saw it. Shall I give him a ring?"

Alan looked at the slip from the paying-in book. "No, that's O.K. So long as it's come out clear and it has. I'm off to lunch now, Joyce."

"Don't get wet," said Joyce. "It's going to pour. It's come over ever so black."

He wondered if she speculated as to where he went. She couldn't suppose he took the car just to the Childon Arms. But perhaps she didn't notice whether he took the car or not. He walked out to it now, the back door locking automatically behind him, and got into the driving seat—and remembered that the three thousand pounds was still in his desk drawer.

She wouldn't open the drawer. But the thought of it there, and not in the safe where it should have been, would spoil for him all the peace and seclusion of Childon Fen. After all, she knew his combination, if she still remembered it, just as he knew hers. Better put it away. He went back and into his office, pushed to but didn't quite close the door into the bank, and softly opened the drawer.

While he was doing so, at precisely one o'clock, Joyce came out from behind the metal grille, crossed the floor of the bank, and came face to face with Marty Foster and Nigel Thaxby. They were between the open oak door and the closed glass door and each was trying to pull a black nylon stocking over his head. They hadn't dared do this before they got into the porch, they had never rehearsed the procedure, and the stockings were wet because the threatening rain had come in a violent cascade during their progress from the van to the bank.

Joyce didn't scream. She let out a sort of hoarse shout and leapt for the glass door and the key that would lock it.

Nigel would have turned and run then, for the stocking was only pulled grotesquely over his head like a cap, but Marty dropped his stocking and charged at the door, bursting it open so that Joyce stumbled back. He seized her and put his hand over her mouth and jammed the gun into her side and told her to shut up or she was dead.

Nigel followed him in quite slowly. Already he was thinking, She's seen our faces, she's seen us. But he closed the oak door behind him and locked and bolted it. He closed and locked the glass door and walked up and stood in front of

Joyce. Marty took his hand from her mouth but kept the gun where it was. She looked at them in silence, and her face was very pale. She looked at them as if she were studying what they looked like.

From the office Alan Groombridge heard Joyce shout and he heard Marty's threat. He knew at once what was happening and he remembered, on a catch of breath, that conversation with Wilfred Summitt last Wednesday. His hands tightened on the bundle of notes, the three thousand pounds.

The Anglian-Victoria directed its staff to put up no resistance. If they could they were to depress with their feet one of the alarm buttons. The alarms were on a direct line to Stantwich police station where they set in motion a flashing-light alert system. If they couldn't reach an alarm, and in Joyce's case it was perhaps impossible, they were to comply with the demands of the intruders. There was an alarm button under each till and another under Alan's desk. He backed his right foot and put his heel to it, held his heel above it, and heard a voice say:

"We know you're on your own. We saw the manager go out."

Where had he heard that voice before, that curious and ugly mixture of cockney and Suffolk? He was sure he had heard it and recently. It was a very memorable voice because the combination of broad flat vowels with slurred or dropped consonants was so unusual. Had he heard it in the bank? Out shopping? Then the sense of the words struck him and he edged his foot forward again. They thought he was out, they must have seen him get into his car. Now he could depress the alarm without their having the faintest idea he had done so, and thereby, if he was very clever, save three thousand of the bank's money. Maybe save all of it once he'd remembered who that strange voice belonged to.

"Let's see what's in the tills, doll."

A different voice, with a disc jockey's intonation. He heard the tills opened. His foot went back again, feeling for the button embedded in the carpet. From outside there came a clatter of coins. A thousand, give or take a little, would be in those tills. He lifted his heel. It was all very well, that plan of his, but suppose he did save the three thousand, suppose he stuffed it in the clothes cupboard before they came in, how was he going to explain to the bank that he had been able to do so?

He couldn't hear a sound from Joyce. He lowered his heel, raised it again.

"Now the safe," the Suffolk or Suffolk-cockney voice said.

To reach it they must pass through the office. He couldn't press the alarm, not just like that, not without thinking things out. There was no legitimate reason why he should have been in his office with three thousand pounds in his hands. And he couldn't say he'd opened the safe and taken it out when he heard them come in because he wasn't supposed to know Joyce's combination. And if he'd been able to save three, why not six?

Any minute now and they would come into the office. They would stuff the notes and the coins—if they bothered with the coins—into their bag and then come straight through here. He pulled open the door of the cupboard and flattened himself against its back behind Joyce's evening dress, the hem of which touched the floor. Madam, is there any armour in your chamber that I might cover my poor body withal . . . ?

He had scarcely pulled the door closed after him when he heard Joyce cry out:

"Don't! Don't touch me!" And there was a clatter as of something kicked across the floor.

Lancelot's words reminded him of the questions he had asked himself on Saturday night. Would he ever have such panache, such proud courage? Now was the time. She was only twenty. She was a girl. Never mind the bank's suspicions, never mind now what anyone thought. His first duty was to rescue Joyce or at least stand with her and support her. He fumbled through the folds of the dress to open the door. He wasn't afraid. With a vague wry amusement, he thought that he wasn't afraid because he didn't mind if they killed him, he had nothing to live for. Perhaps all his life, with its boredom, its pain, and its futility, had simply been designed to lead up to this moment, meeting death on a wet afternoon for seven thousand pounds.

He would leave the money in the cupboard—he had thrust it into the pockets of his raincoat, which hung beside Joyce's dress—and go out and face them. They wouldn't think of looking in his raincoat, and later he'd think up an explanation for the bank. If there was a later. The important thing now was to go out to them, and this might even create a diversion in which Joyce could escape.

But before he touched the door, something very curious happened. He felt into the pockets to make sure none of the notes was sticking out and against his hands the money felt alive, pulsating almost, or as if it were a chemical that reacted at the contact with flesh. Energy seemed to come from it, rays of power, that travelled, tingling, up his arms. There were sounds out there. They had got the safe open. He heard rustling noises and thumps and voices arguing, and yet he did not hear them. He was aware only of the money alive between and around his fingers. He gasped and clenched his hands, for he knew then that he could not leave the money. It was his. By his daily involvement with it, he had made it his and he could not leave it.

Someone had come into the office. The drawers of his

desk were pulled out and emptied onto the floor. He stood
rigid with his hands in the coat pockets, and the cupboard
door was flung open.

He could see nothing through the dark folds of the dress.
He held his breath. The door closed again and Joyce swore
at them. Never had he thought he would hear Joyce use that
word, but he honoured her for it. She screamed and then she
made no more sound. The only sound was the steady roar of
rain drumming on the pantiled roof, and then, after a while,
the noise of a car or van engine starting up.

He waited. One of them had come back. The strange
voice was grumbling and muttering out there, but not for
long. The back door slammed. Had they gone? He could
only be sure by coming out. Loosening his hold on the
money, he thought he would have to go out, he couldn't stay
in that cupboard for the rest of his life. And Joyce must be
somewhere out there, bound and gagged probably. He
would explain to her that when he had heard them enter the
bank he had taken as much money as he had had time to
save out of the safe. She would think him a coward, but that
didn't matter because he knew he hadn't been a coward, he
had been something else he couldn't analyse. It was a
wrench, painful almost, to withdraw his hands from his
pockets, but he did withdraw them, and he pushed open the
door and stepped out.

The desk drawers were on the floor and their contents
spilt. Joyce wasn't in the office or in the room where the safe
was. The door of the safe was open and it was empty. They
must have left her in the main part of the bank. He hesitated. He wiped his forehead, on which sweat was standing.
Something had happened to him in that cupboard, he
thought, he had gone mad, mentally he had broken down.
The idea came to him that perhaps it was the life he led

which at last had broken him. He went on being mad. He took the money out of his coat pockets and laid it in the safe. He went to the back door and opened it quietly, looking out at the teeming rain and his car standing in the dancing, rain-pounded puddles. Then he slammed the door quite hard as if he had just come in, and he walked quite lightly and innocently through to where Joyce must be lying.

She wasn't there. The tills were pulled out. He looked in the lavatory. She wasn't there either. While he was in the cupboard, hesitating, she must have gone off to get help. Without her coat, which was also in the cupboard, but you don't think of rain at a time like that. Over and over to himself he said, I was out at lunch, I came back, I didn't know what had happened, I was out at lunch. . . .

Why had she gone instead of pressing one of the alarm buttons? He couldn't think of a reason. The clock above the currency-exchange rate board told him it was twenty-five past one and the date March 4th. He had gone out to lunch, he had come back and found the safe open, half the money gone, Joyce gone. . . . What would be the natural thing to do? Give the alarm, of course.

He returned to his office and searched with his foot under the desk for the button. It was covered by an upturned drawer. Kneeling down, he lifted up the drawer and found under it a shoe. It was one of the blue shoes with the instep straps Joyce had been wearing that morning. Joyce wouldn't have gone out into the rain, gone running out without one of her shoes. He stood still, looking at the high-heeled, very shiny, patent-leather, dark-blue shoe.

Joyce hadn't gone for help. They had taken her with them.

As a hostage? Or because she had seen their faces? People like that didn't have to have a reason. Did any people have to have a reason? Had he had one for staying in that cupboard? If he had come out they would have taken him too.

Press the button now. He had been out at lunch, had come back to find the safe open and Joyce gone. Strange that they had left three thousand pounds, but he hadn't been there, he couldn't be expected to explain it. If he had been there, they would have taken him too because he too would have seen their faces. He looked at his watch. Nearly twenty to two. Give the alarm now, and there would still be time to put up roadblocks, they couldn't have got far in twenty minutes and in this rain.

The phone began to ring.

It made him jump, but it would only be Pam. It rang and rang and still he didn't lift the receiver. The ringing brought into his mind a picture as bright and clear as something on colour television, but more real. Fitton's Piece and his house and Pam in it at the phone, Pop at the table in the dining recess, drinking tea, Jillian coming home soon, and Christopher. The television. The punk rock. The doors banging. The sports jacket, the army takeover, the gas bill. He let the phone ring and ring, and after twenty rings—he counted them—it stopped. But because it had rung, his madness had intensified and concentrated into a hard nucleus, an appalling and wonderful decision.

His mind was not capable of reasoning, of seeing flaws or hazards or discrepancies. His body worked for him, putting itself into his raincoat, stuffing the three thousand pounds into his pockets, propelling itself out into the rain and into his car. If he had been there they would have taken him with them too. He started the car, and the clear arcs made on the windscreen by the wipers showed him freedom.

6

They took Joyce with them because she had seen their faces. She had opened the safe when they told her to, though at first she said she could only work one of the dials. But when Marty put the gun in her ribs and started counting up to ten, she came out with the other combination. As soon as the lock gave, Nigel tied a stocking round her eyes, and when she cried out he tied the other one round her mouth, making her clench her teeth on it. In a drawer they found a length of clothesline Alan had bought to tie down the boot lid of his car but had never used, and with this they tied Joyce's hands and feet. Standing over her, Marty looked at Nigel and Nigel looked at him and nodded. Without a word, they picked her up and carried her to the back door.

Nigel opened it and saw the Morris 1100 in the yard. He didn't say anything. It was Marty who said, "Christ!" But the car was empty and the yard was deserted. Rain was falling in a thick cataract. Nigel rolled the plastic carrier round the money and thrust it inside his jacket.

"Where the hell's Groombridge?" whispered Marty.

Nigel shook his head. They splashed through the teaming rain, carrying Joyce out to the van, and dropped her on the floor in the back.

"Give me the gun," said Nigel. His teeth were chattering and the water was streaming out of his hair down his face.

Marty gave him the gun and got into the driver's seat with the money on his lap in the carrier bag. Nigel went back into the bank. He stumbled through the rooms, looking for Alan Groombridge. He meant to look for Joyce's shoe too, but it was more than he could take, all of it was too much, and he stumbled out again, the door slamming behind him with a noise like a gunshot.

Marty had turned the van. Nigel got in beside him and grabbed the bag of money and Marty drove off down the first narrow side road they came to, the windscreen wipers sweeping off the water in jets. They were both breathing fast and noisily.

"A sodding four grand," Marty gasped out. "All that grief for four grand."

"For Christ's sake, shut up about it. Don't talk about it in front of her. You don't have to talk at all. Just drive."

Down a deep lane with steep hedges. Joyce began to drum her feet on the metal floor of the van, thud, clack, thud, clack, because she had only one shoe on.

"Shut that racket," said Nigel, turning and pushing the gun at her between the gap in the seats. Thud, clack, thud . . . His fingers were wet with rain and sweat.

At that moment they came face to face, head-on, with a red Vauxhall going towards Childon. Marty stopped just in time and the Vauxhall stopped. The Vauxhall was being driven by a man not much older than themselves, and he had an older woman beside him. There was no room to pass. Joyce began to thrash about, banging the foot with the shoe on it, clack, clack, clack, and thumping her other foot, thud, thud, and making choking noises.

"Christ," said Marty. "Christ!"

Nigel pushed his arm through between the seats right up to his shoulder. He didn't dare climb over, not with those people looking, the two enquiring faces revealed so sharply each time the wipers arced. He was so frightened he hardly knew what he was saying.

With the gun against her hip, he said on a tremulous hiss, "You think I wouldn't use it? You think I haven't used it? Know why I went back in there? Groombridge was there and I shot him dead."

"Sweet Jesus," said Marty.

The Vauxhall was backing now, slowly, to where the lane widened in a little bulge. Marty eased the van forward, hunched on the wheel, his face set.

"I'll kill those two in the car as well," said Nigel, beside himself with fear.

"Shut up, will you? Shut up."

Marty moved past the car with two or three inches to spare, and brought up his right hand in a shaky salute. The Vauxhall went off and Marty said, "I must have been out of my head bringing you on this. Who d'you think you are? Bonnie and Clyde?"

Nigel swore at him. This reversal of roles was unbearable, but enough to shock him out of his panic. "You realise we have to get shot of this vehicle? You realise that? Thanks to you bringing us down a goddamned six-foot-wide footpath. Because that guy'll be in Childon in ten minutes and the fuzz'll be there, and the first thing he'll do is tell them about us passing him. Won't he? Won't he? So have you got any ideas?"

"Like what?"

"Like rip off a car," said Nigel. "Like in the next five minutes. If you don't want to spend the best years of your life inside, little brain."

Mrs. Burroughs phoned her husband at his office in Stantwich and asked him if he thought it would be all right for her to put Aunt Jean's money in the Anglian-Victoria Treasure Trove scheme. He said she was to do as she liked, it was all one to him if she hadn't enough faith in him to let him in-

vest it for her, and she was to do as she liked. So Mrs. Burroughs got into her Scimitar at two and reached the Anglian-Victoria at five past. The doors were still shut. Having
money of her own and not just being dependent on her husband's money had made her feel quite important, a person
to be reckoned with, and she was annoyed. She banged on
the doors, but no one came and it was too wet to stand out
there. She sat in the Scimitar for five minutes and when the
doors still didn't open she got out again and looked through
the window. The window was frosted, but on this, in clear
glass, was the emblem of the Anglian-Victoria, an A and a V
with vine leaves entwining them and a crown on top. Mrs.
Burroughs looked through one of the arms of the V and saw
the tills emptied and thrown on the floor. She drove off as
fast as she could to the police house two hundred yards
down the village street, feeling very excited and enjoying
herself enormously.

By this time the red Vauxhall had passed through Childon
on its way to Stantwich. Its driver was a young man called
Peter Johns who was taking his mother to visit her sister in
Stantwich General Hospital. They met a police car with its
blue lamp on and its siren blaring, indeed they came closer
to colliding with it than they had done with the Mini-van,
and these two near misses afforded them a subject for conversation all the way to the hospital.

At ten to three the police called on Mrs. Elizabeth Culver
to tell her the bank had been robbed and her daughter was
missing. Mrs. Culver said it was kind of them to come and
tell her so promptly, and they said they would fetch her husband, who was a factory foreman on the Stantwich indus-
trial estate. She went upstairs and put back into her wardrobe the dress she had been going to wear that evening,
and then she phoned the Toll House Hotel to tell them to
cancel the arrangements for the silver wedding party. She

meant to phone her sisters too and her brother and the
woman who, twenty-five years before, had been her brides-
maid, but she found she was unable to do this. Her husband
came in half an hour later and found her sitting on the bed,
staring silently at the wardrobe, tears streaming down her
face.

Pamela Groombridge was ironing Alan's shirts and inter-
mittently discussing with her father why the phone hadn't
been answered when she rang the bank at twenty to two
and two o'clock and again at three. In between discussing
this she was thinking about an article she had read telling
you how to put coloured transfers on ceramic tiles.

Wilfred Summitt was drinking tea. He said that he expected Alan had been out for his dinner.

"He never goes out," said Pam. "You know that, you were
sitting here when I was cutting his sandwiches. Anyway,
that girl would be there, that Joyce."

"The phone's gone phut," said Pop. "That's what it is, the
phone's out of order. It's on account of the lines being over-
loaded. If I had my way, only responsible ratepayers over
thirty'd be allowed to have phones."

"I don't know. I think it's funny. I'll wait till half-past and
then I'll try it again."

Pop said to mark his words, the phone was out of order,
gone phut, kaput, which wouldn't happen if the army took
over, and what was wanted was Winston Churchill to come
back to life and Field Marshal Montgomery to help him,
good old Monty, under the Queen of course, under Her Majesty. Or it just could be the rain, coming down cats and dogs
it was, coming down like stair rods. Pam didn't answer him.
She was wondering if the colour on those transfers would be
permanent or if it would come off when you washed them.
She would like to try them in her own bathroom, but not if

the colour came off, no thanks, that would look worse than plain white.

The doorbell rang.

"I hope that's not Linda Kitson," said Pam. "I don't want to have to stop and get nattering to her."

She went to the door, and the policeman and the policewoman told her the bank had been robbed and it seemed that the robbers had taken her husband and Joyce Culver with them.

"Oh, God, oh, God, oh, God," said Pam, and she went on saying it and sometimes screaming it while the policeman fetched Wendy Heysham and the policewoman made tea. Pam knocked over the tea and took the duty-free Bristol Cream out of the sideboard and poured a whole tumblerful and drank it at a gulp.

They fetched Christopher from the estate agent's and when he came in Pam was half drunk and banging her fists on her knees and shouting, "Oh, God, oh, God." Neither the policewoman nor Wendy Heysham could do anything with her. Christopher gave her another tumblerful of sherry in the hope it would shut her up, while Wilfred Summitt marched up and down, declaiming that hanging was too good for them, poleaxing was too good for them. After the electric chair, the poleaxe was his favourite lethal instrument. He would poleaxe them without a trial, he would.

Pam drank the second glass of sherry and passed out.

Wiser than those who had made his escape possible, Alan avoided the narrow lanes. He met few cars, overtook a tractor and a bus. The rain was falling too heavily for him to see the faces of people in other vehicles, so he supposed they would not be able to see his. There wasn't much petrol in the tank, only about enough to get him down into north

Essex, and of course it wouldn't do to stop at a petrol station.

His body was still doing all the work, and that level of consciousness which deals only with practical matters. He couldn't yet think of what he had done, it was too enormous, and he didn't want to. He concentrated on the road and the heavy rain. At the Hadleigh turn he came out onto the A.12 and headed for Colchester. The petrol gauge showed that his fuel was getting dangerously low, but in ten minutes he was on the Colchester By-pass. He turned left at the North Hill roundabout and drove up North Hill. There was a car park off to the left here behind St. Runwald's Street. He put the car in the car park, which was unattended, took out his sandwiches, locked the car, and dropped the sandwiches in a litter bin. Now what? Once they had found his car, they would ask at the station and the booking-office clerk would remember him and remember that he had passed through alone. So he made for the bus station instead where he caught a bus to Marks Tey. There he boarded a stopping train to London. His coat, which was of the kind that is known as showerproof and anyway was very old, had let the rain right through to his suit. The money had got damp. As soon as he had got to wherever he was going, he would spread the notes out and dry them.

There were only a few other people in the long carriage, a woman with two small boys, a young man. The young man looked much the same as any other dark-haired boy of twenty with a beard, but as soon as Alan saw him he remembered where he had heard that ugly Suffolk-cockney accent before. Indeed, so great was the resemblance that he found himself glancing at the boy's hands, which lay slackly on his knees. But of course the hands were whole, there was no mutilation of the right forefinger, no distortion of the nail.

The first time he had heard that voice it had asked him

for twenty five-pence pieces for a pound note. He had pushed the coins across the counter, looked at the young bearded face, thought, Am I being offhand, discourteous, because he's *young?* So he had put the coins into a bag and for a brief instant, but long enough to register, seen the deformed finger close over it and scoop it into the palm of the hand.

Suppose he had remembered sooner, this clue the police would seize on, would it have stopped him? He thought not. And now? Now he was in it as much as the man with the beard, the strange voice, the walnut fingernail.

Some sort of meeting was in progress in the village hall at Capel St. Paul, and among the cars parked in puddles on the village green were two Ford Escorts, a yellow and a silver-blue. The fifth key that Marty tried from his bunch unlocked the yellow one, but when he switched on the ignition he found there was only about a gallon of petrol in the tank. He gave that up and tried the silver-blue one. The tenth key fitted. The pointer on the gauge showed the tank nearly full. The tank of a Ford Escort holds about six gallons, so that would be all right. He drove off quickly, correctly guessing—wasn't he a country lad himself?—that the meeting had begun at two and would go on till four.

The van he had parked fifty yards up the road. They made Joyce get out at gunpoint and get into the Ford, and Marty drove the van down a lane and left it under some bushes at the side of a wood. There was about as much chance of anyone seeing them on a wet March afternoon in Capel St. Paul as there would have been on the moon. Marty felt rather pleased with himself, his nervousness for a while allayed.

"We can't leave her tied up when we get on the A-

Twelve," he said. "There's windows in the back of this motor. Right?"

"I do have eyes," said Nigel, and he climbed over the seat and undid Joyce's hands and took the gags off her mouth and her eyes. Her face was stiff and marked with weals where the stockings had bitten into her flesh, but she swore at Nigel and she actually spat at him, something she had never in her life done to anyone before. He stuck the gun against her ribs and wiped the spittle off his cheeks.

"You wouldn't shoot me," said Joyce. "You wouldn't dare."

"You ever heard the saying that you might as well be hung for a sheep as a lamb? If we get caught we go inside for life anyway on account of we've killed Groombridge. That's murder."

"Get it, do you?" said Marty. "They couldn't do any more to us if we'd killed a hundred people, so we're not going to jib at you, are we?"

Joyce said nothing.

"What's your name?" said Nigel.

Joyce said nothing.

"O.K., Miss J. M. Culver, be like that, Jane, Jenny, or whatever. I can't introduce us," Nigel said loudly to make sure Marty got the message, "for obvious reasons."

"Mr. Groombridge's got a wife and two children," said Joyce.

"Tough tit," said Nigel. "We'd have picked a bachelor if we'd known. If you gob at me again I'll give you a bash round the face you won't forget."

They turned onto the A.12 at twenty-five past two, following the same route Alan Groombridge had taken twenty minutes before. There was little traffic, the rain was torrential, and Marty drove circumspectly, neither too fast nor too slow, entering the fast lane only to overtake. By the time the police had set up one of their checkpoints on the Colchester By-pass, stopping all cars and heavier vehicles, the Ford Escort was passing Witham, heading for Chelmsford.

Joyce said, "If you put me out at Chelmsford I promise I won't say a thing. I'll hang about in Chelmsford and get something to eat, you can give me five pounds of what you've got there, and I won't go to the police till the evening. I'll tell them I lost my memory."

"You've only got one shoe," said Marty.

"You can put me down outside a shoe shop. I'll tell the police you had masks on and you blindfolded me. I'll tell them"—the greatest disguise Joyce could think of—"you were old!"

"Forget it," said Nigel. "You say you would but you wouldn't. They'd get it out of you. Make up your mind to it, you come with us."

The first of the rush traffic was leaving London as they came into it. This time Marty got on to the North Circular Road at Woodford, and they weren't much held up till they came to Finchley. From there on it was crawling all the way, and Marty, who had stood up to the ordeal better than Nigel, now felt his nerves getting the better of him. Part of the trouble was that in the driving mirror he kept his eye as much on those two in the back of the car as on the traffic behind. Of course it was all a load of rubbish about Nigel killing that bank manager, he couldn't have done that, and he wouldn't do anything to the girl either if she did anything to attract the attention of other drivers. It was only a question of whether the girl knew it. She didn't seem to. Most of the time she was hunched in the corner behind him, her head hanging. Maybe she thought other people would be indifferent, pass by on the other side like that bit they taught you in Sunday school, but Marty knew that wasn't so from the time when a woman had grabbed him and he'd only just escaped the store detective. He began to do silly things like cutting in and making other drivers hoot, and once he actually touched the rear bumper of the car in front with the front bumper of the Escort. Luckily for them, the car he touched had bumpers of rubber composition and its driver was easygoing, doing no more than call out of his window that there was no harm done. But it creased Marty up all the same, and by the time they got to Brent Cross his hands were jerking up and down on the steering wheel and he had stalled out twice because he couldn't control his clutch foot properly.

Still, now they were nearly home. At Staples Corner he turned down the Edgware Road, and by ten to five they were outside the house in Cricklewood, the Escort parked among the hundred or so other cars that lined the street on both sides.

Nigel didn't feel sympathy, but he could see Marty was spent, washed up. So he took the gun and pushed it into Joyce's back and made her walk in front of him with Marty by her side, his arm trailing over her shoulder like a lover's. On the stairs they met Bridey, the Irish girl who had the room next to Marty's, on her way to work as barmaid in the Rose of Killarney, but she took no notice of them beyond saying an offhand hallo. She had often seen Nigel there before and she was used to Marty bringing girls in. If he had brought a girl's corpse in, carrying it in his arms, she might have wondered about it for a few minutes, but she wouldn't have done anything, she wouldn't have gone to the police. Two of her brothers had fringe connections with the I.R.A. and she had helped overturn a car when they had carried the hunger-strike martyr's body down from the Crown to the Sacred Heart. She and her whole family avoided the police.

Marty's front door had a Yale lock on it and another, older, lock with a big iron key. They pushed Joyce into the room and Nigel turned the iron key. Marty fell on the mattress, face-downwards, but Joyce just stood, looking about her at the dirt and disorder, and bringing her hands together to clasp them over her chest.

"Next we get shot of the vehicle," said Nigel.

Marty didn't say anything. Nigel kicked at the mattress and lit the wick of the oil heater—it was very cold—and then he said it again. "We have to get shot of the car."

Marty groaned. "Who's going to find it down there?"

"The fuzz. You have to get yourself together and drive it some place and dump it. Right?"

"I'm knackered." Marty heaved himself up and pushed a pile of dirty clothes onto the floor. "I got to have a drink."

"Yeah, right, later, when we've got that car off our backs."

"Christ," said Marty, "we've got four grand in that bag and I can't have a fucking drink."

Nigel gritted his teeth at that. He couldn't understand why there hadn't been seven like that guy Purford said. But he managed, for Jane or Jenny's benefit, a mid-Atlantic drawl. "I'll drive it. You stay here with her. We'll tie her up again, put her in the kitchen. You'll go to sleep, I know you, and if she gets screeching the old git next door'll freak."

"No," said Joyce.

"Was I asking you? You do as you're told, Janey."

They got hold of Joyce and gagged her again and tied her hands behind her and tied her feet. Marty took off her shoe to stop her making noises with her feet and shut the kitchen door on her. She made noises, though not for long.

The rain had stopped and the slate-grey sky was barred with long streaks of orange. Nigel and Marty got as far away from the kitchen door as they could and talked in fierce whispers. When the traffic slackened Nigel would take the car and dispose of it. They looked longingly at Marty's radio, but they dared not switch it on.

7

For a couple of hours the police suspected Alan Groombridge. No one had seen the raiders enter the bank. They set
up roadblocks just the same and informed the Groombridge
and Culver next of kin. But they were suspicious. According
to his son and his father-in-law, Groombridge never went
out for lunch, and the licencee of the Childon Arms told
them he had never been in there. At first they played with
the possibility that he and the girl were in it together, and
had gone off together in his car. The presence of Joyce's
shoe made that unlikely. Besides, this theory presupposed
an attachment between them which Joyce's father and
Groombridge's son derided. Groombridge never went out in
the evenings without his wife, and Joyce spent all hers with
Stephen Hallam.

A girl so devoted to her family as Joyce would never have
chosen this particular day for such an enterprise. But had
Groombridge taken the money, overturned the tills, left the
safe open, and abducted the girl by force? These were ideas
about which a detective inspector and a sergeant hazily
speculated while questioning Childon residents. They were
soon to abandon them for the more dismaying truth.

By five they were back where they had started, back to a
raid and a double kidnapping. A lot of things happened at
five. Peter Johns, driver of the red Vauxhall, heard about it
on the radio and went to the police to describe the white
Mini-van with which he had nearly collided. Neither he nor

his mother could describe the driver or his companion, but Mrs. Johns had something to contribute. As the van edged past the Vauxhall, she thought she had heard a sound from the back of the van like someone drumming a heel on the floor. A single clack-clack-clack, Mrs. Johns said, as of one shoe drumming, not two.

The next person to bring them information was the driver of a tractor who remembered meeting a Morris 1100. The tractor man, who had a vivid imagination, said the driver had looked terrified and there had certainly been someone sitting beside him, no doubt about it, and his driving had been wild and erratic. There had been three bank robbers then, the police concluded, two to drive the van with Joyce in it, the third in Alan Groombridge's car, compelling him to drive. The loss of the silver-blue Ford Escort was reported by its owner, a Mrs. Beech.

By then Nigel Thaxby and Marty Foster and Joyce Culver were in Cricklewood and Alan Groombridge was in the Maharajah Hotel in the Shepherds Bush Road.

Literature had taught him that there were all sorts of cheap hotels and houses of call and disreputable lodging places in the vicinity of Paddington Station, so he went there first on the Metropolitan Line out of Liverpool Street. But times had changed, the hotels were all respectable and filled up already with foreign tourists and quite expensive. The reception clerk in one of them recommended him to Mr. Aziz (who happened to be his cousin) and Alan liked the name, feeling it was right for him. It reminded him of *A Passage to India* and seemed a good omen.

Staying in hotels had not played an important part in his life. Five years before, when Mrs. Summitt had died, she had left Pam two hundred pounds and they had spent it on a proper holiday, staying at a hotel in Torquay. Luggage they had had, especially Pam and Jillian, an immense amount of it, and he wondered about his own lack of even a suitcase. He had read that hotelkeepers are particular about that sort of thing.

The Maharajah was a tall late-nineteenth-century house built of brown brick with its name on it in blue neon, the first H and the J being missing. Yes, Mr. Aziz had a single room for the gentleman, Mr. Forster, was it? Four pounds, fifty, a night, and pay in advance if he'd be so kind. Alan need not have worried about his lack of luggage because Mr. Aziz, who was only after a fast buck, wouldn't have cared what he lacked or what he had done, so long as he paid in advance and didn't break the place up.

Alan was shown to a dirty little room on the second floor where there was no carpet or central heating or washbasin, but there was a sink with a cold tap, a gas ring and kettle and cups and saucers, and a gas fire with a slot meter. He locked himself in and emptied his bulging pockets. The sight of the money made his head swim. He closed his eyes and put his head onto his knees because he was afraid he would faint. When he opened his eyes the money was still there. It was real. He spread it out to dry it, and he hung his raincoat over the back of a chair and kicked off his wet shoes and looked at the money. Nearest to him lay the portrait of Florence Nightingale which he had torn in half and mended with Sellotape.

Outside the window the sky was like orangeade in a dirty glass. The noise was fearful, the roar and throb and grind and screeching of rush traffic going round Shepherds Bush Green and into Chiswick and up to Harlesden and over to Acton and down to Hammersmith. The house shook. He lay on the bed, tossed about like someone at the top of a tree in a gale. He would never sleep, it was impossible that he would ever sleep again. He must think now about what he had done and why and what he was going to do next. The madness was receding, leaving him paralysed with fear and a sensation of being incapable of coping with anything. He must think, he must act, he must decide. Grinding himself to a pitch of thinking, he shut his eyes again and fell at once into a deep sleep.

Nigel delayed till half-past six, waiting for the traffic to ease up a bit. As far as he was concerned, when you drove a car your right foot was for the accelerator and the brake and your left one for nothing. He got into the Escort and started it and it leapt forward and stalled, nearly hitting the Range Rover in front of it because Marty had left it in bottom gear. Nigel tried again and more or less got it right, though the gears made horrible noises. He moved out into the traffic, feeling sick. But there was no time for that sort of thing because it was a full-time job ramming his left foot up and down and doing exercises with his left hand. He didn't know where he was aiming for and it wouldn't have been much use if he had. His knowledge of London was sparse. He could get from Notting Hill to Oxford Street and from Notting Hill to Cricklewood on buses, and that was about all.

The traffic daunted him. He could see himself crashing the car and having to abandon it and run, so he turned it into a side road in Willesden and sat in it for what seemed like hours, watching the main road until there weren't quite so many cars and buses going past. It hadn't been hours at all, it was still only a quarter past seven. He had some idea where he was when he found himself careering uncertainly down Ladbroke Grove, and after that signs for south of the river began coming up. He would take it over one of the bridges and dump it in South London.

He was scared stiff. He wished he had some way of knowing what was going on and how much the police had found out. The way to have found out was from Marty's radio which the girl would have heard, and heard too that Groombridge was alive. Luckily, he'd managed to whisper to Marty not to switch it on. He was so thick, that one, you never knew what he'd do next.

The manual gear shift was getting easier to handle. He tried breathing deeply to calm himself, and up to a point it worked. What he really ought to do was hide the car somewhere where it wouldn't be found for weeks. He knew he was a conspicuous person, being six feet tall and with bright fair hair and regular features, not little and dark and ordinary like Marty. People wouldn't be able to remember Marty but they'd remember him.

He turned right out of Ladbroke Grove and drove down Holland Park Avenue to Shepherds Bush and along the Shepherds Bush Road, thus passing the Maharajah Hotel and forming one of the constituents of the noise that throbbed in Alan Groombridge's sleeping brain. On to Hammersmith and over Putney Bridge. There were still about two gallons in the tank. In Wandsworth he put the car down an alley which was bounded by factory walls and where there was no one to see him. It was a relief to get out of it, though he knew he couldn't just leave it there. He had grabbed a handful of notes out of the carrier. In these circumstances, Marty would have wanted a drink, but stress had made Nigel ravenously hungry. There was a Greek cafe just down the street. He went in and ordered himself a meal of kebab and *taramasalata*.

He might just as easily have chosen the fish and chip place or the Hong Kong Dragon, but he chose the Greek cafe and it gave him an idea. Beginning on his kebab, Nigel glanced at a poster on the cafe wall, a coloured photograph of Heraklion. This reminded him that before he had worked round to the subject of a loan, he had listened with half an

ear to his mother's usual gossip about her friends. This had
included the information that the Boltons were going off for
a month to Heraklion. Wherever that might be, Nigel
thought, Greece somewhere. Dr. Bolton, now retired, and
his Greek wife, whom he was supposed to (or had once
been supposed to) call Uncle Bob and Auntie Helena, lived
in a house near Epping Forest. He had been there once,
about seven years before, and now he recalled that Dr. Bolton kept his car in a garage, a sort of shed really, at the bottom of his garden. An isolated sort of place. The car would
now be in the airport car park, for his mother had said they
were going last Saturday. Would the garage be locked?
Nigel tried to remember if there had been a lock on the door
and thought there hadn't been, though he couldn't be certain after so long. If there was and he couldn't use the garage, he would push the car into one of the forest ponds.
Thinking about the Boltons brought back to him that visit
and how he, aged fourteen, had listened avidly to Dr. Bolton's account of a stolen car that had been dumped in a
pond and not found for weeks.

He left the cafe at nine and returned cautiously to the
alley. The Ford Escort was still there and no other car was.
He got quickly into the car and drove off, this time crossing
the river by Wandsworth Bridge.

It took him nearly an hour to get out to Woodford, and he
had some very bad moments when a police car seemed to be
following him after the lights at Blackhorse Road. But the
police car turned off and at last he was approaching the Boltons' house, which was down a sort of lane off the Epping
New Road. The place was as remote and lonely as he remembered it, but right outside the garage, on the miserable
little bit of pavement that dwindled away into a path a few
yards on, four men were digging a hole. They worked by the
light of lamps run from a generator in a Gas Board van

parked close by. Nigel thought he had better back the car out and pretend to be using the entrance to the lane only as a place for turning. It was only the second time he had got into reverse gear, and he bungled it, getting into first instead and nearly hitting the Gas Board van. But he tried again and managed a reasonable three-point turn, observing exultantly that there was no lock on the garage door and no padlock either. But he couldn't park on the Epping New Road itself, which was likely, he thought, to be a favourite venue for traffic-control cars.

He drove a bit further, stuck the Escort under some bushes off the Loughton Road, and went into a phone box to phone Marty.

The receiver was handed to Marty by the pale red-haired girl, who looked as if she were permanently kept shut up in the dark. She passed it to him without a word. He didn't say anything to Nigel except yes and no and all right and see you, and then he went back to do as he was told and untie Joyce.

She was cramped and cold and stiff, and for the first time her spirit was broken. She said feebly, "I want to go to the toilet."

"O.K., if you must," said Marty, not guessing or even wondering what it had cost her to lie out there for hours, controlling her bladder at all costs, hoping to die before she disgraced herself in that way.

He went out first, making sure there was no one there, and brandishing the gun. He stood on the landing while she was in the lavatory. Bridey was out, and no light showed under Mr. Green's door. He always went to bed at eight-thirty, besides being deaf as a post. Marty took Joyce back and locked the door again with the big iron key, which he pocketed. Joyce sat on the mattress, rubbing her wrists and her ankles. He would have liked a cup of coffee, would have liked one hours ago, but something in him had baulked at making coffee for himself in front of a bound and gagged girl. Nor could he make it now and keep her covered with the gun. So he fetched in a half-full bottle of milk and poured it into two cups.

"Keep your filthy milk," Joyce mumbled.

"Be like that." Marty drank his and reached for the other cup.

"No, you don't," said Joyce, and swigged hers down. "When are you going to let me go?"

"Tomorrow," said Marty.

Joyce considered this. She looked around her. "Where am I supposed to sleep?"

"How about on here with me?"

The remark and the circumstances would immediately have recalled to Alan Groombridge's mind Faulkner's *Sanctuary* or even *No Orchids for Miss Blandish*, but in fact Marty had said what he had out of bravado. Being twenty-one and healthy, he naturally fancied pretty well every girl he saw, and in a different situation he would certainly have fancied big-busted long-legged Joyce. But he had never felt less sexy in his adult life, and he had almost reached a point where, if she had touched him, he would have screamed. Every sound in the house, every creak of stair and click of door, made him think it was the police coming. The sight of the unusable radio tormented him. Joyce, however, was resolved to sell her honour dear. She summoned up her last shreds of scorn, told him he had to be joking, she was engaged to someone twice his size who'd lay him out as soon as look at him, and she'd sleep on the sofa, thanks very much. Marty let her take two of the four pillows off his bed, watched her sniff them and make a face, and grab for herself his thickest blanket.

She lay down, fully clothed, covered herself up, and turned her face to the big greasy back of the sofa. Under the blanket she eased herself out of her skirt and her jumper, but kept her blouse and her slip on. Marty sat up, holding the gun and wishing there was some wine.

"Put the light out," said Joyce.

"Who're you giving orders to? You can get stuffed."

He was rather pleased when Joyce began to cry. She was deeply ashamed of herself but she couldn't help it. She was thinking about poor Mr. Groombridge and about her mother and father not having their party, and about Stephen. It was much to her credit that she thought about herself hardly at all. But those others, poor Mum and Dad, Stephen going to announce their engagement at the Toll House that night, Mr. Groombridge's poor wife, so devoted to him and ringing him at the bank every day. Joyce sobbed loudly, giving herself over to the noblest of griefs, that which is expended for others. Marty had been pleased at first because it showed his power over her, but now he was uneasy. It upset him, he'd never liked seeing birds cry.

"You'll be O.K.," he said. "Belt up, can't you? We won't hurt you if you do what we say. Honest. Get yourself together, can't you?"

Joyce couldn't. Marty switched the light off, but the room didn't get dark, never got dark, because of the yellow lamps outside. He got into bed and put the gun under the pillow and stuffed his fingers in his ears. He felt like crying himself. What the hell was Nigel doing? Suppose he didn't come back? The room vibrated with Joyce's crying. It was worse than the traffic when the lorries and the buses went by. Then it subsided, it stopped, and there was silence. Joyce had cried herself to sleep. Marty thought the silence worse than the noise. He was terribly hungry, he craved for a drink, and he hadn't been to bed at this hour since he was fifteen.

At the point when he had almost decided to give up, to get out of there and run away somewhere, leaving the money to Joyce, there came a tapping at the door. He jumped out of his skin and his heart gave a great lurch. But the tap came again and with it a harsh tired whisper. It was only Nigel, Nigel at last.

Joyce didn't stir but he kept his voice very low.

"Had to hang about till the goddamned gasmen went. The car's in the garage. I walked to Chingford and got a bus. Christ!"

Nigel dropped the bunch of Ford keys into the carrier bag with the money. He found a bit of string in the kitchen and threaded it through the big iron key and hung it round his neck. They turned off the oil heater. They put the gun under the pillows and got into bed. It was just after midnight, the end of the longest day of their lives.

8

When Alan woke up he didn't know where he was. The room was full of orange light. Great God (as Lord Byron had remarked the morning after his wedding, the sun shining through his red bed curtains) I am surely in hell! Then he remembered. It all came back to him, as Joyce would have said. The time, according to his watch, was five in the morning, and the light came from streetlamps penetrating a tangerine-coloured blind which he must have pulled down on the previous evening. He had slept for eleven hours. The money, now dry and crinkly, glimmered in the golden light. Great God, I am surely in hell. . . .

He got out of bed and went into the passage and found the bathroom. There was a notice inside his bedroom door which said in strange English: *The Management take no responsibilities for valuable left in rooms at owners risks.* He put the money back in his raincoat pockets, afraid now of walking about with his pockets bulging like that. All night he had slept in his clothes, and his trousers were as crumpled as the notes, so he took them off and put them under the mattress, which was a way of pressing trousers advocated by Wilfred Summitt. He took off the rest of his clothes and got back into bed, listening to the noise outside that had begun again. The noise seemed to him symptomatic of the uproar which must be going on over his disappearance and Joyce's and the loss of the money, the whole world up in arms.

It struck him fearfully that, once Joyce was set free or rescued, she would tell the police he hadn't been in the bank when the men came. He thought about that for a while, sweating in the cold room. She would tell them, and they would begin tracing his movements from the car to the bus station, the bus to the train. He saw himself as standing out in all those crowds like a leper or a freak or—how had Kipling put it?—a mustard plaster in a coal cellar. But she might not know. It all depended on whether they had blindfolded her and also on how many of them there had been. If she had seen his car still in the yard, and then they had blindfolded her and put her in their car or van for a while before driving away . . . He clung on to that hope, and he thought guiltily of Pam and his children. In her way, Pam had been a good wife to him. It seemed to him certain that, whatever came of this, he would never live with her again, never again share a bed with her or go shopping with her to Stantwich or yield to her for the sake of peace. That was past and the bank was past. The future was liberty or the inside of a jail.

At seven he got up and, wearing his raincoat as a dressing gown, went to have a bath. The water was only lukewarm because, although he had three thousand pounds in his pockets, he hadn't got a ten-pence piece for the meter. Shivering, he put his clothes on. The trousers didn't look too bad. He packed the money as flat as he could, putting some of it into his jacket pockets, some into his trouser pockets, and the rest in the breast pocket of his jacket. It made him look fatter than he was. Mr. Aziz didn't provide breakfast or, indeed, any meals, so he went out to find a place where he could eat.

Immediately when he was in the street, he felt a craven fear. He must be a marked man, he thought, his face better known than a royal prince's or a pop star's. It didn't occur to him then that it had never been a habit in the Groombridge or Summitt families to sit for studio portraits or go in for ambitious amateur photography, and therefore no large recognisable image of his face could exist. By some magic or some feat of science, it would be brought to the public view. He slunk into a newsagent's, trying to see without being seen, but the tall black headlines leapt at him. He stood looking at a counter full of chocolate bars until he dared to face those headlines again.

It was Joyce's portrait, not his own, that met his eyes, Joyce photographed by Stephen Hallam to seem almost beautiful. *Bank Girl Kidnap*, said one paper; another, *Manager and Girl Kidnapped in Bank Raid*. He picked up both papers in hands that shook and proffered a pound note. The man behind the counter asked him if he had anything smaller. Alan shook his head, he couldn't speak.

He had forgotten about breakfast and wondered how he could ever have thought of it. He sat on a bench on Shepherds Bush Green and forced himself to look at those papers, though his instinct, now he had bought them, was to throw them away and run away from them himself. But he took a deep breath and forced his eyes onto those headlines and that smaller type.

Before he could find a picture of himself, he had to look on the inside pages. They had put it there, he thought, because it was such a poor likeness, useless for purposes of identification, and adding no character to the account. Christopher had taken the snapshot of himself and Pam and Wilfred Summitt in the garden of the house in Hillcrest. Enlarged, and enlarged only to about an inch in depth, Alan's face was a muzzy grinning mask. It might equally well have been Constable Rogers or P. Richardson standing there beside the pampas grass.

The other newspaper had the same picture. Were there

any others in existence? More vague snapshots, he thought. At his wedding, that shotgun affair, gloomy with disgrace, there had been no photographers. He became aware that the paralysis of terror was easing. It was sliding from him as from a man healed and made limber again. He saw the mist and the pale sun, the grass, other people, felt the renewal of hunger and thirst. If he couldn't be recognised, identified, he had little to fear. The relief of it, the slow easing that was now quickening and acquiring a sort of excitement, drove away any desire to read any more of the newspaper accounts. He forgot Joyce, who even now might be safe, might be at home once more with only a vague memory of events. He was safe and free, and he had got what he wanted.

A cup of tea and eggs and toast increased his sense of well-being. The papers he dropped thankfully into a bin. After a few minutes' exploration, he found the tube station and got a train to Oxford Circus. Oxford Street, he knew, was the place to buy clothes. Every Englishman, no matter how sheltered the life he has led, knows that. He bought two pairs of jeans, four tee-shirts, some socks and underpants and a windcheater, two sweaters and a pair of comfortable half boots. Jeans had never been permitted him in the past, for Pam said they were only for the young, all right for Christopher but ridiculous on a man of his age. He told himself he was buying them as a disguise, but he knew it wasn't only that. It was to recapture—or to discover, for you cannot recapture what you have never had—his youth.

He came out of the shop wearing his new clothes, and this transformation was another step towards ridding him of the fear of pursuit. People, even policemen, passed him without a second glance. Next he bought a suitcase, and in a public lavatory deep below the street, he filled it with his working suit and that money-loaded raincoat.

The case was too cumbersome to carry about for long. No ardent reader of fiction could for long be in doubt about where temporarily to rid himself of it. He caught a train to Charing Cross, and there deposited the case in a left-luggage locker. At last he and the money were separated. Walking away, with only his wallet filled as he had so often filled it during those secret indulgences in his office, he felt a lightness in his step as if, along with the money, he had disburdened himself of culpability. So he made his way up to Trafalgar Square. He went into the National Gallery and the National Portrait Gallery and looked at the theatres in St. Martin's Lane and the Charing Cross Road, and had a large lunch with wine. Tonight he would go to the theatre. In all his life he had never really been to the theatre except once or twice to Stantwich Rep. and to pantomimes in London when the children were younger. He bought himself a ticket for the front row of the stalls, row A and right in the middle, for Marlowe's *Faustus*.

Next to the theatre was a flat agency. It reminded him that he would need somewhere to live, he wasn't going to stay at the Maharajah longer than he had to. But it wouldn't be a flat. A few seconds spent studying the contents of the agency's window told him anything of that nature would be beyond his means. But a room at sixteen to twenty pounds a week, that he could manage.

The girl inside gave him two addresses. One was in Maida Vale and the other in Paddington. Before he could locate either of them, Alan had to buy himself a London guide. He went to the Paddington address first because the room to let there was cheaper.

The landlord came to the door with an evening paper in his hand. Alan saw that he and Joyce were still the lead story, and his own face was there again, magnified to a featureless blur. The sight of it revived his anxiety, but the landlord put the paper down on a table and invited him in.

Alan would have taken the room, though it was sparsely furnished and comfortless. At any rate, it would be his to improve as he chose, and it was better than the Maharajah. The landlord too seemed happy to accept him as a tenant so long as he understood he had to pay a month's rent in advance and a deposit. Alan had got out his wallet and was preparing to sign the agreement as A. J. Forster when the landlord said:

"I take it you can let me have a bank reference?"

The blood rushed into Alan's face.

"It's usual," said the landlord. "I've got to protect myself."

"I was going to pay you in cash."

"Maybe, but I'll still want a reference. How about your employer or the people where you're living now? Haven't you got a bank?"

In the circumstances, the question held a terrible irony. Alan didn't know what to say except that he had changed his mind, and he got out of the house as fast as he could, certain the landlord thought him a criminal, as indeed he was. No one knew more than he about opening bank accounts. It was impossible for him to open one, he had no name, no address, no occupation, and no past. Suddenly he felt frightened, out there in the alien street with no identity, no possessions, and he saw his act not so much as an enormity as an incredible folly. In all those months of playing with the bank notes, he had never considered the practicalities of an existence with them illicitly in his possession. Because then it had been a dream and now it was reality.

He could go on living, he supposed, at the Maharajah. But could he? At four pounds, fifty, a night, that little hole with its sink and its gas ring was going to cost him as much as one of the flats he had seen on offer in the agency window.

He couldn't go on staying there, yet he wouldn't be able to find anywhere else because it was "usual" to ask for a bank reference.

Occasionally in the past he had received letters asking for such a reference, and his replies had been discreet, in accordance with the bank's policy of never divulging to any outsider the state of a customer's account. He had merely written that, yes, so-and-so banked at his branch of the Anglian-Victoria, and that apparently had been satisfactory. He felt sick at the thought of where his own account was—with the Childon subbranch and in a name that today was familiar to every newspaper reader.

An idea came to him of returning home. It wasn't too late to go back if he really wanted to. He could say they had taken him and had let him go. He had been blindfolded all the time, so he hadn't seen their faces or where they had taken him. The shock had been so great that he couldn't remember much, only that he had saved some of the bank's money which he had deposited in a safe place. Perhaps it would be better not to mention the money at all. Why should they suspect him if he ·gave himself up now?

It was a quarter past three. It was not on his watch but on a clock on a wall ahead of him that he saw the time. And beside the clock, on a sheet of frosted glass, were etched the A and the V, the vine leaves and the crown, that were the emblems of the Anglian-Victoria Bank. The Anglian-Victoria, Paddington Station Branch. Alan stood outside, wondering what would happen if he went in and told the manager who he was.

He went into the bank. Customers were waiting in a queue behind a railing until a green light came on to tell them a till was free. A tremendous impulse took hold of him to announce that he was Alan Groombridge. If he did that now, in a few days' time he would be back behind his own till, driving his car, listening to Pam talking about the cost of living, to Pop quarrelling with Christopher, reading in the evenings in his own warm house. He set his teeth and clenched his hands to stop himself yielding to that impulse, though he still stood there at the end of the queue.

Steadily the green lights came on, and one customer moved to a till, then another. Alan stayed in the queue and shifted with it as it passed a row of tables spread with green blotters. A man was sitting at one of the tables, making an entry in his paying-in book. Alan watched him, envying him his legitimate possession of it.

The time was half-past three, and the security man moved to the door to prevent any late-comer from entering. Alan began framing words in his mind, how he had lost his memory, how the sight of that emblem had recalled to him who he was. But his clothes? How could he explain his new clothes?

Looking down at those jeans brought his eyes again to the man at the table. The paying-in book was open for anyone to see that two hundred and fifty pounds was about to be paid in, though Paul Browning hadn't been so imprudent as actually to place notes or cheques on it. Alan knew he was called Paul Browning because that was the name he had just written on a cheque-book request form. And now he added under it, in the same block capitals, his address: 15 Exmoor Gardens, London N.W.2.

As a green light came up for the woman immediately in front of Alan in the queue, Paul Browning joined it to stand behind him. With a muttered "Excuse me," Alan turned and made for the door.

He had found a bank reference and an identity, and with the discovery he burned the last fragile boat that could have taken him back. The security man let him out politely.

9

Joyce woke up first. With sleep, her confidence and her courage had come back. The fact that the others—those two pigs, as she called them to herself—still slept on, made her despise more than fear them. Fancy sleeping like that when you'd done a bank robbery and kidnapped someone! They must want their heads tested. But while she despised them, she also felt easier with them than she would have done had they been forty or fifty. Disgusting and low as they were, they were nevertheless young, they belonged with her in the great universal club of youth.

She got up and put on her clothes. She went into the kitchen and washed her hands and face under the cold tap, a good cold splash like she always had in the mornings, though she usually had a bath first. Pity she couldn't clean her teeth. What was there to eat? No good waiting for those pigs to provide something. Like the low people they were, they had no fridge, but there was an unopened packet of back bacon on a shelf of that bookcase thing, and some eggs in a box and lots of tins of baked beans. Joyce had a good look at the bacon packet. It might be a year old, for all she knew, you never could tell with people like that. But, no. *Sell by March 15th*, it said. She put the kettle on, and Flora margarine into a frying pan, and lit all the other gas burners and the oven to warm herself up.

The misery of Mum and Dad and Stephen she had got into better perspective. She wasn't dead, was she? Stephen

would value her all the more when she turned up alive and
kicking. They were going to let her go today. She wondered
how and where, and she thought it would be rather fun telling it all to the police and maybe the newspapers.

The roaring of the gas woke Marty and he saw Joyce
wasn't on the sofa. He called out, "Christ!" and Joyce came
in to stand insolently in the doorway. There are some people
who wake up and orient themselves very quickly in the
mornings, and there are others who droop about, half asleep,
for quite a long time. Joyce belonged in the first category and Marty in the second. He groaned and fumbled for
the gun.

"For all you know," said Joyce, "I might have a couple of
detectives out here with me, waiting to arrest you."

She made a big pot of strong tea and found a packet of
extended-life milk. Nasty stuff, but better than nothing. She
heard Marty starting to get up and she kept her head
averted. He might be stark naked for all she could tell,
which was all right when it was Stephen or one of her
brothers coming out of the bathroom, but not that pig. However, he was wearing blue pants with mauve bindings, and
by the time he had come into the kitchen he had pulled on
jeans and a shirt.

"Give us a cup of tea."

"Get it yourself," said Joyce. "You can take me to the toilet first."

She was a full five minutes in there, doing it on purpose,
Marty thought. He was on tenterhooks lest Bridey came out
or old Green. But there was no one. The lavatory flushed
and Joyce walked back, not looking at him. She passed
Nigel, who was sitting on the mattress with his head in his
hands, and went straight to the sink to wash her hands. All
the bacon in the pan, two eggs, and a saucepanful of baked

beans went onto the plate she had heated for herself. She sat
down at the kitchen table and began to eat.

Nigel was obliged to pour tea for both of them and start
cooking more bacon. He did it clumsily because he too was
a slow waker. "One of us'll have to go out," he said, "and
get a paper and more food."

"And some booze, for Christ's sake," said Marty.

"How about me going?" said Joyce pertly.

"Be your age," said Nigel, and to Marty, "You can go. I'll
be better keeping an eye on her."

Joyce ate fastidiously, trying not to show how famished
she was. "When are you going to let me go?"

"Tomorrow," said Marty.

"You said that yesterday."

"Then he shouldn't have," snapped Nigel. "You stay here.
Get it? You stay here till I'm good and ready."

Joyce had believed Marty. She felt a little terrible tremor,
but she said with boldness, "If he's going out he can get me
a pair of shoes."

"You what? That'd be marvellous, that would, me getting
a pair of girl's shoes when they know you've lost one."

"Get her a pair of flip-flops or sandals or something. You
can go to Marks in Kilburn. She'll only get a hole in her
tights and then we'll have to buy goddamned tights."

"And a toothbrush," said Joyce.

Marty pointed to a pot, encrusted with blackened soap, in
which reposed a toothbrush with splayed brown tufts.

"Me use that?" said Joyce indignantly. She thought of the
nastiest infection she could, of one she'd seen written on the
wall in the ladies' on Stantwich Station. "I'd get crabs."

Nigel couldn't help grinning at that. They ate their breakfast and Marty went off, leaving Nigel with the gun.

Joyce wasn't used to being idle, and she had never been

in such a nasty dirty place before. She announced, without asking Nigel's permission, that she intended to clean up the kitchen.

Marty would have been quite pleased. He didn't clean the kitchen himself because he was too lazy to do so, not because he disapproved of cleaning. Nigel did. He had left home partly because his parents were always cleaning something. He sat on the mattress and watched Joyce scrubbing away, and for the first time he felt some emotion towards her move in him. Until then he had thought of her as an object or a nuisance. Now what he felt was anger. He was profoundly disturbed by what she was doing, it brought up old half-forgotten feelings and unhappy scenes, and he kept the gun trained on her, although her back was turned and she couldn't see it.

About an hour later Marty tapped at the door, giving the four little raps that was their signal to each other. He threw a pair of rubber-thonged sandals onto the floor and dropped the shopping bag. His face was white and pinched.

"Where's Joyce?"

"That's her name, is it? In the kitchen, spring-cleaning. What's freaking you?"

Marty began taking a newspaper, folded small, out of his jacket pocket. "No," said Nigel. "Outside." They went out onto the landing and Nigel locked the door behind them. He spread out a copy of the same newspaper Alan Groombridge had read some hours before. "I don't get it," he said. "What does it mean? We never even saw the guy."

"D'you reckon it's some sort of trick?"

"I don't know. What would be the point? And why do they say seven thousand when there was only four?"

Marty shook his head. "Maybe the guy did see us and got scared and went off somewhere and lost his memory." He voiced a fear that had been tormenting him. "Look, what you said to the girl about killing him—that wasn't true, was it?"

Nigel looked hard at him and then at the gun. "How could it be?" he said slowly. "The trigger doesn't even move."

"Yeah, I meant—well, you could have hit him over the head, I don't know."

"I never saw him, he wasn't there. Now you tear up that paper and put the bits down the bog. She's got to go on thinking we've killed Groombridge and we've got to get out of here and get her out. Right?"

"Right," said Marty.

Joyce finished cleaning the kitchen and then she cleaned her teeth with the toothbrush Marty had bought. She had to use soap for this, and she had heard that cleaning your teeth with soap turned them yellow, but perhaps that was only if you went on doing it for a long time. And she wasn't going to be there for a long time because tomorrow they were going to let her go.

Nigel sharply refused to allow her to go down to the bathroom, so she washed herself in the kitchen with a chair pushed hard against the door. Her mother used to make a joke about this fashion of getting oneself clean, saying that one washed down as far as possible and up as far as possible, but what happened to poor possible? Thinking of Mum brought tears to Joyce's eyes, but she scrubbed them away and scrubbed poor possible so hard that it gave her a reason for crying. After that she washed for herself to wear tomorrow the least disreputable of Marty's tee-shirts from the pile on the bed. She wasn't going to confront the police and be reunited with her family in a dirty dishevelled state, not she.

Marty went out again at seven and came back with whisky and wine and Chinese takeaway for the three of

them. Joyce ate hers in the kitchen, at the table. The boys
had theirs sitting on the living-room floor. The place was
close and fuggy and smelly from the oil heater and the oven,
which had been on all day, and condensation trickled down
the inside of the windows. When she had finished eating,
Joyce walked in and looked at Nigel and Marty. The gun
was on the floor beside the plastic pack with chow mein in
it. They didn't use plates, pigs that they were, thought
Joyce.

She had never been the sort of person who avoids issues
because it is better not to know for certain. She would
rather know.

"You're going to let me go tomorrow," she said.

"Who said?" Nigel put his hand over the gun. He forgot
to be a mid-Atlantic-cum-sixties-hippy-drop-out and spoke,
to Marty's reluctant admiration, in the authoritative public
school tone of his forbears. "There's no question of your
leaving here tomorrow. You'd go straight to the police and
describe us and describe this place. We took you with us to
avoid that happening and the situation hasn't changed." He
remembered then and added, with a nasal intonation, "No
way."

"But the situation won't change," said Joyce.

"I could kill you, couldn't I? Couldn't I?" He watched her
stiffen and then very slightly recoil. It pleased him. "You be
a good girl," he said, "and do what we say and stop asking
goddamned silly questions, and I'll think of a way to work it
for the lot of us. I just need a bit of hush. Right?"

"Have a drop of scotch," said Marty, who was cheered
and made affable by about a quarter of a pint of it. Joyce
wouldn't. Nor would she accept any of the Yugoslav Ries-
ling that Nigel was drinking. If the situation hadn't changed
and wasn't going to change, she would have to think of
ways to change it. The first duty of a prisoner is to escape.

Her uncle who had been a prisoner of war always said that, though he had never succeeded in escaping from the *Stalag Luft* in which for four years he had been incarcerated. She had never thought of escaping before because she had believed they would release her, but she thought about it now.

When they had settled down for the night and the boys were asleep, Marty snoring more loudly than her father did —Joyce had formerly thought young people never snore—she got up off the sofa and tiptoed into the kitchen. Earlier in the day she had found a ballpoint pen while scraping out thick greasy dirt from under the sink, and she had left it on the draining board, not supposing then that she would have any use for it. She hadn't much faith in this pen, which had probably been there for years, perhaps before the time of the present tenant. But once she had wiped the tip of it carefully on the now clean dishcloth and scribbled a bit on the edge of a matchbox to make the ink flow, she found it wrote quite satisfactorily. Enough light came in from outside to make writing, if not reading, possible. Like Alan Groombridge, Joyce found the constant blaze of light shining in from streetlamps throughout the night very strange, but it had its uses. She sat at the table and wrote on a smoothed-out piece of the paper bag in which the sandals had been:

"They have killed Mr. Groombridge. They are keeping me in a room in London." She crossed out "London" and wrote "in this street, I do not know the name of the street or the number of the house. There are two of them. They are young, about twenty. One of them is little and dark. The first finger on his right hand has been injured. The nail is twisted. The other one is tall and fair. Please get me out. They are dangerous. They have a gun. Signed, Joyce Marilyn Culver."

Joyce thought she would wrap her message round the piece of pumice stone from the draining board and drop it out of the window. But she couldn't open the window, though neither of the boys seemed to hear her struggling with it. Never mind, the lavatory window opened and she would throw it out of there in the morning. So for the time being she put the note in that traditional repository favoured by all heroines in distress, her bosom. She put it into the cleft between her breasts, and went back to the sofa. But first she favoured her captors with a look of contempt. If she had been in their place, she thought, she would have insisted on staying awake while her partner slept, and only sleeping while he stayed awake to watch. Look where getting drunk and passing out had got them! But in the yellow light the string with the key on it showed round the dark one's neck, and the black barrel of the gun gleamed dully against the fair one's slack hand.

At nine she was up and washed and dressed and shaking Marty, who woke with a blinding headache and much hung over.

"Go away. Leave me alone," said Marty, and he buried his face in the dirty pillow.

"If you don't get up and take me to the toilet I'll bang and bang at that door with a chair. I'll break the window."

"Do that and you're dead," said Nigel, elbowing Marty out of the way and fishing out the gun. He had gone to bed fully clothed, and it was out of distaste for the smell of him that Joyce looked in the other direction. Nigel took her out onto the landing and leaned against the wall, seeing stars and feeling as if an army of goblins in hobnailed boots were forming fours inside his head. He mustn't drink like that again, it was crazy. He wasn't hooked on the stuff like that little brain, was he? He didn't even really like it.

Joyce had her message wrapped round the pumice stone. She stood on the lavatory seat, wishing she could see something of what lay outside and below the window, but it was only a frosted fanlight that opened and this above her head, though not above the reach of her hand. The pumice dropped, and she trembled least it make a bang which the fair one might hear when it touched the ground. She pulled the flush hard to drown any other sound.

The other one glowered at her when they were back in the room. "What d'you think you're doing, wearing my tee-shirt?"

"I've got to change my clothes, haven't I? I'm not going to stay in the same thing day after day like you lot. I was brought up to keep myself nice. You want to take all that lot round the launderette. What's the good of me cleaning the place up when it just pongs of dirty clothes?"

Neither of them answered her. Marty took the radio to the lavatory with him, but he couldn't get anything out of it except pop music. Then he went off shopping without waiting for Nigel's command. The open air comforted him. He was a country boy and used to spending most of his time outside, all his jobs but the parcel-packing one had been outdoor jobs, and even when living on the dole he had spent hours wandering about London each day and walking on Hampstead Heath. He couldn't stand being shut up, scared as he was each time he saw a policeman or a police car. Nigel, on the other hand, liked being indoors, he didn't suffer from claustrophobia. He liked dirty little rooms with shut windows where he could loaf about and dream grandiose Nietzschean dreams of himself as the Superman with many little brains and stupid women to cringe and do his bidding. The stupid woman was cleaning again, the living room this time. Let her get on with it if that was all she was fit for.

On her knees, washing the skirting board, Joyce said, "Have you thought yet? Have you thought when I'm going to get out of here?"

"Look," said Nigel, "we're looking after you O.K., aren't we? You're getting your nosh, aren't you? And you can drink as much liquor as you want, only you don't want. I know this pad isn't amazing, but it's not that bad. You aren't getting ill-treated."

"You must be joking. When are you going to let me go?"

"Can't you say anything else but when are you going to get out of here?"

"Yes," said Joyce. "What's your name?"

"Robert Redford," said Nigel, who had been told he resembled this actor in his earliest films.

"When am I going to get out of here, Robert?"

"When I'm ready, Joyce. When my friend and I see our opportunity to get ourselves safely out of the country and don't have to worry about you giving the police a lot of damaging information."

Joyce stood up. "Why don't you talk like that all the time?" she said with an ingenuous look. "It sounds ever so nice. You could have a really posh accent if you liked."

"Oh, piss off, will you?" said Nigel, losing his temper. "Just piss off and give me a bit of hush."

Joyce smiled. She had never read Dr. Edith Bone's account of how, when condemned in Hungary to seven years' solitary confinement, she never missed a chance to needle and provoke her guards, while never in the slightest degree co-operating with them. She had not read it, but she was employing the same tactics herself.

10

The police were told of a silver-blue Ford Escort seen on the evening of Monday, 4 March, in the Epping New Road. Their informant was one of the gang of gasmen who had been working on a faulty main outside Dr. Bolton's house, and the car he had seen had in fact been Mrs. Beech's car and its driver Nigel Thaxby. But when the police had searched Epping Forest for the car and dragged one of the gravel-pit ponds, they abandoned that line of enquiry in favour of a more hopeful one involving the departure of a silver-blue Escort from Dover by the ferry to Calais on Monday night. This car, according to witnesses, had been driven by a middle-aged man with a younger man beside him and a man and a girl in the back. The man in the back seemed to have been asleep, but might have been unconscious or drugged. No one had observed the registration plates.

Alan Groombridge's car was found in the car park in Colchester. His fingerprints were on its interior and so were those of his wife. There were several other sets of fingerprints, and these came from the hands of a Stoke Mill farm worker to whom Alan had given a lift home on the previous Tuesday. But the police didn't know this, and it didn't occur to the farm worker to tell them. By that time they had questioned Christopher and Jillian Groombridge about their friends and anyone to whom they might have talked and given information about the Childon branch of the Anglian-Victoria Bank.

At first it seemed likely that the leak had come from Christopher, he being male and the elder. But it was soon clear that Christopher had never shown the slightest interest in any of the bank's arrangements, was ignorant as to how much was kept in the safe, and hadn't those sort of friends anyway. All his friends were just like himself, law-abiding, prosperous salesmen, or belonging to fringe professions like his own, well-dressed, affluent, living at home in order the better to live it up. They regarded crime as not so much immoral as "a mug's game." As for Jillian, she made an impression on them of naïve innocence. All her time away from home, she said, had been spent with Sharon and Bridget, and Sharon and Bridget backed her up. They wouldn't, in any case, have been able to give the name of John Purford because they didn't know it. Perhaps there had been no leak, for nothing need have been divulged which local men couldn't have found out for themselves. On the other hand, the Mini-van, located soon after Mrs. Beech's complaint, had been hired in Croydon by a man with a big black beard who spoke, according to the Relyacar Rentals girl, with a North Country accent. So the police, having turned Stantwich and Colchester and quite a large area of South London upside down, turned their attention towards Humberside and Cleveland.

Wilfred Summitt and Mrs. Elizabeth Culver appeared on television, but neither put up satisfactory performances. Mrs. Culver broke down and cried as soon as the first question was put to her, and Pop, seeing this as an opportunity to air his new dogmas, launched into a manifesto which opened with an appeal for mass public executions. He went on talking for a while after he had been cut off in midsentence, not realising he was no longer on view.

Looking for somewhere to live, Alan left the suitcase in a locker at Paddington Station. At the theatre he had put it under his seat where it annoyed no one because he was sitting in the front row. He had enjoyed *Faustus,* identifying with its protagonist. He too had sold his soul for the kingdoms of the earth—and, incidentally, for three thousand pounds. See, see where Christ's blood streams in the firmament! He had felt a bit like that himself, looking at the sunset while earlier he was walking in Kensington Gardens. Would he also find his Helen to make him immortal with a kiss? At that thought he blushed in the dark theatre, and blushed again, thinking of it, as he walked from Paddington Station down towards the Bayswater Road.

Notting Hill, he had decided, must be his future place of abode, not because he had ever been there or knew anything about it, but because Wilfred Summitt said that wild horses wouldn't drag him to Notting Hill. He hadn't been there either, but he talked about it as a sort of Sodom and Gomorrah. There had been race riots there in the fifties and some more a couple of years back, which was enough to make Pop see it as a sinful slum where everyone was smashed out of their minds on hashish, and black people stuck knives in you. Alan went to two agencies in Notting Hill and was given quite a lot of hopeful-looking addresses. He went to three of them before lunch.

It was an unpleasant shock to discover that London landlords call a room ten feet by twelve, with a sink and cooker in one corner, a flatlet. He could hardly believe in the serious, let alone honest, intent behind calling two knives and two forks and two spoons from Woolworth's "fully equipped with cutlery" or an old three-piece suite in stretch nylon covers "immaculate furnishings." Having eaten his lunch in a pub—going into pubs was a lovely new experience—he bought an evening paper and a transistor radio, and read the

paper sitting on a seat in Kensington Gardens. It told him
that the Anglian-Victoria Bank was offering a reward of
twenty thousand pounds for information leading to the arrest of the bank robbers and the safe return of himself and
Joyce. A girl came and sat beside him and began feeding pigeons and sparrows with bits of stale cake. She was so much
like his fantasy girl, with a long slender neck and fine delicate hands and black hair as smooth and straight as a skein
of silk, that he couldn't keep from staring at her.

The second time she caught his eye, she smiled and said it
was a shame the way the pigeons drove the smaller birds
away and got all the best bits, but what could you do? They
also had to live.

Her voice was strong and rich and assured. He felt shy of
her because of her resemblance to the fantasy girl, and because of that too he was aware of an unfamiliar stirring of
desire. Was she his Helen? He answered her hesitantly and
then, since she had begun it, she had spoken to him first,
and anyway he had a good reason for his question, he asked
her if she lived nearby.

"In Pembroke Villas," she said. "I work in an antique
shop, the Pembroke Market."

He said hastily, not wanting her to get the wrong idea—
though would it be the wrong idea?—"I asked because I'm
looking for a place to live. Just a room."

She interrupted him before he could explain how disillusioned he had been. "It's got much more difficult in the past
couple of years. A good way used to be to buy the evening
papers as soon as they come on the streets and phone places
straightaway."

"I haven't tried that," he said, thinking of how difficult it
would be, using pay phones and getting enough change, and
more and more nights at the Maharajah, and thinking too

how exciting and frightening it would be to live in the same house as she.

"You sometimes see ads in newsagents' windows," she said. "They have them in the window of the place next to the Market."

Was it an invitation? She had got up and was smiling encouragingly at him. For the first time he noticed how beautifully dressed she was, just the way his private black-haired girl had been dressed in those dreams of his. The cover of *Vogue*, which he had seen in Stantwich paper shops but which Pam couldn't afford to buy—coffee-coloured suede suit, long silk scarf, stitched leather gloves, and nut-brown boots as shiny as glass.

"May I walk back with you?" he said.

"Well, of course."

It was quite a long way. She talked about the difficulty of getting accommodations and told anecdotes of the experiences of friends of hers, how they had found flats by this means or that, their brushes with landlords and rent tribunals. She herself owned a floor of the house in which she lived. He gathered that her father was well-off and had bought it for her. Her easy manner put him at his ease, and he thought how wonderful it was to talk again, to have found, however briefly, a companion. Must their companionship be brief?

Outside the Pembroke Market she left him.

"If you're passing," she said, "come in and let me know how you've got on." Her smile was bold and inviting, yet not brazen. He wouldn't have cared if it had been. He thought, he was sure, she was waiting for him to ask if he could see her before that, if he could see her that evening. But paralysis overcame him. He could be wrong. How was he to know? How did one ever tell? She might simply be being helpful and friendly, and from any overture he made, turn on her heel in disgust.

So he just said, "Of course I will, you've been very kind," and watched her walk away, fancying he had seen disappointment in her face.

There were no ads for accommodations in the newsagent's window, only cards put there by people who wanted rooms or had prams and pianos and kittens for sale, and an unbelievable one from a girl offering massage and "very strict" French lessons. As he was turning away, the back of the case in which the cards were was suddenly opened inwards and a hand appeared. When he looked back, he saw that a new card had been affixed. Doubtfully—because what sort of an inhabitable room could you get for ten pounds a week?— he read it: 22 Montcalm Gardens, W.11. He looked up Montcalm Gardens in his London guide, and found that it turned off Ladbroke Grove at what he was already learning to think of as the "nice" end. A boy of about twenty was looking over his shoulder. Alan thought he too must be looking for a room, and if that was so he knew who was going to get there first. The room might be all right, it was bound to be better than the Maharajah. His legs were weary, so he did another first-time thing and, copying gestures he had seen successfully performed by others, he hailed and acquired a taxi.

The name on the card had been Engstrand and it had immediately brought to Alan's mind old man Jacob and Regina in Ibsen's *Ghosts*. One branch of the Forsyte family had lived in Ladbroke Grove. Such literary associations were pleasant to think of. He himself was like a character in a book on the threshold of adventure and perhaps of love.

In Montcalm Gardens two long terraces of tall early Victorian houses eyed each other austerely across a straight wide roadway. The street was treeless, though thready branches of planes could be seen at the far end of it. It had an air of dowdy, but not at all shabby, grandeur. There were little balconies on the houses with railings whose supports were like the legs of Chippendale chairs, and each house had, at the top of a flight of steps, a porch composed of pilasters and a narrow flat roof. The first thing he noticed about number twenty-two was how clean and sparkling its windows were, and that inside the one nearest the porch stood surely a hundred narcissi in a big copper bowl.

The door was opened to him by a woman he supposed must be Mrs. Engstrand. She looked inquiringly at him, her head a little on one side.

"I saw your advertisement . . ." he began.

"Already? I only put it in half an hour ago. I've just got back."

"They were putting it in when I saw it."

"Well, you mustn't stand there. Do come in." Her voice was both vague and intense, an educated voice which he wouldn't have expected from the look of her. She wore no make-up on her pale small face that seemed to peep out from, to be engulfed by, a mass of thick brown curly hair. Had she really been out, dressed like that, in denims with frayed hems and a sweater with a hole at one elbow? She looked about thirty, maybe more.

He went in, and she closed the door behind him. "I'm afraid the room's in the basement," she said. "I'm telling you that now in case you've got any sort of *thing* against basements."

"I don't think so," said Alan. From what he could see of the hall, and, through an open door, of the interior of a room, the house was very beautifully, indeed luxuriously, furnished. There were those things in evidence that make for an archetype of domestic beauty: old carefully polished

furniture, precious ornaments, pictures in thin silver frames,
a Chinese lacquer screen, chairs covered in wild silk, long
and oval mirrors, more spring flowers in shallow bowls. And
there was exquisite cleanliness. What would he be offered
here for ten pounds a week? A cupboard under the stairs?

Downstairs in the basement was a kind of hall, with white
walls and carpeted in red haircord. He waited to be shown
the cupboard. She opened a door and he saw instead something like that which he had expected to see at the first
house he had visited, before he was disillusioned.

She said, "It's big, at any rate, and it really isn't very
dark. The kitchen's through there. Tenants have the use of
the garden. I'm afraid anyone who took this room would
have to share the bathroom with Mr. Locksley, but he's very
very nice. He's got the front room."

This one was large, with french windows. One wall was
hung all over with shelves, and the shelves were full of
books. The furniture wasn't of the standard of upstairs, but
it was good Victorian furniture, and on the floor was the
same haircord as in the passage. It looked new, as if no one
had ever walked on it. He looked out of the window at a
lawn and daffodils and two little birch trees and a peaked
black-brick wall, overgrown with ivy.

"That's the chapel of a convent. There are lots of con-
vents round here. It's Cardinal Manning country. The Ob-
lates of St. Charles, you know."

He said, "Like in that essay by Lytton Strachey."

"Oh, have you read *that?*" He turned round and saw that
her intense birdlike little face was glowing. "Isn't it lovely?"
she said. "I read it once every year. *Eminent Victorians* is
up there on the top shelf. Oh, do you mind the books?
They're nearly all novels, you see, and there isn't anywhere
else for them because my father-in-law can't bear novels."

He was bewildered. "Why not?"

"He says that fiction causes most of our troubles because

it teaches us to fantasise and lead vicarious lives instead of
coming to terms with reality. He's Ambrose Engstrand, you
know."

Alan didn't know. He had never heard of Ambrose Engstrand. Did she mean he could have the room? "I can give
you a bank reference," he said. "Will that do?"

"I *hate* having to ask for one at all," she said earnestly. "It
seems so awfully rude. But Ambrose said I must. As far as
I'm concerned, anyone who likes *Eminent Victorians* is all
right. But it's Ambrose's house and I do have to do what he
says."

"My name is Browning," Alan said. "Paul Browning. Fifteen, Queens Vale, Highgate—that's my present address. My
bank's the Anglian-Victoria, Paddington Station Branch."
He hesitated. "D'you think I could move in this week?"

"Move in today if you like." She pushed back her thick
massy hair with both hands, smiled at his amazement. "I
didn't mean I was really going to write to that bank. I shall
just let Ambrose think I have. Caesar—that's Mr. Locksley—
hasn't even got a bank. Banks don't mean anything. I've
proved that because he always pays his rent on the dot, and
I knew he'd be lovely because he knows all Shakespeare's
sonnets by heart. Can you believe it?"

His head swimming, Alan said he was very grateful and
thank you very much, and he'd move in that evening. He
went back to Paddington Station and fetched the suitcase
and went into a cafe to have a cup of tea. He was Paul
Browning, late of Northwest Two (wherever that might be),
now of Montcalm Gardens, Notting Hill. It was by this
name that he would introduce himself to the black-haired
girl tomorrow when he went to the Pembroke Market to tell
her what had happened. Tomorrow, though, not today.
Quite enough had happened today. He needed peace and
quiet to collect his thoughts and make himself a design for
living.

11

Joyce Culver's father offered his house, or the price that house would fetch when sold, for the safe return of his daughter. It was all he had.

Marty and Nigel saw it in the paper.

"What's the good of a house or the bread it'll fetch," said Nigel, "if you're inside?"

"We could make him promise not to tell the fuzz. And then he could sell the place and give us the money."

"Yeah? And just why would he do that thing once he'd got her back? Be your age."

They were talking in low voices on the landing. Joyce was in the lavatory, dropping another note out of the window, this time wrapped round the metal lid of a glass jar. Even in a normal dwelling house, and Marty's place was far from that, it is difficult to find an object which is at the same time heavy enough to drop, unbreakable, and small enough to conceal on one's person. She couldn't see where it fell. She didn't know that under the window was an area containing five dustbins, and that Brent Council refuse collectors had already thrown the pumice stone and the paper round it into the crushing machine at the back of their truck. One of the dustbin lids had blown off, and Joyce's second note dropped into the bin on top of a parcel of potato peelings deposited there by Bridey on the previous night.

"When am I going to get out of here?" said Joyce, emerging.

"Keep your voice down." Nigel was aghast, in spite of the absence of Bridey and the deafness of Mr. Green.

"When am I going to get out of here!" yelled Joyce at the top of her voice.

Marty clapped his hand over her mouth and manhandled her back into the room. She felt the gun thrust against her ribs, but she was beginning to have her doubts about the gun, she was beginning to get ideas about that.

"If you do that again," said Marty, "you can pee in a pot in the kitchen."

"Charming," said Joyce. "I suppose that's what you're used to, I suppose that's what goes on in whatever home you come from. Or pig sty, as I should call it. Got an Elsan in a hut at the end of your garden, have you? I shouldn't be at all surprised."

She held up her head and glared at him. Marty was beginning to hate her, for the shot had gone home. She had precisely described the sanitary arrangements in his father's cottage. It was Thursday, and they had been shut up in here since Monday night. Why shouldn't they just get out and leave her here? They could tie her up to the gas stove or something so she couldn't move. And then when they'd got safe away they could phone the police, make one of those anonymous calls, and tell them where she was. He thought that would work. It was Nigel, whispering out there on the landing or when Joyce was washing—she was always washing—who said it wasn't on. Where could they go, he said, where the call couldn't be traced from? Once give them this address, anyway, and they'd know who Marty was and very soon who Nigel was. They might just as well go and give themselves up now. Nigel had said he had a plan, though he didn't say what it was, and Marty thought the plan must be all hot air and Nigel didn't know what to do any more than he did.

His only consolation was that he could have an unlimited amount to drink. Yesterday he had drunk more than half a bottle of whisky and today he was going to finish it and start on the next one. He couldn't understand why Nigel had begun being nice to Joyce, buttering her up and flattering her. What was the point when it was obvious the only way was to put the fear of God into her? Nigel had got him to buy her *Woman* and *Nineteen* and made him take the sheets and pillowcases to the launderette on the corner. Nigel, who liked dirt and used to say being clean was bourgeois! He poured himself a cupful of whisky.

"You can get me some wool and some needles next time you go out," said Joyce. "I need a bit of knitting to pass the time."

"I'm not your slave."

"Do as she says," said Nigel. "Why not if it keeps her happy?"

The room was spotlessly clean. Joyce had even washed the curtains, and Nigel, with the aid of sign language and a pencil and paper, had borrowed an iron from Mr. Green so that she could iron them and iron her own freshly washed blouse. Marty thought he must be off his head, that wasn't the way to break her spirit. He glowered at her resentfully. She looked as if she were just about to set off for work in a job where one's appearance counted for a lot.

Two hours earlier she had washed her hair. She had on a crisp neat blouse and a creaseless skirt, and now she was filing her nails. That was another thing Nigel had got him to fetch in, a nail file, and he'd said something about mascara. But Marty had jibbed at that. He wasn't buying bloody silly mascara, no way.

Nigel didn't say much all that day. He was thinking. Marty made him sick with his silly ideas and the way, most

of the time, he was smashed out of his mind on whisky. He
ought to be able to see they couldn't get shot of Joyce.
Where they went she must go. Only he knew they couldn't
take her out into the street with them, couldn't steal another
car while she was with them. Yet she must be with them,
and the only way she could was if she could somehow be
made to be on their side. It was with some vague yet
definite aim of getting her on his side that Nigel had started
being nice to her. That was why he made Marty buy things
for her and praised her appearance and the cleanliness of
the place—though he hated it—and why, that evening he got
Marty to fetch in three great hunks of T-bone because Joyce
said she liked steak.

There had been robberies, he thought, in which hostages
had been so brainwashed by their captors that they had
gone over to the kidnappers' side and had even assisted in
subsequent raids. Nigel didn't want to do any Symbionese
Liberation Army stuff, he had no doctrines with which to in-
doctrinate anyone, but there must be other ways. By Friday
morning he had thought of another way.

He lay on the mattress in the yellow light that was the
same at dawn as at midnight, shifting his body away from
Marty, who snored and smelt of sweat and whisky, and
looking at the plump pale curve of Joyce's cheek and her
smooth pink eyelids closed in sleep. He got up and went
into the kitchen and looked at himself in Marty's bit of broken mirror over the sink. Beautiful blue eyes looked back at
him, a straight nose, a mobile delicately cut mouth. Any
polone'd go for me in a big way, thought Nigel, and then he
remembered he mustn't use that word and why he mustn't,
and he was flooded with fear.

Marty went out and brought back brown knitting wool
and two pairs of needles and some proper toilet soap and
toothpaste—and two more bottles of whisky. They didn't

bother to count the money or ration it or note what they had spent. Marty just grabbed a handful of notes from the carrier each time he left. He bought expensive food and things for Joyce and, in Nigel's opinion, quantities of rubbish for himself, pornography from the Adult Book Exchange and proper glasses to put his whisky in and, now he could afford to smoke again, cartons of strong king-size cigarettes. And he stayed out longer and longer each day. Skiving off his duties, leaving him to guard Joyce, thought Nigel. It maddened him to see Marty sitting there, making them all cough with the smoke from his cigarettes, and gloating over those filthy magazines. He found he was embarrassed for Joyce when Marty looked at those pictures in front of her, but he didn't know why he should be, why he should care.

Joyce scarcely noticed and didn't care at all. She had the attitude of most women to pornography, that it was disgusting and boring and its lure beyond her comprehension. She was having interesting ideas about the gun. One of them was that it wasn't loaded, and the other that it wasn't a real gun. She had written on all her notes—there was a third one tucked inside her bra—that they had killed Alan Groombridge, but now she wondered if this were true. She only had their word for it, and you couldn't believe a word they said. It might be a toy gun. She had read that robbers used toy guns because of the difficulty of getting real ones. It would be just like them to play about with a toy gun. If she could get her hands on that gun and find out that it was only a toy or not loaded, she would be free. She might not be able to unlock the door because the key was on a string round Nigel's neck, but she would be able to run when they took her to the lavatory, or break one of the windows at night and scream.

But how was she ever going to get hold of the gun? They kept it under their pillows at night, and though Marty was a

heavy sleeper, Nigel wasn't. Or Robert, as she thought of
him, and the dark one, as she thought of Marty. Sometimes
she had awakened in the night and looked at them, and
Robert had stirred and looked back at her. That was unnerv-
ing. Maybe one night, if the police didn't come and no one
found her notes, Robert would get drunk too and she would
have her chance. She had stopped thinking much about
Mum and Dad and Stephen, for when she did so she
couldn't keep from crying. And she wasn't going to cry, not
even at night, not in front of them. She thought instead
about the gun and ways of getting hold of it, for she had as
little faith in any plan Robert might concoct as the dark one
had. They would keep her there forever unless she escaped.

They ate smoked trout and Greek takeaway and cream
trifle from Marks and Spencers on Friday night, and Marty
drank half a bottle of Teacher's. Everything was bought
ready-cooked because Marty and Nigel couldn't cook and
Joyce wouldn't cook for them. Joyce sat on the sofa with her
feet up to stop either of them sitting there too. She had already completed about six inches of the front of her jumper,
and she knitted away resolutely.

"The fact is," she said, "you don't know what to do with
me, do you? You got yourselves in a right mess when you
brought me here and now you don't know how to get out of
it. My God, I could rob a bank single-handed better than
the two of you did. No more than a pair of babes in arms
you are."

Nigel kept his temper and even smiled. He could look
pleasantly little-boyish when he smiled. "Maybe you've got
something there, my love. We made a mistake about that.
We all make mistakes."

"I don't," said Joyce arrogantly. "If you do what's right
and keep to the law and face up to your responsibilities and
get steady jobs you don't make mistakes."

"Shut up!" screamed Marty. "Shut your trap, you bitch! Who d'you think you are, giving us that load of shit? You want to remember you're our prisoner."

Joyce smiled at him slowly. She made one of the few profound statements she was ever to utter.

"Oh, no," she said. "I'm not your prisoner. You're mine."

12

The man called Locksley came home while Alan was putting his clothes away and stowing the money in one of the drawers of a Victorian mahogany tallboy. The door of the next room closed quietly, and for about an hour there penetrated through the wall soft music of the kind Alan thought was called baroque. He liked it and was rather sorry when it stopped and Locksley went out again.

The house was quiet now, the only sound the distant one of traffic in Ladbroke Grove. This surprised him. Since his landlady had a father-in-law, she must also surely have a husband and very likely, at her age, small children. But Alan felt that he was now alone in the house, though this couldn't be so as, through the french window, he could see light from upstairs shining on the lawn. The two radiators in his room had come on at six, and it was pleasantly warm, but there didn't seem to be any hot water or anything to provide it. After looking in vain for some switch or meter, he went upstairs to find Mrs. Engstrand.

He knocked on the door of the room from which the light was coming. She opened it herself and there was no one with her. She was still wearing the jeans and the sweater, not the long evening skirt he had somehow expected.

"I'm terribly sorry. There's an immersion heater in that cupboard outside your door and you share it with Caesar. I expect he's switched it off. I must tell him to leave it on *all*

the time now you've come. I'll come down with you and
show you."

He only caught a glimpse of the interior of the room, but
that was enough. A dark carpet, straw-coloured satin curtains, silk-papered walls, Chinese porcelain, framed photographs of a handsome elderly man and an even handsomer
young one.

"Caesar's very considerate." She showed him the heater
and the switch. "He's always trying to save me money but it
really isn't necessary. I pay the bills for this part of the
house, you see, so Ambrose won't ever see them."

He didn't understand what she meant and he was too shy
to enquire. Shyness stopped him asking her in for a drink,
though he had drinks, having stocked up with brandy and
vodka and gin on his way there. The bottles looked good on
top of the tallboy. Maybe when the husband turned up,
young Engstrand, he'd invite the two of them and this
Caesar and the black-haired girl. It would give him an excuse for asking her.

That night and again in the morning he listened to his
radio. There was nothing about Joyce or himself, for no
news is not good news as far as the media are concerned. He
bought a paper in which the front page headlines were *Pay
Claim Fiasco* and *Wife-swapping Led to Murder*. Down in
the bottom left-hand corner was a paragraph about Joyce's
father offering his house for the return of his daughter. Alan
wondered what the police and the bank would do if Joyce
turned up safe and told them she had been alone in the
bank when the two men came, that there had been only two
men, and only four thousand in the safe and the tills. It was
very likely that she would tell them that. He asked himself
if, by wondering this, he meant that he didn't want her to
turn up safe. The idea was uncomfortable and disturbing, so
he put it out of his head and walked to the back of this

rather superior newsagent-cum-stationers to where there were racks of paperbacks. There was no need to buy any books as his room was like a little library, but he had long ago got into the habit of always looking at the wares in bookshops, and why break such a good habit as that?

It wasn't really coincidence that among the books on the shelf labelled Philosophy and Popular Science he came upon the name of Ambrose Engstrand. Probably the man's works were in most bookshops but he had never had occasion to notice them before.

He took down *The Glory of the Real* and read on the back of its jacket that its author was a philosopher and psychologist. He had degrees that filled up a whole line of type, had held a chair of philosophy at some northern university, and made his home, when he was not travelling, in West London. His other works included *Neo-Empiricism* and *Dream, the Opiate.*

Alan read the first page of the introduction. "In modern times, though not throughout history, the dream has been all. Think of the contexts in which we use this word. 'The girl of my dreams,' 'It was like a dream,' 'In my wildest dreams.' The real has been discarded by mankind as ugly and untenable, to be shunned and scorned in favour of a shadow land of fantasy." A few pages further on he found: "How has this come about? The cause is not hard to find. Society was not always sick, not always chasing mirages and creating chimeras. Before the advent of the novel, in roughly 1740, when vicarious living was first presented to man as a way of life, and fiction took the lid from the Pandora's Box of fantasy, man had come to terms with reality, lived it and loved it." Alan put the book back. One pound, thirty, seemed a lot to pay for it, especially as—he smiled to himself—there were a lot of novels in Montcalm Gardens he hadn't yet read.

But it was certain that he had sold his soul and run away in order to find what this Engstrand called the real, so he had better begin by going to the Pembroke Market. The black-haired girl wasn't there, she was taking the day off, and Alan didn't dare ask the man who spoke to him for the number of her house. But he learned that her name was Rose. Tomorrow he would come back and see Rose and find the courage to ask her out with him on Saturday night. Saturday night was for going out, he thought, not yet understanding that for him now every night was a Saturday.

The rest of the day he spent at the Hayward Gallery, going on a river trip to Greenwich, and at a cinema in the West End where he saw a Fassbinder film which, though intellectual and obscure, would have made Wilfred Summitt's scanty hair stand on end. There was nothing in the evening paper about Joyce, only *New Moves in Pay Claim* and *Sabena Jet Hi-jacked*. He had been in his room ten minutes when there came a knock at his door.

A man of about thirty with red hair and the kind of waxen complexion that sometimes goes with this colouring stood outside.

"Locksley. I thought I'd come and say hallo."

Alan nearly said his name was Groombridge. He remembered just in time. "Paul Browning. Come in."

The man came in and looked round. "Bit of luck for both of us," he said, "finding this place. By the way, they call me Caesar. Or I should say I call me Caesar. What they called me was Cecil. I had the name part in Julius Caesar at school and I sort of adopted it."

"Do you really know all Shakespeare's sonnets by heart?"

"Una tell you that, did she?" Caesar grinned. "I'm not clever, I've just got a good memory. She's a lovely lady, Una, but she's crazy. She told me she let you have this place because you'd read some essay about Cardinal Manning. Feel

like coming up the Elgin or K.P.H. or somewhere for a slow
one?"

"A slow one?" said Alan.

"Well, it won't be a quick one, will it? No point in euphe-
misms. We have to face the real, as Ambrose would say.
D'you mind if we take Una?"

Alan said he didn't mind, but what about her husband
coming home? Caesar gave him a sidelong look and said
there was no fear of that, thank God. However, he came
back to say she couldn't come because she had to wait in for
a phone call from Djakarta, so they went to the Kensington
Park Hotel on their own.

"Did you mean there isn't a husband?" said Alan when
Caesar had bought them two pints of bitter. It was a strange
experience for him who had never been "out with the boys"
in his life or even into pubs much except with Pam on holiday. "Is she a widow?"

Caesar shook his head. "The beautiful Stewart's alive and
kicking somewhere out in the West Indies with his new
lady. I got it all from Annie, that's my girl friend. She used
to know this Stewart when he was the heart throb of Hampstead. Una's about the loneliest person I know. She's a waif.
But what's to be done? I'd do something about it myself,
only I've got Annie."

"There must be unattached men about," said Alan.

"Not so many. Una's thirty-two. She's O.K. to look at but
she's not amazing, is she? Most guys the right age are married or involved. She doesn't go out much, she never meets
anyone. You wouldn't care to take an interest, I suppose?"

Alan blushed and hoped it didn't show in the pub's murky
light. He thought of Rose, her inviting smile, her elegance,
the girl of his dreams soon to come true. To turn Una down,
he chose what he thought was the correct expression. "I
don't find her attractive."

"Pity. The fact is, she ought to get away from Ambrose. Of course he's saved her. He's probably saved her sanity and her life, but all that dynamic personality—it's like Trilby and Svengali."

"Why does she live in his house?"

"She was married to this Stewart, who's quite something in the looks line. I've seen photos. I tell you, if I wasn't hetero up to my eyebrows, he'd turn *me* on. He and Una had a flat in Hampstead but he was always going off with other ladies. Couldn't resist them, Annie says, and they never left him alone. Una got so she couldn't stand it anymore and they split up. They had this kid, Lucy her name was. She was two. Stewart used to have her at the weekends."

"Was?" Alan interrupted. "You mean she's dead?"

"Stewart took her to his current lady's flat for the weekend. Slum, I should say. He and the lady went out for a slow one and while they were out Lucy overturned an oil heater and her nightdress caught fire."

"That's horrible."

"Yes. Una was ill for months. The beautiful Stewart took himself off after the coroner had laid into him at the inquest. He shut himself up in a cottage his mother had left him on Dartmoor. And that's where Ambrose came in. He fetched Una back here and looked after her. He was writing his *magnum opus* at the time, *Neo-Empiricism*. That's what he calls himself, a Neo-Empiricist. But he dropped that for months and gave himself over to helping her. That was three years ago. And ever since then she's lived here and kept house for him, and before he went off to Java in January he had the basement converted and redecorated and said she was to let it and have the rents for her income. He said it would teach her to assume responsibility and re-face reality."

"What happened to Stewart Engstrand?"

"He turned up after a bit, wanted Una to go back to him. But she wouldn't, and Ambrose said he'd only be retreating into a mother dream, whereas what he needed was to work experientially through the reality of his exceptional looks and his sexuality. So he worked through them by taking up with a new lady who's rich and who carried him off to her house in Trinidad. Another beer? Or would you rather have something shorter and stronger?"

"My turn," said Alan awkwardly, not knowing if this was etiquette when Caesar had invited him out. But it seemed to be, Caesar didn't demur, and Alan knew that he was learning and making friends and working experientially through the reality of what he had chosen back there in Childon with the money in his hands.

Rose was there in the Pembroke Market on Friday. She had wound her long hair about her head in coils and put on a long black dress with silver ornaments. She looked remote and mysterious and seductive. He had his speech prepared, he had been rehearsing it all the way from Montcalm Gardens.

"I said I'd come in and tell you how I got on. I found a place from looking in that window, and it's ideal. But for you I'd never have thought of looking. I'm so grateful. If you're free tomorrow night, if you're not busy or anything, I wondered if I could—well, if we could go out somewhere. You've been so kind."

She said with raised eyebrows, "You want to take me out because I was kind?"

"I didn't just mean that." She had embarrassed him, and embarrassment made his voice tremble. But he was inspired to say, afraid of his own boldness, "No one would think of you like that, no one who had seen you."

She smiled. "Ah," she said, "that's better." Her eyes de-

voured him. He turned his own away, but he seemed beyond blushing.

In as casual a manner as he could muster, he said, "Dinner perhaps and a theatre? Could I fix something and—and
phone you?"

"I'll be in the shop all day tomorrow," she said. "Do
phone anytime." It was strange and fascinating the way
those simple words seemed to imply and promise so much.
It was her voice, he supposed, and her cool poise and the
swanlike way she had of moving her head. She gave a light
throaty giggle. "Haven't you forgotten something?"

"Have I?" He was afraid all the time of committing sol-
ecisms. What had he done now?

"Your name," she said.

He told her it was Paul Browning. Some hours had passed
before he began to get cold feet, and by then he had booked
a table in a restaurant whose phone number he had got from
an advertisement in the evening paper. He stood outside a
theatre, screwing up his courage to go in and buy two stalls
for himself and Rose.

13

Like Alan Groombridge, Nigel lived in a world of dreams. The only thing he liked about Marty's magazines were the advertisements which showed young men of his own age and no better-looking posing with dark glasses on in front of Lotus sports cars, or lounging in penthouses with balloon glasses of brandy in their hands. He saw himself in such a place with Joyce as his slave, waiting on him. He would make her kneel in front of him when she brought him his food, and if it wasn't to his liking he would kick her. She would know of every crime he committed—by that time he would be the European emperor of crime—but she would keep his secrets fanatically, for she worshipped him and received his blows and his insults with a doglike devotion. They would live in Monaco, he thought, or perhaps in Rome, and there would be other women in his life, models and film stars to whom he gave the best part of his attention while Joyce stayed at home or was sent, with a flick of his fingers, to her own room. But occasionally, when he could spare the time, he would talk to her of his beginnings, remind her of how she had once defied him in a squalid little room in North London, until, with brilliant foresight, he had stooped to her and bound her to him and made her his forever. And she would kneel at his feet, thanking him for his condescension, begging for a rare touch, a precious kiss. He would laugh at that, kicking her away. Had she forgotten that once she had talked of betraying him?

Reality was shot through with doubt. His sexual experience had been very limited. At his public school he had had encounters with other boys which had been nasty, brutish, and short, though a slight improvement on masturbation. When he left he found he was very attractive to girls, but he wasn't successful with them. The better-looking they were the more they frightened him. Confronted by youth and beauty, he was paralysed. His father sent him to a psychiatrist—not, of course, because of his failure with the girls, which Dr. Thaxby knew nothing about. He sent him to find out why his son couldn't get a degree or a job like other people. The psychiatrist was unable to discover why not, and this wasn't surprising as he mostly asked Nigel questions about his feelings towards his mother. Nigel said he hated his mother, which wasn't true but he knew it was the kind of thing psychiatrists like to hear. The psychiatrist never told Nigel any of his findings or diagnosed anything, and Nigel stopped going to him after about five sessions. He had himself come to the conclusion that all he needed to make him a success and everything come right was an older and perhaps rather unattractive woman to show him the way. He found older women easier to be with than girls. They frightened him less because he could despise them and feel they must be grateful to him.

Joyce, however, wasn't an older woman. He thought she was probably younger than he. But there was no question of her looks scaring him into impotence. With her big round eyes and thick lips and nose like a small pudgy cake, she was ugly and coarse. And he despised her already. Though he affected to be contemptuous of gracious living and cut-glass and silver and well-laid tables and professional people and dinner in the evening and university degrees, his upbringing had left on him an ineradicable mark. He was a snob at heart. Joyce was distasteful to him because she came from the working class. But he wasn't afraid of her, and as he thought of what he would gain, freedom and escape and her silence, he became less afraid of himself.

On Saturday morning he brought in coffee, a cup for her and one for himself. Marty had stopped drinking anything but whisky and wine.

"What's that you're knitting, Joyce?"

"A jumper."

"Is there a picture of it?"

She turned the page of the magazine and showed him a coloured photograph of a beautiful but flat-chested and skeletal girl in a voluminous sweater. She didn't say anything but flicked the page over after allowing him a five-second glimpse.

"You'll look great in that," said Nigel. "You've got a super figure."

"Mmm," said Joyce. She wasn't flattered. Every boy she had ever been out with had told her that, and anyway she had known it herself since she was twelve. We long to be praised for the beauties we don't have, and Joyce had started to love Stephen when he said she had wonderful eyes.

"I want you to go out tonight," said Nigel to Marty while Joyce was in the lavatory.

"You what?"

"Leave me alone with her."

"That's brilliant, that is," said Marty. "I hang about out in the cold while you make it with the girl. No way. No way at all."

"Think about it if you know how to do that thing. Just think if that isn't the only way to get us out of here. And you don't have to hang about in the cold. You can go see a movie."

Marty did think about it, and he saw it made sense. But

he saw it grudgingly, for if anyone was going to make it with Joyce it ought to be himself. For the *machismo*, if he had known the word, rather from inclination, but still it ought to be he. Not that he had any ideas of securing Joyce's silence by such methods. He was a realist whose ideas of a sex life were a bit of fun with easy pickups until he was about thirty when he would settle down with some steady and get married and live in a semidetached. Still, if Nigel thought he could get them out that way, let Nigel get on with it. So at six he fetched them all some doner kebab and stuffed vine leaves, drank half a tumbler of neat whisky, and set off to see a film called *Sex Pots on the Boil* at a nasty little cinema down in Camden Town.

"Where's he gone?" said Joyce.

"To see his mother."

"You mean he's got a mother? Where does she live? Monkey house at the zoo?"

"Look, Joyce, I know he's not the sort of guy you've been used to. I realise that. He's not my sort either, only frankly, it's taken me a bit of living with him to see that."

"Well, you don't have to talk about him behind his back. I believe in loyalty, I do. And if you ask me, there's not much to choose between the pair of you."

They were in the kitchen. Joyce was washing up her own supper plates. Nigel and Marty hadn't used plates, but they had each used a fork and Marty one of his new glasses. Joyce considered leaving the forks and the glass dirty, but it spoiled the look of the place, so she washed them too. For the first time in his life Nigel took a tea cloth in his hands and started to dry dishes. He put the gun down on the top of the oven.

His lie about Marty's mother had given him an idea. Not that mothers, feared, despised, adored, longed for, were ever far from his thoughts, whatever he might pretend. The rea-

son he had given for Marty's going out had come naturally
and inevitably to him. An hour or so before, Marty had
brought in the evening paper and Nigel had glanced
through it while in the lavatory. *Sabena Hostage Tells of
Torture* and *New Moves in Pay Claim,* and on an inside
page a few lines about Mrs. Culver recovering in hospital
after taking an overdose of sleeping pills. Nigel dried the
glass clumsily, and with an eye to the main chance, told her
what had happened to her mother.

Joyce sat down at the table.

"You're maniacs," she said. "You don't care what you do.
It'll just about kill my dad if anything happens to her."

Using the voice he knew she liked to hear, Nigel said,
"I'm sorry, Joyce. We couldn't foresee it was going to turn
out this way. Your mother's not dead, she's going to get
better."

"No thanks to you if she does!"

He came up close to her. The heat from the open oven
was making him sweat. Joyce was on the point of crying,
squeezing up her eyes to keep the tears back. "Look," he
said, "if you want to get a message to her, like a letter, I'll
see she gets it. I can't say fairer than that, can I? You just
write that you're O.K. and we haven't harmed you and I'll
see it gets posted."

Unconsciously, Joyce quoted a favourite riposte of her
mother's. "The band played 'Believe It if You Like.'"

"I promise. I like you a lot, Joyce. I really do. I think
you're fantastic-looking."

Joyce swallowed. She cleared her throat, pressing her
hands against her chest. "Give me a bit of paper."

Nigel picked up the gun and went off to find a piece.
Apart from toilet paper out in the lavatory, there wasn't any,
so he had to tear one of the end papers off Marty's much-
thumbed copy of *Venus in Furs.* The gun went back on top

of the oven, and Nigel stood behind Joyce, putting on a tender expression in case she looked round.

She wrote, "Dear Mum, you will recognise my writing and know I am O.K. Don't worry. I will soon be home with you. Give my love to Dad." She set her teeth, grinding them together. Later she would cry, when they were asleep. "Your loving daughter, Joyce."

Nigel put his hand on her shoulder. She was going to shout at him, "Get off me!" but the gun was so near, within reach if she put out her left arm. There might be no later for crying, but a time for joy and reunion, if she could only keep her head now. She bowed forward across the table. Nigel came round her. He bent over her, put his other hand on her other shoulder so that he was almost embracing her, and said, "Joyce, love."

Slowly she lifted her face so that it wasn't far from his. She looked at his cold eyes and his mouth that was soft and parted and going slack. It wouldn't be too disgusting to kiss him, he was good-looking enough. If she had to kiss him, she would. No good making a big thing of it. As for going any further . . . Nigel brought his mouth to hers, and she reached out fast for the gun.

He shouted, "Christ, you bitch!" and punched the gun out of her hand and it went skidding across the floor. Then he fell on his knees, scrabbling for it. Retreating from him, Joyce backed against the wall, holding her arms crossed over her body. Nigel pointed the gun at her and flicked his head to indicate she was to go into the living room. She went in. She sat down heavily on the mattress, her letter in her hand.

Presently she said in a hoarse throaty voice, "May as well tear this up."

"You shouldn't have done that."

"Wouldn't you have, in my place?"

Nigel didn't answer her. He was thinking fast. It needn't spoil his plan. She had been willing enough to kiss him, she had been dying for it, he could tell that by the soppy look on her face when he'd held her shoulders. It was only natural that getting hold of the gun came first with her, self-preservation came before sex. But there could be a situation where self-preservation didn't come into it, where the last thing either of them would think of was the gun. Attempting that kiss had brought him a surge of real desire. Having her at his mercy and submitting to him and grateful to him had made him desire her.

"I won't let it make any difference," he said. "Your letter still goes."

Joyce was surprised, but she wasn't going to thank him. That soft slack look was again replacing savagery in his face.

"The thing is," he said, the polite public-school boy. "I thought you really liked me. You see, I've felt like that about you from the first."

She knew what she had to do now, or not *now* but tomorrow when the dark one next went out. It sickened her to think of it, and how she'd feel when she'd done it she couldn't imagine. Dirty, revolting, like a prostitute. Suppose she had a baby? She had been off the Pill necessarily for a week now. But she'd do it and get the gun and think of consequences later when she was home with her mother and father and Stephen. It had never crossed her mind that in all her life she'd make love with anyone but Stephen. She and Stephen would go on making love every night the way they had been doing until they got to be about forty and were too old for it. But needs must when the devil drives, like her father said. She looked up at the devil with the gun.

"What you wanted to do out there in the kitchen just now," she said, "I don't mind. Only not now. I feel funny, it was a shock."

He said, "Joyce," and started to come towards her.

"No. I said not now. Not when he might come back."

"I'll get rid of him for the whole evening tomorrow."

"Not tomorrow," said Joyce, putting off the evil day. "Monday."

14

At the theatre Alan had chosen was a much-praised production of one of Shaw's comedies. He had picked it because there wouldn't be any bedroom scenes or sexy dialogue or four-letter words, which would have embarrassed him in Rose's company. But when he was at the box office he found that they only had upper-circle seats left, and he couldn't take a girl like Rose in the upper circle. All the other theatres round about seemed to be showing the kind of plays he had avoided in choosing *You Never Can Tell*, or Shakespeare, which was too heavy, or musicals, which she might not like.

And then, suddenly, he knew he couldn't face it at all. His cold feet were turning to ice. He couldn't be alone with her in a restaurant, not knowing what to order or how to order or what wine to choose. He couldn't bring her home in the dark, be alone with her in the back of a taxi, after they had seen a play in which people were naked or talked about, or even acted, sex. In the midst of his doubts, a happy thought came to him. When he had gone upstairs to ask Una Engstrand about the water heater, he had considered inviting her and Caesar Locksley in for drinks on Saturday night. Why not do that? Why not ask her and Caesar and this Annie of his for drinks in his room and ask Rose too? It was a much better idea. Rose would see the home her kindness had secured for him, he wouldn't have to be alone with her until he took her home—perhaps she had a car—and he would have the pleasure of creating an evening so different from those encounters with the Kitsons and the Heyshams, what a party should be with real conversation between people who liked each other and wanted to be together. And it would break the ice between him and Rose, it would make their next meeting easier for him.

Would drinks be enough or ought he to get food? He couldn't cook. He thought of lettuce and sardines and madeira cake, of liver and bacon and sausages. It was hopeless. Drinks alone it would have to be, with some peanuts. Next to the wineshop where he bought Bristol Cream and some vermouth was a newsagent's. The evening paper told him—it preceded Nigel's by twenty-four hours—that the Sabena jet had come down in Cairo, the pay-claim negotiations had reached deadlock, and Joyce Culver's mother had been rushed to hospital in a coma. A cloud seemed to pass across him, dulling his happiness and the pale wintry sun. If Mrs. Culver died, could anyone say it was his fault? No. If he had given the alarm and the police had chased Joyce's kidnappers, who could tell what would have happened to her? They would have crashed the car or shot her. Everything went to prove that it was better to take no violent action with people like that. You had only to read what was being done in this aircraft hi-jack business. No threats or armed onslaughts like in that Entebbe affair where a woman had died, but submission to the hi-jackers to be followed by peaceful negotiation.

He met Una in the hall. He and Caesar had to use the front door because, long ago, Ambrose had had the basement door blocked up for fear of burglars. Even he, apparently, had some reservations when it came to reality. Una, an indefatigable housewife, was polishing a brass lamp. She had blackened her fingers with metal polish.

"I'd love to come," she said when he told her of his party.

"How sweet of you to ask me. Caesar's gone to Annie's for the weekend. He mostly does. But I'm sure he'll bring her."

"Does she live in London then?" He had only once been away for the weekend, and that had been to a cousin of Pam's in Skegness, a visit involving days of feverish preparation.

"Harrow or somewhere like that," said Una. "Not very far. I'll ask him when he phones tonight, shall I?" She added in her strange vague complex way, "He's going to phone to find out if he's had a call from someone who knows his number and he wants to talk to but he doesn't know theirs. I'll ask him but I know he'd *love* to."

She was one of those people whose faces are transformed when they smile. She smiled now, and he thought with a little twinge of real pain for her that she was full of gaiety really, of life and fun and zest, only those qualities had been suppressed and nullified by the loathsome Stewart and the death of her child and perhaps too by the Neo-Empiricist.

"As a matter of fact," she said, "it will be very nice to drink some alcohol again. Ambrose doesn't believe in it, you know, because it distorts the consciousness. Oh dear, I don't suppose there's a wineglass in the house."

"I'll buy some glasses," said Alan. He went down to his room and put on his radio. There was nothing on the news about Mrs. Culver. Some Sabena spokesman and some government minister had said they would do nothing to endanger the lives of the hi-jacked hostages.

That night he dreamed about Joyce. Caesar Locksley asked him if he found her attractive, and the implications of that question frightened him, so he hid from her in a cupboard where there was an immersion heater and lots of bottles of sherry and piles of books by Ambrose Engstrand. It was warm in there and safe, and even when he heard Joyce screaming he didn't come out. Then he saw that the cup-

board was really, or had grown into, a large room with many
flights of stairs leading up and down and to the left and the
right. He climbed one of these staircases and at the top
found himself in a great chamber as in a mediaeval castle,
and there fourteen armed knights awaited him with drawn
swords.

The dream woke him up and kept him awake for a long
time, so that in the morning he overslept. What awakened
him then was a woman's voice calling to someone named
Paul. "Paul, Paul!" It was a few minutes before he remembered that Paul was his own name, and understood that it
must have been Una Engstrand calling him from outside his
room. He thought a tapping had preceded the uttering of
that unfamiliar name, but when he opened the door she was
no longer there.

It was after half-past nine. While he was dressing he
heard from above him the sound of the front door closing.
She had gone out. Would she mind if he used her phone?
Apparently, Caesar used it. He made himself tea and ate a
piece of bread and butter and went upstairs to phone Rose
at the Pembroke Market.

It was she who answered. "Why, hallo!" The last syllable
lingered seductively, a parabola of sound sinking to a sigh.
He told her of his alternative plan.

"I thought you were taking me out to dinner."

He found himself stammering because the voice was no
longer enticing. "I've asked these—these people. You'll like
them. There's the man in the next room to me and my—my
landlady. You'll be able to see what a nice place this is."

Very slowly, almost disbelievingly, she said, "You must be
crazy. Or mean. I'm expected to come round and have
drinks with your landlady? Thank you, but I've better
things to do with my Saturday nights."

The phone cut and the dialling tone began. He looked at the receiver and, bewildered, was putting it back when the front door opened and Una Engstrand came in.

"I'm sorry," he said. "I shouldn't have made a call without asking you. I'll pay for it."

"Was it to Australia?"

"No, why should it be? It was a local call."

"Then please don't bother about paying. I said Australia because you couldn't be phoning America, they'd all be asleep." He looked at her despairingly, understanding her no more than he had understood Rose, yet wishing Rose could have had this warmth, this zany openness. "Caesar didn't phone till this morning," she said. "I knocked on your door and called you but you were asleep. He can't come to your party, he's going to another one with Annie. But I expect you've got lots of other people coming, haven't you?"

"Only you," he said, "now."

"You won't want me on my own."

He didn't. He thought of phoning Rose back and renewing the invitation to dinner, but he was afraid of her scorn. He had lost her, he would never see her again. What a mess he had made of his first attempt at a social life! Because he had no experience and no idea of how these people organised their lives or of what they expected, he had let himself in for an evening alone with this funny little woman whose tragic life set her apart. His dreams of freedom and fantasies of love had come to this—hours and hours to be spent in the company of someone no more exciting and no better-looking than Wendy Heysham.

Una Engstrand was looking at him wistfully, meekly awaiting rejection. He answered her, knowing there was no help for it.

"Of course I will," he said.

The day ahead loomed tediously. He went out and

walked around the park, now seeing clearly the cause of
Rose's resentment and wondering why he was such a fool as
not to have foreseen it. He had contemplated a love affair
with her, yet he lacked the courage to make even the first
moves. Retribution had come to him for even thinking of a
love affair while he was married to Pam. The evening paper
cheered him, for it told him that Mrs. Culver was recovering
and that submitting to the hi-jackers' demands had secured
the release of all the hostages unharmed, except one man
who alleged his neck had been burned with lighted cigarettes. Alan had lunch and went to a matinee of a comedy
about people on a desert island. His freedom, so long de-
sired, had come to solitary walks in the rain and sitting in
theatres among coach parties of old women.

Una Engstrand came down at eight-thirty just when he
had decided she wasn't going to bother to come after all,
that she was no more enticed by this dreary tête-à-tête than
he was. She had put on a skirt and tied her hair back with a
bit of ribbon, but had otherwise made no concessions to her
appearance.

"I would like some vodka, please," she said, sitting down
primly in the middle of his sofa.

"I forgot to buy the glasses!"

"Never mind, we can use tumblers."

He poured out the vodka, put some tonic in, racked his
brains for a topic of conversation. Cars, jobs, the cost of living—instinctively he knew that was all nonsense. No free,
real person would ever talk of such things. He said abruptly,
"I saw some of your father-in-law's books in a bookshop."
That wouldn't be news to her. "What's he doing in Java?"

"I suppose Caesar told you he was in Java. He's very
sweet is Caesar, but a *dreadful* gossip. I expect he told you a
lot of other things too." She smiled at him enquiringly. He
noticed she had beautiful teeth, very white and even.

She shrugged, raised her glass, said quaintly, "Here's to you. I hope you'll be happy here." Suddenly she giggled. "He's heard there's a tribe or something in Indonesia that doesn't have any folklore or any legends or mythology and doesn't read books. I expect they *can't* read. He wants to meet them and find out if they've got beautiful free minds and understand the meaning of reality. When he comes back he's going to write a book about them. He's got the title already, *The Naked Mind*, and I'm to type it for him."

He sat down opposite her. The vodka or something was making him feel better. "You're a typist then?"

"No, I'm not. Oh dear, I'm supposed to be learning while he's away, I'm supposed to be doing a course. And I did start, but they made me have a cover over the keys and it gave me claustrophobia. Caesar says that's crazy. Can you understand it?"

Her expression was such a comical mixture of merriment and rue that Alan couldn't help himself, he burst out laughing. That made her laugh too. He realised he hadn't laughed aloud like this since he ran away from Childon, and perhaps for a long time before that. Why did he have this strange feeling that laughter with her too had fallen into disuse? Because he knew her history? Or from another, somehow telepathic cause? The thought stopped his laughter, and by infection hers, but her small flying-fox face stayed alight.

"It doesn't really matter," she said. "Ambrose thinks I'm hopeless, anyway. He'll just say he's very disappointed and that'll be that. But I mustn't keep on talking about him— Ambrose says this and Ambrose says that. It's because I'm with him so much. Tell me about you."

Until then he had had to tell remarkably few lies. Neither Rose nor Caesar had asked him about himself, and he had hardly spoken to anyone else. He had lied only about his name and address. Rather quickly and with uncertainty, he

told her he had been an accountant but had left his job. The
next bit was true, or almost. "I've left my wife. I just walked
out last weekend."

"A permanent break?" she said.

"I shall never go back!"

"And that's all you brought with you? A suitcase?"

"That's all." Involuntarily, he glanced at the tallboy
where the money was.

"Just like me," she said. "I haven't anything of my own either, only a few clothes and books. But I wouldn't need
them here. There's everything you can think of in this house
and lots of things twice over. You name something, the most
way-out thing you can think of. I bet Ambrose has got it."

"Wineglasses."

She laughed. "I asked for that."

"Before you came here," he said carefully, "you must
have had things."

The sudden sharpening of her features, as if she had
winced, distressed him. He was enjoying her company so
much—so surprisingly and wonderfully—that he dreaded
breaking the rapport between them. But she recovered herself, speaking lightly. "Stewart, that's my husband, kept the
lot. Poor dear, he needs to know he's got things even if he
can't use them. Ambrose says it's the outward sign of his in-
security and it's got to be worked through."

Alan burst out, knowing he shouldn't, "Your father-in-law
is worse than mine! He's a monster."

Again she laughed, with delight. She held out her glass.
"More, please. It's delicious. I *am* having a nice time. I suppose he is rather awful, but if I say so people think it's me
that is because everyone thinks he's wonderful. Except you."
She nodded sagely. "I like that."

In that moment he fell in love with her, though it was
some hours before he realised it.

15

Una stayed till eleven, Fitton's Piece Cinderella hour. But she didn't ask him whatever time it was or cry out that, Good heavens, she had no idea it was so late. After she had gone, he tidied up the room and washed the glasses, thinking how glad he was that Caesar and his girl friend hadn't been there. He was even more glad Rose hadn't been there. Una had talked about the books she had read, which were much the same as the books he had read, and he had never before talked on this subject with anyone. There was something heady, more intoxicating than the vodka he had been drinking, about being with someone who talked about a character in a book or the author's style with an intensity he had previously known to be lavished only over saving money and the cost of living. What would Rose have talked about? During the hours with Una, Rose had slipped back into, been engulfed by, the fantasy image from which she had come. He could hardly believe that he had ever met her or that she had been real at all. But he went over and over in his mind the things Una had said and the things he had said to her, and he thought of things he wished he had said. It didn't matter, there would be more times. He had made a friend to whom he could talk.

Before he went to bed he looked at himself carefully in the mirror. He wanted to see what sort of a man she had seen. His hair wasn't greased down anymore, so that it looked more like hair and less like a leather cap, and his face was—well, not exactly brown but healthily coloured. He who had never got a tan while living in the country, had got one in a week of walking round London. His belly didn't sag quite so much. He looked thirty-eight, he thought, instead of going on for fifty. That was what she had seen. And he? He conjured her up vividly, she might still have been sitting there, her small face so vital when she laughed, her eyes so bright, the curly hair escaping from the ribbon until, by the time she left, it had massed once more about her thin cheeks. Tomorrow he'd go upstairs and find her and take her out to lunch. The idea of taking her out and ordering food and wine didn't frighten him a bit. But he was very tired now. He got into bed and fell immediately asleep.

At about three he woke up. The vodka had given him a raging thirst, so he went into the kitchen and drank a pint of water. After that it would have been natural to go back to bed and sleep till, say, seven, but he felt wide awake and entirely refreshed and tremendously happy. It was years since he had felt happy. Had he ever? When he was a child, yes, and when Jillian was born because she was the child he had wanted, and in a strange way when he was driving off with the money. But he hadn't felt like this. This feeling was quite new. He wanted to go out and rush up and down Montcalm Gardens, shouting that he was free and happy and had found the meaning of life. A great joy possessed him. Energy seemed to flow through his body and out at his fingertips. He wanted to tell someone who would understand, and he knew it was Una he wanted to tell.

So this was being in love, this was what it was like. He laughed out loud. He turned on the cold tap and ran his hands under it, he splashed cold water over his face. The room was freezing because the heating went off at eleven, but he was hot, glowing with heat and actually sweating. He fell onto the bed and pulled the sheet over him and thought about Una up there asleep somewhere in the house. Or was she awake too, thinking about him? He thought about her for an hour, reliving their conversation and then fantasising that he and she lived together in a house like this one and were happy all the time, every minute of the day and night. The fantasy drifted off into a dream of that, a long protracted dream that broke and dissolved and began again in new aspects, until it ended in horror. It ended with his hearing Una scream. He had to run up many staircases and through many rooms to find where the screams were coming from and to find her. At last he came upon her and she was dead, burnt to death with charred bank notes lying all around her. But when he took her body in his arms and looked into her face, he saw that it was not Una he held. It was Joyce.

The cold of morning pierced through the thin sheet, and he awoke shivering, his legs numb. All the euphoria of the night was gone. He had no idea of how one went a-courting. It would be as difficult to speak of love to Una as it would have been to Rose, more difficult because he was in love with her—that was unchanged—while for Rose he had felt only the itch of lust. He was alone in the house with Una, he must be, and thinking of it terrified him. Inviting her out to lunch was impossible, making any sort of overtures to her was unthinkable. He was married, and she knew it. He had a notion, gathered more from Pam's philosophy than from novels, that if you told a woman you loved her and she didn't love you, she would slap your face. Especially if you were married and she was married. It was apparently, for no reason he could think of, in some circumstances an insult to tell a woman you loved her. He dressed and went out, thinking he would collapse or weep if he were to meet Una in the hall, but he didn't meet her.

Ex-priest Marries Stripper and *Torture "Hotly" Denied*

said the Sunday papers. They were searching potholes in Derbyshire for the bodies of himself and Joyce. The silver-blue Ford Escort, last observed at Dover, had turned up in Turkey, its passengers blamelessly on their way to an ashram in India. Alan had a cup of coffee and a sandwich, which made him feel sick. He noticed, after quite a long while, that it was a nice day. They were back to the kind of weather of the week before he ran away, just like spring, as Joyce had said. The sun on his face was warm and kind. If he went into the park or Kensington Gardens he might meet Rose, so he made for the nearest tube station, which was Notting Hill, and bought a ticket to Hampstead.

Una had lived in Hampstead. He didn't remember that until he got there. He walked about Hampstead, wondering if she had lived in this street or that, and if she had walked daily where he now was walking. He found the Heath by the simple expedient of following Heath Street until he got to it. All London lay below him, and, standing on the slope beside the Spaniard's Road, he looked down on it as Dick Whittington had looked down and, in the sunshine, seen the city paved with gold.

His gold lay down there, but it was nothing to him if it couldn't give him Una. He turned abruptly and walked in the opposite direction, through the wood that lies between the Spaniard's Road and North End. It wasn't much like Childon Fen. In the woods adjacent to great cities the trees are the same as trees in the deep wild, but at ground level all the plants and most of the grass have been trodden away. A sterile dusty brownness lies underfoot. The air has no moist green sweetness. But on that sunny Sunday morning—it was still morning, he had left so early—the wood seemed to Alan to have a tender, bruised beauty, spring renewing it all for further spoliation, and he knew the authors were right when they wrote of what love does, of how it transforms and glorifies and takes the scales from the eye of the beholder.

When he emerged from the wood he had no idea where he was, but he went on walking roughly westward until he came to a large main road. Finchley Road, N.W.2, he read, and he realised he must be in Paul Browning country. Strange. Paddington was West Two, so he had supposed that Northwest Two must be nearby. It was now evident that Paul Browning banked in Paddington not because he lived but because he worked there. Alan took out his London guide, for even though he would never speak to Una again, never be alone with her again, he ought to know the location of his old home.

The street plan showed Exmoor Gardens as part of an estate of houses where the roads had been quaintly constructed in concentric circles, or really, concentric ovals. Each one was named after a range of mountains or hills in the British Isles. It seemed a long way to walk, but Alan didn't know if there was any other means of getting there, and he felt a strange compulsion to see Paul Browning's home. In the event, the walk didn't take so very long.

Most of the houses in Exmoor Gardens were mock-Tudor, but a few were of newer, plainer design, and number fifteen was one of these. It was bigger than his own house at Fitton's Piece, but otherwise it was very much like it, red brick and with picture windows and a chimney for show not use, and a clump of pampas grass in the front garden. He stood and looked at it, marvelling that by chance he should have chosen for his fictional past so near a replica of his actual past.

Paul Browning himself was cleaning his car on the garage drive. The front door was open and a child of about eight was running in and out, holding a small distressed-looking puppy on a lead. There was a seat on the opposite side of the road. It had been placed at the entrance to a footpath which presumably linked one of those ovals to another. Alan sat down on the seat and pretended to read his paper while the child galloped the puppy up and down the steps. Paul Browning gave an irritable exclamation. He threw down his soapy cloth and went up to the door and called into the hall:

"Alison! Don't let him do that to the dog."

There was no answer. Paul Browning caught the boy and admonished him, but quietly and gently, and he picked the puppy up and held it in his arms. A woman came out of the house, blond, tallish, about thirty-five. Alan couldn't hear what she said but the tone of her voice was protective. He had the impression from the way she put her arm round the boy and smiled at her husband and patted the little dog, that she was the fierce yet tender protector of them all. He folded his paper and got up and walked away down the footpath.

The little scene had made him miserable. He should have had that but he had never had it, and now it was too late to have it with anyone. He felt ridiculously guilty too for taking this man's identity and background, a theft which had turned out to be pointless as well as a kind of slander on Paul Browning, who would never have left his wife. Alan asked himself if his other theft had been equally pointless.

The path brought him out at the opposite end to that where he had entered the oval, and his guide showed him that he wasn't far now from Cricklewood Broadway, which seemed to be part of the northern end of the Edgware Road. He walked towards it through a district that rapidly grew shabbier, that seemed as if it must inevitably run down into squalor. Yet this never happened. Expecting squalor, he found himself instead in an area that maintained itself well this side of the slummy and the disreputable. The street was wide, lined with the emporiums of car dealers, with betting shops, supermarkets, and shops whose windows displayed saris and lengths of oriental silks. On a blackboard outside a pub called the Rose of Killarney a menu was chalked up, offering steak pie and two veg or ham salad or something called a Leprechaun's Lunch. This last appeared to be bread, cheese, and pickles, but the thought of asking for it in the blackboard's terms daunted Alan so he ordered the salad and a half of bitter while he waited for it to come.

The girl behind the bar had the pale puffy face and black circles under her eyes of someone reared on potatoes in a Dublin tenement. She drew Alan's bitter and a pint for an Irishman with an accent as strong as her own, then began serving a double whisky to a thin boy with a pinched face whose carrier bag full of groceries was stuffed between Alan's stool and his own. Alan didn't know what made him look down. Perhaps it was that he was still surprised you could go shopping in London on a Sunday, or perhaps he was anxious, in his middle-class respectable way, not to seem to be touching that bag or encroaching upon it. Whatever it was, he looked down, slightly shifting his stool, and saw the boy's hand go down to take a cigarette packet and a box of matches from inside the bag. It was the right hand. The forefinger had been injured in some kind of accident and the nail was cobbled like the kernel of a walnut.

The shock of what he had seen made Alan's stomach turn with a fluttering movement. He looked sharply away, started to eat his salad as smoke from the boy's cigarette drifted across the sliced hard-boiled eggs, the vinegary lettuce. Reflected in the glass behind the bar was a smooth gaunt face, tight mouth, biggish nose. The beard could have been shaved off, the hair cut. Alan thought he would know for sure if the boy spoke. He must have spoken already to ask

for that whisky, but that was before Alan came in. He
watched him pick up the bag, and this time the finger
seemed less misshapen. It wasn't the same. The finger that
had come under the metal grille and scooped into the palm
the bag of coins he remembered as grotesquely warped and
twisted, tipped with a carapace more like a claw or a bar-
nacled shell than a human nail.

It was a kind of relief knowing they weren't the same so
that he wouldn't have to do anything about it. Do what? He
was the last person who could go to the police. The boy left
the pub and after a few minutes Alan left too, not following
him though, intending never to think of him again. He was
suddenly aware that he was tired, he must have walked
miles, and he was getting thankfully on to a south-bound
bus when he caught his last glimpse of the boy, who was
walking down a side street, walking slowly and swinging his
carrier as if he had all the time in the world and nothing to
go home for.

Alan felt himself in the same situation. For the rest of
that day and most of the next he avoided seeing Una.
Nearly all the time he kept away from Montcalm Gardens.
And he kept away too from North London, from those distant outposts of the Edgware Road where an invented past
had bizarrely met an illusion. It was obviously unwise to
visit venues, shabby districts, and down-at-heel pubs, which
suggested crime and criminals to him and where conscience
worked on his imagination. He sat in parks, rode on the tops
of buses, visited Tussaud's. But he had to go back or settle
for being a vagrant. Should he move on to somewhere else?
Should he leave London and go on to some provincial city?
For years he had longed for love, and now he had found it
he wanted lovelessness back again. He came back to his
room on Monday evening and sat on the bed, resolving that
in a minute, when he had got enough courage, he would go

upstairs and tell her he was leaving, he was going back to his wife, to Alison.

From the other side of the wall, in Caesar Locksley's room, he heard her voice.

Not what she said, just her voice. And he was consumed with jealousy. Immediately he thought Caesar had been deceiving him and she had been deceiving him, and she was even now in bed with Caesar. He began to walk up and down in a kind of frenzy. They must have heard him in there because someone came to his door and knocked. He wasn't going to answer. He stood at the window with his eyes shut and his hands clenched. The knock came again and Caesar said:

"Paul, are you O.K. in there?"

He had to go then.

"Annie and I are going to see the Chabrol film at the Gate," said Caesar. "Una as well." He winked at Alan. The wink meant, take her out of herself, get her out of this house. "Feel like coming too?"

"All right," said Alan. The relief was tremendous, which was why he had agreed. In the next thirty seconds he realised what he had agreed to, and then he couldn't think at all because he was confronting her. Nor could he look at her or speak. He heard her say:

"It *is* good to see you. I've knocked on your door about fifteen times since Saturday night to thank you and say how nice it was."

"I was out," he muttered. He looked at her then, and something inside him, apparently the whole complex labyrinth of his digestive system and his heart and his lungs, rotated full circle and slumped back into their proper niches.

"This is Annie," said Caesar.

It didn't help that the girl looked quite a lot like Pam and Jillian. The same neat, regular, very English features and

peachy skin and small blue eyes. He heard Caesar say she
was a nurse, and he could imagine that from her brisk
hearty manner, but she brought Pam back to him, her calms
and her storms. He felt trapped and ill.

They walked to the cinema. He and Una walked together,
in front of the others.

"They say," said Una, "that if two couples go out together
you can tell their social status by the way they pair off. If
they're working class the two girls walk together, if they're
middle class, husband and wife walk together, and if they're
upper class each husband walks with the other one's
wife."

"Don't make me out middle class, Una," said Caesar.

"Ah, but none of us is married to any of the others."

That made Annie talk about Stewart. She had had a letter
from someone who had met him in Port of Spain. Una didn't
seem to mind any of this and talked quite uninhibitedly to
Annie about Stewart so that the two girls drifted together in
the working-class way, a pairing which settled in advance
the seating arrangement in the cinema. Alan went in first,
then Caesar, then Annie, with Una next to her and as far as
possible from Alan. The film was in French and very subtle
as well, and he didn't bother to read the subtitles. He followed none of it. In a kind of daze he sat, feeling that he
lived from moment to moment, that there was no future and
no past, only instants precisely clicking through an infinite
present.

Afterwards, they all went for a drink in the Sun in Splen-
dour. Caesar wanted Annie to come home with him for the
night, but Annie said Montcalm Gardens was much too far
from her hospital and she wanted her sleep, anyway. There
was a certain amount of badinage, in which Caesar and both
girls took part. Alan had never before heard sexual behaviour so freely and frivolously discussed, and he was embar-

rassed. He tried to imagine himself and Pam talking like this
with the Heyshams, but he couldn't imagine it. And he
stopped trying when it became plain that Annie was going,
and Caesar taking her home, and that this was happening
now.

Una said, after they had left, "I think Annie was one of
Stewart's ladies, though she won't admit it. I expect he 'gave
her a whirl.' That was the way he always put it when he
only took someone around for a week. Poor whirl girls, I
used to feel so sorry for them." She paused and looked at
him. "Let me buy you a drink this time."

He had an idea women never bought drinks in pubs, that
if they tried they wouldn't get served. It surprised him that
she got served, and with a smile as if it were nothing out of
the way. He couldn't finish the whisky she had brought
him. As soon as he felt it on his tongue, he knew that his
gorge would rise at a second mouthful. The landlord called
time, and he and she were out in the street alone together,
walking back to Montcalm Gardens by intricate back ways.
It wasn't dark as it would have been in the country, but
other-worldly bright with the radiance from the livid lamps.
The yellowness was not apparent in the upper air, but only
where the light lay like lacquer on the dewy surface of
metal and gilded the moist leaves of evergreens.

"The night is shiny," said Una.

"You mean shining," he corrected her stiffly.

She shook her head. "No. Shakespeare has a soldier say
that in *Antony and Cleopatra*. It's my favourite line. The
night is shiny. I know exactly what he meant, though I suppose he was talking of moonlight."

He longed for her with a yearning that made him feel
faint, but he could only say stupidly, "There's no moon tonight."

She unlocked the front door and switched on lights, and

they went together into the fragrant polished hall where the
vases were filled with winter jasmine. The sight of it
brought back to him the yard at the back of the bank where
that same flower grew, and he passed his hand across his
brow, though his forehead was hot and dry.

"You're tired," she said. "I was going to suggest making
coffee, but not if you're too tired."

He didn't speak but followed her into the kitchen and sat
down at the table. It was a room about four times as big as
the one at Fitton's Piece. He thought how happy it would
make Pam to have a kitchen like that, with two fridges and
an enormous deep freeze and a cooker halfway up the wall,
and a rotisserie and an infrared grill. With deft swift movements Una started the percolator and set out cups. She
talked to him in her sweet vague way about Ambrose and
his books, about the banishment of all Stewart's mother's
novels to the basement after her death, flitted on to speak of
Stewart's little house on Dartmoor, now empty and neg-
lected. She poured the coffee. She sat down, shaking her
hair into a bright curly aureole, and looked at him, waiting
for him to contribute.

And then something happened to him which was not
unlike that something that had happened when the phone
rang in the office and he had had the money in his hands,
and he knew he had to act now or never. So he said aloud
and desperately, "Una," just hearing how her name sounded
in his voice.

"What is it?"

"Oh, God," he said, "I'll leave, I'll go whenever you say,
but I have to tell you. I've fallen in love with you. I love you
so much, I can't bear it." And he swept out his arms across the
table and knocked over the cup, and coffee flooded in a
stream across the floor.

She gave a little sharp exclamation. Her face went crimson. She fell on her knees with a cloth in her hands and began feverishly mopping up the liquid. He ran down the basement stairs and flung himself into his room and closed the door and locked it.

Up and down the room he walked as he had done earlier. He would never sleep again or eat a meal or even *be*. A kind of rage possessed him, for in the midst of this tempest of emotion, he knew he was having now what he should have had at eighteen, what at eighteen had been denied him. He was having it this way now because he had never had it before. And was he to have it now without its fruition?

Ceasing to pace, he listened to the silence. The light was still on upstairs in the kitchen. He could see it lying in yellow squares on the dark rough lawn. Trembling, he watched the quadrangles of light, thinking that at any moment he might see her delicate profile and her massy hair silhouetted upon them. The light went out and the garden was black.

He imagined her crossing the hall and going up the wide curving staircase to her own room, angry with him perhaps, or shocked, or just glad to be rid of him. He turned off his own light, for he couldn't bear to see any part of himself. Then he unlocked his door and went out into the pitch dark, knowing he must find her before she made herself inaccessible to him now and thus forever.

There was a faint light illuminating the top of the basement stairs. She hadn't yet gone to bed. He began to climb the stairs, having no idea what he would say, thinking he might say nothing but only fall in an agony at her feet. The light from above went out. He felt for the banister ahead of him, and touched instead her extended hand at the light switch. He gasped. They couldn't see each other, but they closed together, his arms encircling her as she held him, and they stood on the stairs in the black dark, silently embraced.

Presently they went down the stairs, crab-wise, awkwardly, clinging to each other. He wouldn't let her put a light on. She opened the door of his room and drew him in, and as it closed they heard Caesar enter the house. Lights came on and Ceasar's footsteps sounded softly. Alan held Una in his arms in a breathless hush until all was silent and dark again.

16

Very little food was kept in stock because Marty hadn't got a fridge. The bookcase held a few tins of beans and spaghetti and soup, half a dozen eggs in a box, a packet of bacon, tea bags and a jar of instant coffee, some cheese and a wrapped loaf. They usually had bread and cheese for lunch, and every day Marty went out to buy their dinner. But when it got to five o'clock on Monday he was still fast asleep on the mattress, where he had been lying since two. Joyce was in the kitchen, washing her hair.

Nigel shook Marty awake.

"Get yourself together. We want our meal, right? And a bottle of wine. And then you're going to do like a disappearing act. Get it?"

Marty sat up, rubbing his eyes. "I don't feel too good. I got a hell of a pain in my gut."

"You're pissed, that's all. You got through a whole goddamned bottle of scotch since last night." Unconsciously, Nigel used the tones of Dr. Thaxby. "You're an alcoholic and you'll give yourself cirrhosis of the liver. That's worse than cancer. They can operate on you for cancer but not for cirrhosis. You've only got one liver. D'you know that?"

"Leave off, will you? It's not the scotch. That wouldn't give me a pain in my gut, that'd give me a pain in my head. I reckon I got one of them bugs."

"You're pissed," said Nigel. "You need some fresh air."

Marty groaned and lay down again. "I can't go out. You
go."

"Christ, the whole point is to leave me alone with her."

"It'll have to be tomorrow. I'll have a good night's kip and
I'll be O.K. tomorrow."

So Marty didn't go out, and they had tinned spaghetti and
bacon for their supper. Joyce unbent so far as to cook it. She
couldn't agree to what she'd agreed to and then refuse to
cook his food. Marty stayed guarding Joyce while Nigel
went down and had a bath. On the way up again, he encountered old Mr. Green in a brown wool dressing gown
and carrying a towel. Mr. Green smiled at him in rather a
shy way, but Nigel took no notice. He flushed Joyce's letter
down the lavatory pan.

Marty was holding the gun and looking reasonably alert.

"You see?" said Nigel. "There's nothing wrong with you
so long as you keep off the booze."

That seemed to be true, for Marty didn't drink any more
that evening and on Tuesday he felt almost normal. It was a
lovely day to be out in the air. On Nigel's instructions, he
bought a cold roast chicken and some prepared salad in cartons and more bread and cheese and a bottle of really good
wine that cost him four pounds. He forgot to get more tea
and coffee or to replenish their supply of tins, but that didn't
matter since, by tomorrow, the three of them would be off
somewhere, Nigel and Joyce all set for a honeymoon.

The fact was, though, that neither of them seemed very
loverlike. Marty wondered what had happened between
them on Saturday. Not much, he thought, but presumably
enough for Nigel to be sure he was going to make it. Marty
observed their behaviour. Joyce sat knitting all day, not
being any nicer to Nigel than she had ever been, and Nigel
didn't talk much to her or call her "sweetheart" or "love,"
which were the endearments he would have used in the cir-

cumstances. Maybe it was just that they fancied each other so much that they were keeping themselves under control in his presence. He hoped so, and hoped they wouldn't expect him to stay out half the night, for his stomach was hurting him again and he felt as if he had a hangover, though he hadn't touched a drop of scotch for twenty-four hours.

At just after six he went off. It was a fine clear evening, preternaturally warm for the time of year. Or so Marty supposed from the way other people weren't wearing coats, and from seeing a couple of girls walking along in thin blouses with short sleeves. He didn't feel warm himself, although he had a sweater and his leather jacket on. He stood shivering at the bus stop, waiting for the number sixteen to come and take him down to the West End.

The two in the room in Cricklewood were self-conscious with each other. Nigel put his arm round Joyce and wondered how it would be if she were thirty-seven or thirty-eight and grateful to him for being such a contrast to her dreary old husband. The fantasy helped, and so did some of Marty's whisky. Joyce said she would have some too, but to put water with it.

They took their glasses into the living room.

"Did you send my letter?" said Joyce.

"Marty took it this morning."

"So that's his name? Marty."

Nigel could have bitten his tongue out. But did it matter now?

"You'd better tell me yours, hadn't you?"

Nigel did so. Joyce thought it a nice name, but she wasn't going to say so. She had an obscure feeling that some part of herself would be saved inviolate if, even though she slept with Nigel, she continued to speak to him with cold indifference. The whisky warmed and calmed her. She had

never tasted it before. Stephen said it was gin that was the
woman's drink, and once or twice she had had a gin and
tonic with him in the Childon Arms, but never whisky.
Nigel was half-sitting on the gun. It was beside him but not
between them. She let Nigel kiss her and managed to kiss
him back.

"We may as well eat," Nigel said, and he took the gun
with him to the table. The wine would put the finishing
touch to a pleasant muzziness that was overcoming his inhi-
bitions. He liked Joyce's shyness and her ugliness. It meant
she wouldn't know whether he acquitted himself well or
badly. She ate silently, returning the pressure of his knee
under the table. But, God, she was ugly! The only good
thing about her was her hair. Her eyelashes were white—no
wonder she'd nagged him to get her mascara—and her skin
was pale and coarse and her features doughy. In Marty's
tee-shirt and pullover she looked shapeless.

He started talking to her about the things he had done,
how he had been to university and got a first-class honours
degree, but had thrown it all up because this society was
rotten, rotten to the core, he didn't want any part of it, no
way. So he had gone to live in a commune with other young
people with ideals, where they had a vegetarian diet and
made their own bread and the girls wove cloth and made
pots. It was a free sexuality commune and he had been
shared by two girls, a very young one called Samantha and
an older one, Sarah.

"Why did you rob a bank then?" said Joyce.

Nigel said it had been a gesture of defiance against this
rotten society, and they were going to use the money to start
a Raj Neesh community in Scotland.

"What's that when it's at home?"

"It's my religion. It's a marvellous Eastern religion with
no rules. You can do what you like."

"Sounds right up your street," said Joyce, but she didn't say it unpleasantly, and when she got up to put the plates on the draining board beside Marty's whisky bottles, she let Nigel run his hand down her thigh. Then she sat down closer to him and they drank up the last of the wine. By now it was dark outside, but for the light from the yellow lamps. Nigel drew the curtains, and when Joyce came through from the kitchen he put his arms round her and began kissing her violently and hungrily, pushing her head back and chewing at her face.

She had very little feeling left, just enough to know from the feel of Nigel pressed like iron up against her that it was going to happen. But she felt no panic or despair, the whisky and the wine had seen to that, and no compulsion to break a window or scream when, for the first time since she had been there, she was left quite alone and free to move. Nigel went out to the lavatory, taking the gun with him. Joyce got onto the mattress and took all her clothes off under the sheet. The third note was still inside her bra. She pushed it into one of the cups and hid the bra on the floor under her pullover. Nigel came back, closing the door on the Yale but not bothering with the other lock. He switched off the light. For a little while he stood there, surprised that the lamps outside lit the room so brightly through the threadbare curtains, as if he hadn't seen that same thing for many nights. Then he stripped off his clothes and pulled back the blankets and the sheet that covered Joyce.

Her head was slightly turned away, the exposed cheek half-covered by her long fair hair. He stared at her in amazement, for he hadn't known any real woman could look like that. Her body was without a flaw, the full breasts smooth and rounded like blown glass, her waist a fragile and slender stem, the bones and muscles of her legs and arms veiled in an extravagant silkiness of plump tissue and white

skin. The yellow light lay on her like a patina of gilding,
shining in a gold blaze on those roundnesses and leaving the
shallow hollows sepia brown. She was like one of the nudes
in Marty's magazines, only she was more superb. Nigel had
never thought of those as real women, but as contrivances of
the pornographer's skill, assisted by the pose and the cun-
ning camera. He looked down on her with appalled wonder,
with a sick shrinking awe, while Joyce lay motionless and
splendid, her eyes closed.

At last he said, "Joyce," and lowered his body onto hers.
He too shut his eyes, knowing he should have shut them before or never have pulled back that sheet. He tried to think
of Samantha's mother, stringy and thin and thirty-two, of
Sarah in her black stockings. With his right hand he felt for
the gun, imagining how it would be if he were raping Alan
Groombridge's wife at gunpoint. But the damage was done.
In the last way he would have thought possible, Joyce had
taken away his manhood without moving, without speaking.
Now she shifted her body under his and opened her eyes
and looked at him.

"I'll be O.K. in a minute," said Nigel, his teeth clenched.
"I could use a drink."

He went out into the kitchen and took a swig out of the
whisky bottle. He shut his eyes so that he couldn't see Joyce
and tied himself round her, his arms and legs gripping her.

"You're hurting!"

"I'll be O.K. in a minute. Just give me a minute."

He rolled off her and turned on his side. His whole body
felt cold and slack. He concentrated on fantasies of Joyce as
his slave, and on the importance of this act which he must
perform to make her so. After a while, after the minutes he
had asked her to give him, he turned to her once more to
look at her face. If he could just look at her face and forget
that wonderful terrifying body. . . . She was asleep. Her

head buried in her arms, she had fallen into a heavy drunken sleep.

Nigel would have liked to kill her then. He held the gun pressed to the back of her neck. Perhaps he would have killed her if the gun had been loaded and the trigger not stiff and immovable. But the gun, like himself, was just a copy or a replica. It was as useless as he.

He took it with him into the kitchen and closed the door. Suddenly he was visited by a childhood memory, a vision from some fifteen or sixteen years in the past. He was sitting at the table and his father was spoon-feeding him, forcibly feeding him, while his mother crawled about the floor with a cloth in her hand. His mother was mopping up food that he spilt or spat out, reaching up sometimes to wipe his face with the flannel in her other hand, while his father kept telling him he must eat or he would never grow up, never be a man. The adult Nigel bent his head over the table in Marty's kitchen, as he had bent it over that other one, and began to weep as he had wept then. It was only the thought of Marty coming back and finding him there that stilled his sobs and made him get up again, choking and cursing. Reality was unbearable, he wanted oblivion. He put the mouth of the bottle to his own mouth, closed his lips right round it, and poured a long steady stream of whisky down his throat. There was just time to get back to that mattress and stretch himself out as far as possible from Joyce before the spirit knocked him out.

Marty looked at the shops in Oxford Street, thinking of the clothes he would buy when he was free to buy them. He had never had the money to be a snappy dresser but he would like to be one, to wear tight trousers and velvet jackets and shirts with girls' faces and pop stars' names on them. A couple of passing policemen looked at him, or he fancied they looked at him, so he stopped peering in windows and walked off down Regent Street to Piccadilly Circus.

In the neighbourhood of Leicester Square he visited a couple of amusement arcades and played the fruiters, and then he wandered around Soho. He had always meant to go into one of those strip clubs, and now, when he had wads of money in his pocket, was surely the time. But the pain which had troubled him on Monday was returning. Every few minutes he was getting a twinge in the upper part of his stomach, with cramps which made him break wind and taste bile when the squeezing vice released. He couldn't go into a club and enjoy himself, feeling like that and liable to keep doubling up. It wasn't his appendix, he thought, he'd had that out when he was twelve. Withdrawal symptoms, that's what it was. Alcohol was a drug, and everyone knew that when you came off a drug you got pains and sweats and felt rotten. He should have done it gradually, not cut it off all of a sudden.

How long were those two going to take over it? Nigel hadn't said what time he was to get back, but midnight ought to be O.K. for God's sake. He hadn't eaten since breakfast, no wonder he felt so queasy. He'd best get a good steak and some chips and a couple of rolls inside him. The smell in the steak house made his throat rise, and he stumbled out, wondering what would happen if he collapsed in the street and the police picked him up with all that money in his pockets.

He'd feel safer nearer home, so he got into the Tube, which took him up to Kilburn. Luckily the thirty-two bus came along at once. Marty got on it, slumped into a downstairs seat, and lit a cigarette. The Indian conductor asked him to put it out, and Marty said to go back to the jungle and told him what he could do to himself when there. So they stopped the bus and the big black driver came round and together, to the huge glee of the other passengers, they put Marty off. He had to walk all the way up Shoot-up Hill and he didn't know how he made it.

But it was too early to go back yet, only a quarter to eleven. Whether his trouble was withdrawal symptoms or a bug, he had to have a drink, and they did say whisky settled the stomach. His father used to say it, the old git, and if anyone knew about booze he should. A couple of doubles, thought Marty, and he'd sleep like a log and wake up all right tomorrow.

The Rose of Killarney was about halfway along the Broadway. Marty walked in a bit unsteadily, wincing with pain as he passed between the tables. Bridey and the licencee were behind the bar.

"Double scotch," said Marty thickly.

Bridey said to the licencee, "This fella lives next to me. Will you listen to his manners?"

"O.K., Bridey, I'll serve him."

"In the same house he lives and can't say so much as a civil 'please.' If you ask me, he's had too much already."

Marty took no notice. He never spoke to her if he could help it, any more than he did to any of these foreigners, immigrants, Jews, spades, and whatever. He drank his scotch, belched, and asked for another.

"Sorry, son, you've had enough. You heard what the lady said."

"Lady," said Marty. "Bloody Irish slag."

It was only just eleven, but he was going home anyway. The light in his room was out. He could see that from the street where he had to sit down on a wall, he felt so sick and weak. The stairs were the last phase in his ordeal and they were the worst. Outside his door he thought he'd rather just lie down on the landing floor than go through all the hassle of waking Nigel to let him in. He peered at the keyhole but couldn't see through because the iron key was blocking it. Maybe Nigel hadn't bothered to lock it because things had gone right and there was no longer any need to. He tried the key in the Yale and the door opened.

After the darkness of the landing, the yellow light made him blink. From force of habit he locked the door and hung the string the key was on round his neck. The light lay in irregular patches on the two sleeping faces. Great, thought Marty, he's made it, we'll be out of here tomorrow. Holding his sore stomach, breathing gingerly, he curled up on the sofa and pulled the blanket over him.

Joyce hadn't been aware of his arrival. It was three or four hours later that she awoke with a banging head and a dry mouth. But she came to herself quickly and remembered what her original purpose in going to bed with Nigel had been. She looked at him with feelings of amazement and distaste, and with pity too. Joyce thought she knew all about sex, far more than her mother did, but no one had ever told her that what had happened with Nigel is so usual as to be commonplace, an inhibition that affects all men sometimes and some men quite often. She thought of virile, confident Stephen, and she decided Nigel must have some awful disease.

Both her captors were deeply asleep, Marty snoring, Nigel with his right hand tucked under the pillow. Joyce put her clothes on. Then she lay down beside Nigel and put her right hand under the pillow too, feeling the hard warm metal of the gun. Immediately her hand was gripped hard, but not, she thought, because he was aware of what she was after. Rather it was as if he needed a woman's hand to hold in his troubled sleep, as a child may do. With her left hand she slid the gun out and eased her right hand away. Nigel gave a sort of whimper but he didn't wake up.

Taking a deep breath and wishing the thudding in her head would stop, she raised the gun, pointed it at the kitchen wall, and tried to squeeze the trigger. It wouldn't move. So it was a toy, as she had hoped and lately had often supposed. She was filled with exultation. It was a toy, as you could tell really by the plasticky look of it, that handle part seemed actually made of plastic, and by the way it said *Made in W. Germany*.

Her future actions seemed simple. She wouldn't try to get the key from Marty, for the two of them could easily overpower her and might hurt her badly. But in the morning, when one of them took her to the lavatory, she would run down the stairs, yelling at the top of her voice.

She decided not to take her clothes off again in case Nigel woke up and started pawing her about. That was a horrible thought when you considered that he was ill or not really a man at all. She came back and looked at him, still sleeping. Wasn't it rather peculiar to make a toy gun with a trigger that wouldn't move? The point with having a toy gun, she knew from her younger brother, was that you could press the trigger and fire caps. She wondered how you put the caps into this one. Perhaps by fiddling with that handle thing at the back? She pushed it but it wouldn't move.

Joyce carried the gun to the kitchen window where the light was brightest. In that light she spotted a funny little knob on the side of the gun, and she pushed at it tentatively with the tip of her finger. It moved easily, sliding forward towards the barrel and revealing a small red spot. Although the handle thing at the back had also moved and dropped forward, no space for the insertion of caps had been revealed. But there wouldn't be any point in putting caps in, thought Joyce, if you couldn't move the trigger. Perhaps it was a real gun that had got broken. She raised it again, smiling to herself because she'd really been a bit of a fool, hadn't she, letting herself be kept a prisoner for a week by two boys with a gun that didn't work? She felt quite ashamed.

Levelling the gun at Nigel made her giggle. She enjoyed the sensation of threatening him, even though he didn't know it, as for days he had threatened her. They'd killed Mr. Groombridge with that, had they? Like hell they had. Like this, had they, squeezing a broken trigger that wouldn't move?

Joyce squeezed it, almost wishing they were awake to see her. There was a shattering roar. Her arm flew up, the gun arced across the room, and the bullet tore into the rotten wood of the window frame, lodging there, missing Nigel's ear by an inch.

Joyce screamed.

17

Marty was off the sofa and Nigel off the mattress before the reverberations of the explosion had died away. Nigel seized Joyce and pulled her down on the bed, his hand over her mouth, and when she went on screaming he stuffed a pillow over her face. Marty knelt on the end of the mattress, holding his head in both hands and staring at the hole the bullet had made in the window frame. In all their heads the noise was still ringing.

"Oh, Christ," Marty moaned. "Oh, Christ."

Nigel pulled the pillow off Joyce and slapped her face with the flat of his hand and the back of his hand.

"You bitch. You stupid bitch."

She lay face-downwards, sobbing. Nigel crawled over the mattress and reached out and picked up the gun. He pulled a blanket round himself like a shawl and sat hunched up, examining the gun with wonder and astonishment. The room stank of gunpowder. Silence crept into the room, heavier and somehow louder than sound. Marty squatted, taut with fear, waiting for the feet on the stairs, the knock on the door, the sound of the phone down below being lifted, but Nigel only held and turned and looked at the gun.

The German writing on the side of it made sense now. With a thrill of excitement, he read those words again. This was a Bond gun he held in his hands, a Walther P.P.K. He didn't want to put it down even to pull on his jeans and his sweater, he didn't want ever to let it out of his hands again.

He brooded over it with joy, loving it, wondering how he could ever have supposed it a toy or a replica. It was more real than himself. It worked.

"That's quite a weapon," he said softly.

In other circumstances, Marty would have been quite amused to have fooled Nigel about the gun for so long, and elated to have received his praise. But he was frightened and he was in pain. So he only muttered, "Course it is. I wouldn't pay seventy-five quid for any old crap," and winced as a twinge in his stomach doubled him up. "Going to throw up," he groaned and made for the door.

"Just check what the scene is while you're out there," said Nigel. He was looking at the small circular red indentation the moving of the safety catch had exposed. Carefully he pushed the catch down again and that thing on the back, which had always puzzled him but which he now knew to be the hammer, dropped down. Now the trigger would hardly move. Nigel looked at Joyce and at the hole in the window frame and he sighed.

Marty vomited for some minutes. Afterwards he felt so weak and faint that he had to sit down on the lavatory seat, but at last he forced himself to get up and stagger down the stairs. His legs felt like bits of wet string. He crept down two flights of stairs, listening. The whole house seemed to be asleep, all the doors were shut and all the lights off except for a faint glimmer under the red-haired girl's front door. Marty hauled himself back up, hanging onto the banisters, his stomach rotating and squeezing.

He lurched across the room to the kitchen and took a long swig from the whisky bottle. Warm and brown and reassuring, it brought him momentary relief so that he was able to stand up properly and draw a deep breath. Nigel, hunched over Joyce, though she was immobile and spent and crying feebly, ordered him to make coffee.

"What did your last slave die of?" said Marty. "I'm sick and I'm not a bloody woman. She can make it."

"I'm not letting her out of my sight, no way," said Nigel.

So no one made any coffee, and no one went to sleep again before dawn. Once they heard the siren of a police car, but it was far away up on the North Circular. Marty lay across the foot of the mattress, holding his stomach. By the time the yellow lamps had faded to pinky-vermilion and gone out, by the time a few birds had begun to sing in the dusty planes of the churchyard, they had all fallen asleep in a spread-eagled pile, like casualties on a battlefield.

Bridey went down with a bag of empty cans and bottles before she went to work. The red-haired girl, who had been lying in wait for her, came out.

"Did you hear that funny carry-on in the night?"

"What sort of carry-on?" said Bridey cautiously.

"Well, I don't know," said the red-haired girl, "but there was something going on up the top. About half three. I woke up and I said to my fella, 'I thought I heard a shot,' I said. 'From upstairs,' I said. And then someone came down, walked all the way down and up again."

Bridey too had heard the shot, and she had heard a scream. For a moment she had thought of doing something about it, get even with that filthy-spoken bit of rubbish, that Marty. But doing something meant the police. Fetching the guards, it meant. No one in Bridey's troubled family history had ever done so treacherous a thing, not even for worthy motives of revenge.

"You were dreaming," said Bridey.

"That's what my fella said. 'You were dreaming,' he said. But I don't know. You know you sleep heavy, Bridey, and old Green's deaf as a post. I said to my fella, 'You don't reckon we ought to ring the fuzz, do you?' and he said,

'Never,' he said. 'You were dreaming.' But I don't know. D'you reckon I ought to have rung the fuzz?"

"Never do that, my love," said Bridey. "What's in it for you? Nothing but trouble. Never do that."

They would never get out now, Nigel thought, they would just have to stick there. For weeks or months, he didn't know how long, maybe until the money ran out. He found he didn't dislike the idea. Not while he had that beautiful effective weapon. He nursed the gun as if it were a cuddly toy or a small affectionate animal, his fear of losing it to Marty, whose possession it was, keeping it always in his hands. If Marty tried to take it from him, he thought he would threaten Marty with it as he threatened Joyce, if necessary kill him. During that night, what with one thing and another, something in Nigel that had always been fragile and brittle had finally split. It was his sanity.

Looking at the gun, passionately admiring it, he thought how they might have to stay in that room for years. Why not? He liked the room, it had begun to be his home. They would have to get things, of course. They could buy a fridge and a TV. The men who brought them up the stairs could be told to leave them on the landing. Joyce would do anything he said now, and there wouldn't be any more snappy back answers from her. He could tell that from one glance at her face. Not threats or privation or uncongenial company or separation from her family had broken her, but the reality of the gun had. That was what it had been made for.

He would have two slaves now, for Marty looked as shaken by what had happened as she did. One to shop and run errands and one to cook and wait on him. He, Nigel, wasn't broken or even shaken. He was on top of the world and king of it.

"We need bread and tea bags and coffee," he said to Marty, "and a can of paraffin for the stove."

"Tomorrow," said Marty. "I'm sick."

"I'd be bloody sick if I boozed the way you do. While you're out you can go buy us a big fridge and a colour TV."

"Do what? You're crazy."

"Don't you call me crazy, little brain," shouted Nigel. "We've got to stay here, right? Thanks to her, we've got to stay here a long, long time. The three of us can stay here for years, I've got it all worked out. Once we've got a fridge you won't have to go out more than once a week. I don't like it, you going to the same shops over and over, shooting your mouth off to guys in shops, I know you. We'll all stay in here like I said and keep quiet and watch the TV. So you don't blue all our bread on fancy stuff, right? We go careful and we can live here two years, I've got it all worked out."

"No," Joyce whimpered. "No."

Nigel rounded on her. "Nobody's asking you, I'm telling you. If I get so much as a squeak out of you, you're dead. A bomb could go off in this place and they wouldn't hear. You know that, don't you? You've had the experience."

On Thursday morning Marty made a big effort and got as far as the corner shop. He bought a large white loaf and some cheese and two cans of beans, but he forgot the tea bags and the coffee. Carrying the paraffin would have been too much for him, he knew that, so he didn't even bother to take the can. Food didn't interest him, anyway, he couldn't keep a thing on his stomach. He had some whisky and retched. When he came back from the lavatory he said to Nigel:

"My pee's gone brown."

"So what? You've only got cystitis. You've irritated your bladder with the booze."

"I'm dead scared," said Marty. "You don't know how bad

I feel. Christ, I might die. Look at my face, my cheeks are sort of fallen in. Look at my eyes."

Nigel didn't answer him. He sat cobbling for himself a kind of holster made from a plastic jeans belt of Marty's and a bit of towelling. He sewed it together with Joyce's brown knitting wool while Joyce watched him. He needn't have bothered, for Joyce would have died before she touched that gun again. She had given up her knitting, she had given up doing anything. She just sat or cringed on the sofa in a daze. Nigel was happy. All the time he was doing mental arithmetic, working out how much they would be able to spend on food each week, how much on electricity and gas. The summer was coming, he thought, so they wouldn't need any heat. When the money ran out, he'd make Marty get a job to keep them all.

The next day there was no paraffin left and no tea or butter or milk. The bookcase in the kitchen contained only a spoonful of coffee in the bottom of the jar, half the cheese Marty had bought and most of the bread, two cans of soup and one of beans, and three eggs. The warm weather had given place to a chilly white fog, and it was very cold in the room. Nigel put the oven on full and lit all the burners, angry because it would come expensive on the gas bill and upset his calculations. But even he could see Marty was no better, limp as a rag and dozing most of the time. He considered going out himself and leaving Marty with the gun. Joyce wouldn't try anything, all the fight had gone out of her. She was the way he had always wanted her to be, cowed, submissive, trembling, dissolving into tears whenever he spoke to her. She made beans on toast for their supper without a murmur of protest while he stood over her with the gun, and she gobbled her share up like a starving caged animal which has had a lump of refuse thrown to it. No, it wasn't the fear of her escaping that kept him from

going. It was the idea of having to relinquish even for ten
minutes—he could see from the kitchen window the corner
shop, open and brightly lit—the precious possession of the
gun.

That evening, while he was thinking about what kind and
what size of fridge they should buy, whether they could
afford a colour television or should settle for black and
white, Joyce spoke to him. It was the first time she had really spoken since she fired the gun.

"Nigel," she said in a small sad voice.

He looked up at her impatiently. Her hair hung lank and
her nails were dirty and she had a spot, an ugly eruption,
coming out at the corner of her mouth. Marty lay bundled
up, with all the blankets they possessed wrapped round him.
What a pair, he thought. A good thing they had him to manage them and tell them what to do.

"Yeah?" he said. "What?"

She put her hands together and bowed her head. "You
said," she whispered, "you said we could stay here for years.
Nigel, please don't keep me here, *please*. If you let me go I
won't say a word, I won't even speak. I'll pretend I've lost
my memory, I'll pretend I've lost my voice. They can't make
me speak! Please, Nigel. I'll do anything you want, but don't
keep me here."

He had won. His dream of what he might achieve with
her had come true. He smiled, raised his eyebrows, and
lightly shook his head. But he said nothing. Slowly he drew
the gun out of its holster and pointed it at her, releasing the
safety catch. Joyce rewarded him by shrinking, covering her
face with her hands, and bursting into tears. In a couple of
days, he thought, he'd have her pleading with him to be
nice to her, begging him to find her tasks to do for his comfort. He laughed then, remembering all the rudeness and insults he'd had to put up with from her. Without announcing

his intention, he switched the light off and stretched out on the mattress beside Marty.

"You smell like a Chink meal," he said. "Sweet and sour. Christ!"

Joyce couldn't sleep. She lay staring at the ceiling in despair. With a curious kind of intuition, for she had never known any mad people, she sensed that Nigel was mad. Sooner or later he would kill her and no one would ever know, no one would hear the shot or care if they did, and wounded perhaps, she would lie in that room till she died. The thought of it made her cry loudly, she couldn't help herself. She would never see her mother again or her father and her brothers, or kiss Stephen or be held in his arms. Nigel hissed at her to shut up and give them all a bit of hush, so she cried quietly until the pillow was wet with tears and, exhausted, she drifted off into dreams of home and of sitting with Stephen in the Childon Arms and talking of wedding plans.

Marty's anguished voice woke her. It was still dark.

"Nige," he said. He hardly ever used Nigel's name or its ugly diminutive. "Nige, what's happening to me? I went out to the bog and I had to crawl back on my hands and knees. I can't hardly walk. My guts are on fire. My eyes have gone yellow."

"First your pee, now your eyes. D'you know what the bloody time is?"

"I went down the bathroom, I don't know how I made it. I looked at myself in the mirror. I'm yellow all over, my whole body's gone yellow. I'll have to go see the doc."

That woke Nigel fully. He lurched out of bed, the gun hanging in its holster against his naked side. He stood over Marty and gripped his shoulders.

"Are you out of your goddamned mind?"

Marty made noises like a beaten puppy. Sweat was

streaming down his face. The blankets were wet with sweat, but he was shivering.

"I'll have to," he said, his teeth chattering. "I've got to do something." He met Nigel's cold glittering eyes, and they made him cry out, "You wouldn't let me die, Nige? Nige, I might die. You wouldn't let me die?"

18

He could hear her talking to Caesar outside the room. She must have gone out to the bathroom. He looked at his watch. Half-past seven. He was embarrassed because Caesar had seen her—dressed in what? the bedspread that he saw was missing?—and he was afraid of Caesar's censure because all his life every friend or acquaintance or relative had appeared to him in the guise of critical authority. She came back and stepped naked out of wrappings of red candlewick, and into his arms.

"What did he say to you?" Alan whispered.

"'Good luck, my darling,'" said Una, and she giggled.

"I love you," he said. "You're the only woman I ever made love to apart from my wife."

"I don't believe it!"

"Why would I say it, then? It's nothing to be proud of."

"Well, but Paul, it is *quite* amazing."

A horrid thought struck him. "And you?"

"I never made love to any women."

"You know I don't mean that. Men."

"Oh, not so many, but more than *that*."

And a horrider one. "Not Ambrose?"

"Silly, you are. Ambrose is a celibate. He says that at his age you should have experienced all the sex you need and you must turn your energy to the life of the mind."

"'Leave me, O Love, that reachest but to dust.'"

"Well, I don't think it does. I really think it reacheth to

much nicer things than that. You know, it wasn't just incredulity that made me say it was quite amazing."

He considered. He blushed. "Honestly?"

"Honestly. But if it's true, what you said, don't you think you need some more practice? Like now?"

That was the best week he had ever known.

He took Una to the theatre and he took her out to dinner. They hired a car. They had to hire it in her name because he was Paul Browning who had left his licence at home in Cricklewood. Driving up into Hertfordshire, they played the lovers' game of looking at houses and discussing whether this one or that one would best suit them to live in for the rest of their lives. He already knew that he wanted to live with her. The idea of even a brief separation was unthinkable. He couldn't keep his eyes off her, and the memory that he had told Caesar he didn't find her attractive was a guilty reproach, though she would never know of it. The word, anyway, was inadequate to describe the effect she had on him. He was glad now that she didn't wear make-up or dress well, for these things would have been an obscuring of herself. More than anything, he liked to watch the play of emotion in her face, that small intense face that screwed itself into deep lines of dismay or surprise, and relaxed to a child's smoothness with delight.

"Paul," she said gently, "the lights are green. We can go."

"I'm sorry. I can't keep from looking at you. I do look at the road while I'm driving."

When they got home that night and were in his room—she slept with him every night in his room—she asked him about his wife.

"What's her name?"

"Alison," he said. He had to say that because he was Paul Browning.

"That's nice. You haven't told me if you've got any children."

He thought of dead Lucy, who had never been mentioned between them. How many children had Paul Browning? In this case there could be no harm in telling the truth. "I've got two, a boy and a girl. They're more or less grown up. I was married very young." Not just to change the subject, but because a greater truth, never before realised, came suddenly to him, "I was a very bad father," he said. Of course he had been, a bad father, a bad husband, whose energies went, not into giving love, but to indulging in self-pity. "They won't miss me."

Una looked at him with a wistfulness in which there was much trepidation. "You said you wanted to live with me."

"So I do! More than anything in the world. I can't imagine life without you now."

She nodded. "You can't imagine it but you could live it. Will you tell Alison about me?"

He said lightly, because "Alison" merely conjured for him an unknown blond woman in Cricklewood, "I don't suppose so. What does it matter?"

"I think it matters if you're serious."

So he took her in his arms and told her his love for her was the most serious thing that had ever happened to him. Alison was nothing, had been nothing for years. He would support her, of course, and do everything that was honourable, but as for seeing her and talking to her, no. He piled lie upon lie and Una believed him and smiled and they were happy.

Or he would have been happy, have enjoyed unalloyed happiness, had it not been for Joyce. The man he had seen in the Rose of Killarney was certainly not the man who had asked him for twenty five-pence pieces for a pound and therefore not one of the men who had raided the bank and kidnapped Joyce. True, they both had mutilated forefingers on their right hands, but those mutilations were quite different, the men were quite different. And yet the sight of that man, or really the sight of that finger, so similar to the other and so evocative, had reawakened all his conscience about Joyce and all his shame. The bitterness of love unattained had kept that guilt at bay, the happiness of love triumphant had temporarily closed his mind to it, but it was back now, weighing on him by day, prodding him in the night.

"Is Joyce your daughter's name?" Una asked him.

"No. Why?"

"You kept calling that name in the night. You called, 'Joyce, it's all right, I'm here.'"

"I knew a girl called Joyce once."

"It was as if you were talking to a frightened child," said Una.

He should have done something in the Rose of Killarney, he thought, to make the boy speak. It would have been quite easy. He could have asked him where the buses went or the way to the nearest Tube station. And then when he had heard the ordinary North London voice he would have known for sure and wouldn't be haunted like this. He understood now why he was haunted. The sight of that finger had brought him fear, disbelief, a need to react against it by pretending to himself that the similarity was an illusion—but it had also brought him hope. Hope that somehow this could open a way to redeeming himself, to vindicating himself for what he had done in leaving Joyce to her fate.

On Friday morning he locked his door and took out the money and counted it. He could hardly believe that he had got through, in this short time, nearly two hundred pounds. Without really appalling him, the discovery brought home to him how small a sum three thousand

pounds actually was. Since finding Una, he was no longer
content vaguely to envisage one crowded hour of glorious
life with disgrace or death at the end of it. He had known
her for a week and he wanted a lifetime with her. He would
have to get a job, something that didn't need credentials or
qualifications or a National Insurance card. Optimistically,
not doubtfully or desperately at all, he thought of taking her
away from London and working as a gardener or a decora-
tor or even a window cleaner.

The door handle turned. "Paul?"

He thrust the money back into the drawer and went to let
Una in.

"You'd locked your door." Her eyes met his in bewildered
rejection, and in that look of fear, of distrust, she suddenly
seemed to him to represent other women that he had disappointed, that he had failed, Pam and Joyce. Trying to think
of an explanation for that locked door, he understood that
here was something else which eluded explanation. But she
didn't ask. "I've had a letter from Ambrose," she said. "He's
coming home on Saturday week."

Alan nodded. He was rather pleased. Somehow he felt
that hope for them lay with Ambrose Engstrand, though he
didn't know why or in what form. Perhaps it was only that
he thought of the philosopher as prepared to do anything to
ensure Una's happiness.

"I don't want to be here when he comes back," Una said.

"But why not?"

"I don't know. I'm afraid—I'm afraid he'll spoil this." She
moved her hand in an embracing gesture to contain her and
himself and the room. "You don't know him," she said. "You
don't know how he can probe and question and get hold of
things that are beautiful and—well, fragile—and make them
mundane. He does it because he thinks it's for the best, but
I don't, not always."

"There's nothing fragile about my feeling for you."

"What's in that drawer, Paul? What were you doing that you had to lock me out?"

"Nothing," he said. "It was force of habit."

She made no acknowledgement of this. "I felt," she said, "I thought you might have things of your wife's there, of Alison's. Letters, photographs, I don't know." She gave him a look of fear. Not the kind of fear that is based on imaginings and has in it a counterweight of hope, but settled despair. "You'll go back to Alison."

"I'll never do that. Why do you say that?"

"Because you never see her. You never communicate with her."

"I don't follow that logic."

"It is logic, Paul. You'd phone her, you'd write to her, you'd go and see her, if you weren't afraid that once you'd seen her you'd go back. With me and Stewart it's different. I haven't seen him for months but he'll turn up, he always does. And we'll talk and discuss things and not care because we're indifferent. You're not indifferent to your wife. You daren't see her or hear her voice."

"D'you *want* me to see her?"

"Yes. How can I feel I'm important to you if you won't tell her about me? I'm a holiday for you, I'm an adventure you'll look back on and sentimentalise about when you're back with Alison. Isn't it true? Oh God, if you went to see her I'd go mad, I'd be sick with fear you wouldn't come back. But when you did, if you did, I'd know where we were."

He put his arms round her and kissed her. It was all nonsense to him, a fabric of chimeras based on nothing. Fleetingly he thought of Alison Browning with her husband and her little boy and her puppy and her nice house.

"I'll do anything you want," he said. "I'll write to her today."

"Ambrose," she murmured, "would be so angry with me. He'd say I'd no precedent·for reasoning the way I do about you and Alison except what I'd got out of books. He'd say we should never conjecture about things we've no experience of."

"And he'd be so right!" said Alan. "I said he was a monster, but I'm not so sure. I wish you'd let me meet him."

"No."

"All right. I don't meet him and I write to Alison today, now. Will that make you happy, my darling? I'll write my letter and then we'll hire the car again and I'll take you out to Windsor for lunch."

She smiled at him, thrusting back her hair with both hands. "The lights are green and we can go?"

"Wherever you want," he said.

She left him alone to write the letter, and this time he didn't lock the door. He had nothing to hide from her because he really did write a letter beginning "Dear Alison." It gave him a curious pleasure to write Una's name and to describe her and explain that he loved her and she loved him. He even addressed the envelope to Mrs. Alison Browning, 15 Exmoor Gardens, N.W.2, in case Una should catch sight of it as he passed through the hall on his way to the post.

His pillar box was a litter bin. He tore the envelope and the letter inside it into pieces and dropped them into the bin, noticing that the last scrap to go was that on which he had written the postal district, Northwest Two. Not half a mile away from Alison's house he had seen the boy with the mutilated finger. Suppose he had asked him that question about the buses and the Tube and had got an answer and the voice answering had been Suffolk-cockney? What next?

What could he have done? Written an anonymous letter to
the police, he thought, or, better than that, made an anonymous phone call. They would have acted on that, they
wouldn't dare not to. Why hadn't he made the boy speak? It
was the obvious thing to have done and it would have been
so easy, so easy. . . .

Walking back to Montcalm Gardens and Una, he was
forced to ask himself something that made him wince. Had
he kept silent and fed his incredulity and condemned his
overactive imagination because he didn't *want* to know? Because all that talk of redemption and vindication was nonsense. He didn't want to know because he didn't want Joyce
found. Because if Joyce were found alive she would immediately tell the police he hadn't been in the bank, he hadn't
been kidnapped, and they would hunt for him and find him
and take him away from freedom and happiness and Una.

19

"You haven't even got a goddamned doctor," said Nigel.

But there he was wrong, for Marty had needed a doctor in the days when he had worked. Medical certificates had frequently been required for imaginary gastritis or nervous debility or depression.

"Course I have," said Marty. "Yid up Chichele." He clutched his stomach and moaned. "I got to see him and get some of them antibiotics or whatever."

Nigel wrapped a blanket round himself and padded out and lit the oven. He contemplated the bookcase: half a dozen slices of stale bread, two cans of soup and three eggs, four bottles of whisky and maybe eighty cigarettes. Having made a face to these last items, he squatted down to warm himself at the open oven. He didn't want Marty coming into contact with any form of official authority, and into this category the doctor would come. On the other hand, the doctor would reassure Marty—Nigel was sure there was nothing really wrong with him—and that ignorant peasant was just the type to start feeling better the minute anyone gave him a pill. Aspirin would cure him, Nigel thought derisively, provided it came in a bottle labelled tetracycline. He wanted Marty fit again and biddable, his link and go-between with the outside world, but he didn't want him shooting his mouth off to this doctor about not needing a medical certificate, thanks, and his mate he was sharing with who'd look after him and the girl they'd got staying with them and whatever. Above all, he didn't want this doctor remembering that last time he'd seen him Marty had sported a bushy beard like the guy who had hired the van in Croydon.

A groan from the mattress fetched him back into the living room. Joyce was sitting up, looking warily at Marty. Nigel took no notice of her. He said to Marty, not too harshly for him:

"Give it another day and keep off the booze. If your belly's still freaking you tomorrow, I reckon you'll have to go see the doctor. We'll like wait and see."

They had bread and the last of the cheese for lunch, and a tin of scotch broth and the three eggs for supper. Marty didn't eat anything, but Nigel, who wasn't usually a big eater, felt ravenous and had two of the eggs himself. The main advantage of getting Marty to the doctor would mean that he could do their shopping on his way back. A lot more cans, thought Nigel hungrily, and a couple of large loaves and milk and butter and some of that Indian takeaway, Vindaloo curry and dhal and rice and lime pickle. He wanted Marty to go to the doctor now, he was almost as keen as Marty himself had been on Thursday night.

He didn't seem keen any more when Nigel woke him at eight in the morning.

"Come on, get dressed," he said to Marty. "Have a bit of a wash too if you don't want to gas the guy."

Marty groaned and rolled over, turning up the now yellow whites of his eyes. "I don't reckon I've got the strength. I'll just lay here a bit. That'll be better in a day or two."

"Look, we said if your belly's still freaking you you'd go see the doctor, right? You get down there now and do our shopping on the way back. You can do it at the corner shops, you don't need to go down the Broadway."

Marty crawled off the mattress and into the kitchen, where he ran water over his hands and slopped a little onto

his face. The kitchen walls and floor were moving and slant-
ing like in a crazy house at a fair. He took a swig of whisky
to steady himself and managed to struggle into his clothes. It
didn't help that Joyce, sitting up on the sofa with the blanket cocooned around her, was watching him almost with
compassion or as if she were genuinely afraid he might fall
down dead any minute.

An icy mist, thick, white, and still, greeted him when he
opened the front door. It wasn't far to Dr. Miskin's, not
more than a couple of hundred yards, but it felt more like
five miles to Marty, who clung to lampposts as he staggered
along and finally had to sit down on the stone steps of a
chapel. There he was found by a policeman on the beat.
Marty felt too ill to care about being spoken to by a policeman, and the policeman could see he was ill, not drunk.

"You're not fit to be out in this," said the policeman.

"On my way to the doc," said Marty.

"Best place for you. Here, I'll give you a hand."

So Marty Foster was conducted into Dr. Miskin's waiting
room on the kindly arm of the law.

Nigel knew Marty would be quite a long time because he
hadn't made an appointment. That sort of morning surgery—
he knew all about it from the giving if not the receiving end
—could well go on till noon, so he didn't get worried. Marty
would be back by lunchtime with some food. He was hungry and Joyce kept whimpering that she was hungry, but so
what? Nobody got malnutrition because they hadn't eaten
for twelve hours.

At one o'clock they shared the can of chicken soup, eating
it cold because it was thicker and more filling that way.
There was now no food left. Marty was fool enough, Nigel
thought, to have taken his prescription to a chemist who
closed for lunch. That would be it. He had gone to the

chemist at five to one, and now he was having to wait till two when they opened again. Probably wouldn't even have the sense to do the shopping in the meantime.

"Suppose he doesn't come back?" said Joyce.

"You missing him, are you? I didn't know you cared."

The mist had gone and it was a beautiful clear day, sunshine making the room quite warm. Soon they could stop using any heat, and when the fridge came and the TV . . . Nigel saw himself lounging on the sofa with a long glass of martini and crushed ice in his hand, watching a film in glorious colour, while Joyce washed his clothes and polished his shoes and grilled him a steak. Half-past two. Any time now and that little brain would be back. If he'd had the sense to take a couple of pills straightaway he might be fit enough to get down to the electrical discount shop before it closed.

Nigel told himself he was standing by the window because it was nice to feel a bit of sun for a change. He watched old Green coming back from the Broadway with shopping in a string bag. He saw a figure turning into the street from Chichele Road, and for a minute he thought it was Marty, the jeans, the leather jacket, the pinched bony face, and the cropped hair. It wasn't.

"Watching for him won't bring him," said Joyce, who was forcing herself, rather feebly, to knit once more.

"I'm not watching for him."

"He's been gone nearly seven hours."

"So what?" Nigel shouted at her. "Is it any goddamned business of yours? He's got things to get, hasn't he? Him and me, we can't sit about on our arses all day."

They both jumped at the sound of the phone. Nigel said, "You come down with me," pointing the gun, but by the time they were out on the landing the bell had stopped. No one had come up from the lower floors of the house. In the heavy warm silence, Nigel propelled Joyce back into the room and they sat down again. Past three and Marty hadn't come.

"I'm hungry," Joyce said.

"Shut up."

Nothing happened for an hour, two hours. Although Nigel had turned off the oven, the heat was growing oppressive, for the room faced west. If the police had got Marty, Nigel thought, they would have been here by now. But he couldn't still be wandering about Cricklewood with a prescription, could he? The knitting fell from Joyce's fingers, and her head went back and she dozed. With a jerk she came to herself again, and seeing that neither Nigel nor the gun were putting up any opposition, she dragged herself over to the mattress and lay down on it. She pulled the covers over her and buried her face.

Nigel stood at the window. It was half-past five and the sun was going down into a red mist. There were a lot of people about, but no Marty. Nigel felt hollow inside, and not just from hunger. He started to pace the room, looking sometimes at Joyce, hating her for sleeping, for not caring what happened. Presently he took advantage of her sleeping to go out to the lavatory.

The phone screamed at him.

He left the door wide open and ran down. Keeping the gun turned on that open door, he picked up the receiver. Pip-pip-pip, then the sound of money going in and, Christ, Marty's voice.

"What the hell goes?" Nigel hissed.

"Nige, I rung before but no one answered. Listen, I'm in hospital."

"Jesus."

"Yeah, listen. I'm really sick, Nige. I got hepa- something, something with my liver. That's why I'm all yellow."

"Hepatitis."

"That's him, hepatitis. I passed out in the doc's and they brought me here. God knows how I got it, the doctor don't know, maybe from all that takeaway. They give me the phone trolley to phone you and they want my gear brought in. They want a razor, Nige, and a *toothbrush* and I don't know what. I wouldn't tell them who you was or where and . . ."

"*You've got to get out right now*. You've got to split like this minute. Right?"

"Are you kidding? I can't bloody walk. I got to be in here a week, that's what they say, and you're to bring . . ."

"Shut up! Will you for fuck's sake shut up? You've got to get dressed and get a taxi and come right back here. Can't you get it in your thick head we've got no food?"

Pip-pip-pip.

"I haven't got no more change, Nige."

Nigel bellowed into the phone, "Get dressed and get a taxi and come home *now*. If you don't, Christ, I'll get you if it's the last . . ." The phone went dead and the dialling tone started. Nigel closed his eyes. He leant against the bathroom door. Then he trailed upstairs again. Joyce woke up, coming to herself at once as she always did.

"What's happening?"

"Marty got held up. He'll be here in an hour."

But would he? He always did what he was told, but that was when he was here in this room. Would he when he was miles away in a hospital bed? Nigel realised he didn't even know what hospital, he hadn't asked. He heard the diesel throb of a taxi from the street below several times in the next hour. Joyce washed her face and hands and looked at the empty bookcase and drank some water.

"What's happened to him? He isn't going to come, is he?"

"He'll come."

Joyce said, "He was ill. He went to the doctor's. I bet he's in hospital."

"I told you, he's coming back tonight."

When it got to ten, Nigel knew for certain that Marty wouldn't come. He came back from the window where he had been standing for an hour, and turning to look at Joyce, he found that her eyes were fixed on him. Her eyes were animal-like and full of panic. He and she were alone together now, each the prisoner of the other. He had never seen her look so frightened, but instead of gratifying him, her fear made him frightened too. He no longer wanted her as his slave, he wanted her dead, but he heard the red-haired girl on the phone and then Bridey coming in, and he only fingered the gun, keeping the safety catch on.

Sunday passed very slowly, beginning and ending in fog with hot spring sunshine in between. Nigel thought Marty would phone in the morning, would be bound to, if only to go in for more bloody silly nonsense about having a toothbrush brought in. And when he did, he, Nigel, would find out just what hospital he was in, and then he'd phone for a mini-cab and send it round to fetch Marty out. He couldn't believe that Marty would defy him.

When it got to the middle of the afternoon and Marty hadn't phoned, Nigel's stomach was roaring hunger at him. The bookcase cupboard was bare but for the four bottles of whisky and the eighty cigarettes. For the sake of the nourishment, Nigel drank some whisky in hot water, but it knocked him sideways and he was afraid to repeat the experiment in case he passed out. Most of the time he stood by the window, no longer watching for Marty but eyeing the corner shop, which he could see quite clearly and whose interior, with its delicatessen counter and rack of Greek bread and shelves and shelves of cans and jars, he could recall from previous visits. Pointing the gun at Joyce, he forced her to swallow some neat whisky in an attempt to render her unconscious. She obeyed because she was so frightened of the gun. Or, rather, her will obeyed but not her body. She gagged and threw up and collapsed weeping on the mattress.

Nigel had been thinking, when he wasn't simply thinking about the taste and smell and texture of food, of ways to tie her up. He could gag her and tie her hands and feet and then somehow anchor her to the gas stove. "Somehow" was the word. How? In order to begin he would have to put the gun down. Nevertheless, late in the afternoon, he tried it, seizing her from behind and clamping his hand over her mouth. Joyce fought him, biting and kicking, tearing herself away from him to crouch and cower behind the sofa. Nigel swore at her. She was only a few inches shorter than he and probably as heavy. Without Marty's assistance, he was powerless.

Bridey went out, old Green went out most days. Nigel thought of telling one of them he was ill and getting them to fetch him in some food. But he couldn't cover Joyce with the gun while he was doing so. If he left Joyce she would break the windows, if he took her with him—that didn't bear considering. He could knock her out. Yes, and if he went at it too heavily he'd be left with a sick girl on his hands, too lightly and she'd come to before he got back.

The shop was so near he could easily have struck its windows if he had thrown a stone. His mouth kept filling with saliva and he kept swallowing it down into his empty stomach.

By Monday morning Nigel knew Marty wasn't going to phone or come back. He didn't think he would ever come back now. Even when they let him out of hospital he wouldn't come back. He'd go and hide out with his mother and forget about his share of the money and the two people he'd abandoned.

"What are we going to do for food?" Joyce said.

Nigel was forced to plead with her. It was to be the first of many times. "Look, I can get us food, if you'll guarantee not to scream or try and get out."

She looked at him stonily.

"Five minutes while I go down to the shop."

"No," said Joyce.

"Why don't you fuck off?" Nigel shouted. "Why don't you starve to death?"

20

Alan happened to be in the hall when the phone rang. Una was in the kitchen, getting their lunch. He picked up the phone and said, "Sorry, you've got the wrong number," when a man's voice asked if he was Lloyd's Bank. Maybe if he'd been asked if he was the Anglian-Victoria he would have said yes out of force of habit.

"Who was that on the phone?" said Una.

"Alison."

"Oh."

"She wants to see me . . ." It was the only excuse he could think of for getting himself up to Cricklewood without Una. Wherever he went she went, and he wanted it that way, only not this time. "She was quite all right, nice, in fact," he said with an effort. "I said I'd go over and see her this afternoon."

Una, who had been looking a little dismayed, the flow of her vitality checked, suddenly smiled. "I'm *so* glad, Paul. That makes me feel real. Be kind to her, won't you? Be generous. D'you know, I pity her so much, I feel for her so. I keep thinking how, if it was me, I couldn't bear to lose you."

"You never will," he said.

He had dreamed in the night of the boy with the mutilated finger. In the dream he was alone with the boy in the room at the bank where the safe was, and he was desperately trying to make him speak. He was bribing him to

speak with offers of bank notes which he removed, wad by
wad, from the safe. And the boy was taking the money,
stuffing it into his pockets and down the front of his jacket,
but all the time the boy remained silent, staring at him. At
last Alan came very close to him to see why he didn't speak,
and he saw that the boy couldn't speak, his mouth wouldn't
open, for the lips were fused together and cobbled like the
kernel of a walnut.

When he awoke and reached for Una to touch her and lie
close up against her, the dream and the guilt it carried with
it wouldn't go away. He kept telling himself that the boy in
the pub couldn't be the same as the boy who had come into
the bank and who later had robbed the bank, the coincidence would be too great. Yet when he examined this, he
saw that there wasn't so very much of a coincidence at all.
In the past three weeks he had wandered all over London.
He had been in dozens of pubs and restaurants and cafes and
bars. Nearly all the time he had been out and about, explor-
ing and observing. Very likely, if that boy was also a frequenter of pubs and eating places, sooner or later they would
have encountered each other. And if the boy turned out to
be a different boy, which was the way he wanted it to be,
which was what he longed to know for certain, there would
be no coincidence at all. It would be just that he was very
sensitive to that particular kind of deformity of a finger.
What he really wanted was for someone to tell him that the
boy was an ordinary decent citizen of Cricklewood, out
doing some emergency Sunday-morning shopping for his
wife or his mother, and when he spoke it would be with a
brogue as Irish as that barmaid's.

It was just before the phone rang that the idea came to
him of going back to the Rose of Killarney and asking the
barmaid if she knew who the boy was. Just possibly she
might know because it looked as if the boy lived locally.

Surely you wouldn't go a journey to do Sunday-morning
shopping, would you, when there was bound to be a shop
open in your own neighbourhood? Even if she didn't know,
he would have tried, he thought. He would have done his
best and not have to fail this shame and self-disgust at doing
nothing because he was afraid of what might happen if
Joyce were found. He should have thought of that, he told
himself with bravado, before he hid and left her to her fate
and escaped.

It was half-past one when he walked into the Rose of
Killarney. There were about a dozen people in the saloon
bar, but the boy with the distorted finger wasn't among
them. All the way up in the bus Alan had been wondering if
he might be, but of course he wouldn't, he'd be at work.
Behind the bar was the Irish girl, looking sullen and tired.
Alan asked her for a half of bitter and when it came he said
hesitantly:

"I don't suppose you happen to know"—it seemed to him
that she was looking at him with a kind of incredulous
disgust—"the name of the young man who was in here last
Sunday week?" Was it really as long ago as that? The distance in time seemed to add to the absurdity of the enquiry.
"Early twenties, dark, clean-shaven," he said. He held up
his own right hand, grasping the forefinger in his left. "His
finger . . ." he was beginning when she interrupted him.

"You the police?"

A more self-confident man might have agreed that he was.
Alan, trying to think up an excuse for wanting a stranger's
name and address, disclaimed any connection with the law
and thrust his hand into his pocket, seeking inspiration. All
he could produce was a five-pound note, a portrait of the
Duke of Wellington.

"He dropped this as he was leaving."

"You took your time about it," said the girl.

"I've been away."

She said quickly, greedily, "Sure and I'll give it him. Foster's his name, Marty Foster, I know him well."

The note was snatched from his fingers. He began to insist, "If you could just tell me . . . ?"

"Don't you trust me, then?"

He shrugged, embarrassed. Several pairs of eyes were fixed on him. He got down off his stool and went out. If the girl knew him well, spoke of him therefore as a frequenter of the pub, he couldn't be Joyce's kidnapper, could he? Alan knew he could, that all that meant nothing. But at least he had the name, Foster, Marty Foster. What he could do now was phone the police and give them Marty Foster's name and describe him. He crossed the road and went into a phone box and looked in the directory. There was no police station listed for Cricklewood. Of course he could phone Scotland Yard. A superstitious fear took hold of him that as soon as he spoke they would know at once where he was and who he was. He came hurriedly out of the phone box and began to walk away in the direction of Exmoor Gardens, towards Alison, where he was supposed to be, and looked for another phone box in a less exposed and vulnerable place.

By the time he had found it he knew he wasn't going to make that call. It was more important to him that the police shouldn't track him down than that they should be alerted to hunt for a Marty Foster who very likely had no connection at all with the Childon bank robbery. So he continued to walk aimlessly and to think. In the little shopping parade among the ovals named after mountain ranges, he went into a newsagent's and bought an evening paper. As far as he could see, there was nothing in it about Joyce. At three-fifteen he thought he might reasonably go back to Una now, and he retraced his steps to Cricklewood Broadway to wait for a bus going south.

The bus was approaching and he was holding out his hand to it when he saw the girl from the Rose of Killarney. She had come out of a side door of the pub, and crossing the Broadway, walked off down a side street. Alan let the bus go. He thought, maybe she'll go straight to this Foster's home with the money, that's what I'd do, that's what any honest person would do, and then he gave a little dry laugh to himself at what he had said. He followed her across the road, wishing there were more people about, not just the two of them apparently, once the shopping place and the bus routes were left behind. But she didn't look round. She walked with assurance, cutting corners, crossing streets diagonally. Suddenly there were more shops, a launderette, a Greek delicatessen; on the opposite side a church in a churchyard full of plane trees, on this a row of red-brick houses, three storeys high. The girl turned in at the gate of one of them.

Alan hurried, but by the time he reached the gate the girl had disappeared. He read the names above the bells and saw that the topmost one was M. Foster. Had Foster himself let her in? Or had it been the mother or wife with whom his imagination had earlier invested the man with the mutilated finger? He crossed the road and stood by the low wall of the churchyard to wait for her. And then? Once she had left, was he also going to ring that bell? Presumably. He hadn't come as far as this to abandon his quest and go tamely home.

Time passed very slowly. He pretended to read the notice board and then really read it for something to do. He walked up the street as far as he could go while keeping the house in sight, and then he walked back again and as far in the other direction. He went into the churchyard and even

examined the church, which he was sure was of no archi-
tectural merit whatsoever. Still the girl hadn't come out,
though by now half an hour had gone by.

M. Foster's was the topmost bell. Did that mean he lived
on the top floor? It might not mean that he occupied the
whole of the top floor. For the first time Alan lifted his eyes
to the third storey of the house with its three oblong windows. A young man was standing up against the glass, immobile, flaccid, somehow even from that distance and
through that glass giving an impression of a kind of hopeless
indolence. But he wasn't Foster. His hair was blond. Alan
stopped staring at him and, making up his mind, he went
back across the road and rang that bell.

Nobody came down. He rang the bell again, more insist-
ently this time, but he felt sure it wasn't going to be answered. On an impulse he pressed the one below it, B.
Flynn.

The last person he expected to see was the barmaid from
the Rose of Killarney. Her appearance at the door, not in
her outdoor coat but with a cup of tea in one hand and a
cigarette in the other, made him feel that he had walked
into one of those nightmares—familiar to him these days—in
which the irrational is commonplace and identities bizarrely
interchangeable.

She said nothing and he had no idea what to say. They
stared at each other and as he became aware that she was
frightened, that in her look was awe and fear and repulsion,
she put her hand into the pocket of her trousers and pulled
out the five-pound note.

"Take your money." She thrust it at him. "I've done nothing. Will you leave me alone?" Her voice trembled. "Give it
him yourself if that's what you're wanting."

Alan still couldn't understand, but he questioned, "He
does live here?"

"On the top, next to me. Him and his pal." She began to retreat, rubbing her hands as if to erase the contamination of that money from them. The cigarette hung from her mouth.

Alan knew she thought he was the police in spite of his denial. She thought he was a policeman playing tricks. "Listen," he said. "How does he talk? Has he got an accent?"

She threw the cigarette end into the street. "Bloody English like you," she said, and closed the door.

Una was waiting for him in the hall. The front door had yielded under the pressure of his hand, she had left it on the latch, presumably so that she could the more easily keep running out to see if he were coming.

She rushed up to him. "You were so long." She sounded breathless. "I was worried."

"It's only just gone five," he said vaguely.

"Did you have a bad time with Alison?"

He had almost forgotten who Alison was. It seemed ridiculous to him that Una should be concerned about that happy secure woman who had nothing to do with him or her, but he seized on what might have happened that afternoon as an excuse for his preoccupation.

"She was quite reasonable and calm and nice," he said, and he added, not thinking this time of Paul Browning's wife, "She thinks I shouldn't have left. She says I've ruined her life."

Una said nothing. He followed her through the big house to the kitchen, where she began to busy herself making tea for him. Her flying-fox face was puckered so that the lines on it seemed to presage the wrinkles of age. He put his arms round her.

"What is it?"

"Did it make you unhappy, seeing Alison?"

"Not a bit. Let's forget her." He held Una tight, thinking what a bore it was, all this pretence. He was going to have to fabricate so much, interviews with solicitors, financial arrangements. Why had he ever said he was married? Una was herself married, so the question of marriage between them couldn't have arisen. It seemed to him that she must have read at least some part of his thoughts, for she moved a little aside from him and said:

"I heard from Stewart. By the second post."

She gave him the letter. It was happy and affectionate. Stewart said he had had a call from his father all about her and her new man, and why didn't she and her Paul go and live in the cottage on Dartmoor?

"Could we, please, Paul?"

"I don't know . . ."

"We could just go and see if you liked it. I could write to the woman in the village who looks after it and get her to air it and warm it, and we could be there by the weekend. Ambrose'll be home on Saturday but I'd leave the house *immaculate* for him. He won't mind my not being here, he'll be glad to be rid of me at last. Paul, can we?"

"I'll do whatever you want," he said. "You know that."

He began to drink the tea she had made him. She sat opposite him at the table, her elbows on it, her chin in her hands, her eyes sparkling with anticipation. He smiled back at her and his smile was full of tenderness, yet much as he loved being with her, much as he wanted to share his whole life with her, he wished then that he could briefly be alone. It was impossible. There would be a cruelty in broaching it, he thought, after he had supposedly been all those hours with his wife. But he longed very much for solitude in which to think about what course of action next to take.

Una began talking to him about Dartmoor and the cottage itself. It would be a good place to hide in, he thought, after he had phoned the police and they had rescued Joyce and Joyce had told them the truth about him. They would never look for him in a private house in so remote a place. But before he could phone and certainly before he could leave, he must have more information. He must know for sure that Joyce's kidnapper, the boy whose walnut-nailed finger had scooped up the change, and Marty Foster were one and the same.

"Shall we go on Friday?" said Una.

He nodded. It gave him three days.

As their eyes met across the table, his troubled, hers excited, anxious, hopeful, some twenty miles to the south of them John Purford's aircraft was touching down at Gatwick.

21

Nigel and Marty had never thought of counting the notes they had stolen. They would only have done so if the question of dividing it had come up. Soon after he awoke on the morning of Tuesday, 26 March, after he had drunk some warm water, Nigel took the money out, spread it on the kitchen table, and counted it. He didn't know how much they had spent but there was over four thousand left—four thousand and fifteen pounds, to be precise. The amount they had taken, therefore, had been somewhat in excess of what he had supposed. He divided it into two equal sums and tied up each of the resultant wads with a black stocking. Then he put them back into the bag with the bunch of Ford Escort keys.

He and Joyce had eaten nothing since the chicken soup at midday on Saturday, and not much for two days before that. Nigel was no longer hungry. Nor did he feel particularly weak or tired, only light-headed. The visions of a future in which he dominated Joyce had been replaced by even more highly coloured ones in which he had Marty at his mercy in some mediaeval torture chamber. He saw himself in a black cloak and hood, tearing out Marty's fingernails with red-hot pincers. Once he was out of there he was going to get Marty, hunt him if necessary to the ends of the earth, and then he was going to come back and finish Joyce. He didn't know whom he hated most, Joyce or Marty, but he hated

them more than he hated his parents. The former had succeeded the latter as responsible for all his troubles.

Since Sunday Joyce had spent most of the time lying on
the sofa. She hadn't washed or combed her hair or cleaned
her teeth. Dust lay everywhere once more and the bed linen
smelt sour. Once she had understood that Marty wasn't
coming back, that she was alone with Nigel, that there
wasn't going to be anything to eat, she had retreated into a
zombielike apathy, a kind of fugue, from which she was
briefly aroused only by the ringing of the doorbell on Monday afternoon. She had wanted to know who it was and had
tried to get to the window, but Nigel had caught her and
thrown her back, his hand over her mouth. And then they
had both faintly heard a bell ringing in the next room and
Bridey going downstairs, and she had known to her despair
what Nigel had known to his relief, that it had only been
some salesman or canvasser at the door.

On the following morning it was nearly twelve before she
dragged herself to the kitchen and, having drunk a cup of
water, leant back against the sink, her face going white.
When she drank water she could always feel the shock of it,
teasingly trickling down, tracing its whole passage through
her intestines. She hadn't looked directly at Nigel, much less
spoken to him, since Monday morning, for whenever she allowed her eyes to meet his it only brought on a spasm of
hysterical crying. Twice a day perhaps she would go limply
towards the door, and Nigel would take this as a signal to
escort her to the lavatory. She was weak and broken, a butt
for Nigel's occasional violence. She believed that everything
had been destroyed in her, for she no longer thought with
longing or anguish of Stephen or her parents, or of escape or
of keeping herself decent and nice. Aeons seemed to have
passed since she had been defiant and bold. She was starving to death, as Nigel had told her to, and she supposed—for

this was all she thought of now—that she would grow weaker and weaker and less and less conscious of herself and her surroundings until finally she did die. She walked to the door and waited there until Nigel slouched over to take her outside.

When they were both back in the room, Nigel spoke to her. He spoke her name. She made no answer. He didn't use her name again, it was almost painful to him to bring it out, but said:

"We can't stay here. You said once, you said if we let you go you wouldn't talk to the police."

Stress and starvation had taken from Nigel's speech that disc-jockey drawl and those eclectic idioms, and tones of public school and university reasserted themselves. Joyce wondered vaguely at the voice, which was beautiful and like someone in a serious play on the television, but she hardly took in the sense of the words. Nigel repeated them and went on:

"If you meant that, straight up, we can get out of here." He looked at her hard, his eyes glittering. "I'll give you two thousand," he said, "to get out of here and go and stop in a hotel for two weeks. Give me two weeks to get out of the country, get clear away. Then you can go home and squeal all you want."

Joyce absorbed what he had said. She sat in silence, nervously fingering her chin where a patch of acne had developed. After a while she said, "What about him? What about Marty?"

"Who's Marty?" shouted Nigel.

It was hard for Joyce to speak. When she spoke her mouth filled with saliva and she felt sick, but she did her best.

"What's the good of two thousand to me? I couldn't spend it. I couldn't tell my fiancé. It'd be like Monopoly money, it'd be just paper."

"You can save it up, can't you? Buy shares with it." Memories of his father's advice, often derided in the commune, came back to Nigel. "Buy goddamned bloody National Savings."

Joyce began to cry. The tears trickled slowly down her face. "It's not just that. I couldn't take the bank's money. How could I?" She wept, hanging her head. "I'd be as bad as you."

With a gasp of rage, Nigel came at her, slapping her face hard, and Joyce fell down on the mattress, shaking with sobs. He turned away from her and went into the kitchen, where the money was in the carrier bag. The bunch of car keys was there too, but Nigel had forgotten all about the silver-blue Ford Escort he had hidden in Dr. Bolton's garage twenty-two days before.

While still in Crete, Dr. and Mrs. Bolton had received a telegram announcing that Dr. Bolton's mother had died. Old Mrs. Bolton had been ninety-two and bedridden, but nevertheless when one's mother dies, whatever the circumstances, one can hardly remain abroad enjoying oneself. Dr. Bolton found the Ford Escort before he had even taken the suitcases out of his own car. He unpacked one of these in order to retrieve from where it was wrapped round his sandals the relevant copy of the *Daily Telegraph*. Having checked that his memory wasn't tricking him, he phoned the police.

They were with him in half an hour. Dr. and Mrs. Bolton were asked to make a list of all the people who knew they had no lock on their garage and also knew they were to be away on holiday.

"Our friends," said Dr. Bolton, "are not the kind of people who rob banks."

"I don't doubt that," said the detective inspector, "but your friends may know people who know people who are less respectable than they are, or have children who have friends who are not respectable at all."

Dr. Bolton was obliged to agree that this was possible. The list was a very long one and the Thaxbys were added by Mrs. Bolton only as an afterthought and not until the Thursday morning. She couldn't remember whether or not she had told Mrs. Thaxby. In this case, said the detective inspector, it wasn't a matter of when in doubt leave out, but when in doubt be on the safe side. Mrs. Bolton said it was laughable, the Thaxbys of all people. Maybe they had children? said the inspector. Well, one boy, a very nice intelligent responsible sort of young man who was at present a student at the University of Kent.

Which went to show that Nigel's mother had not been strictly honest when recounting her son's activities to her friends.

A few hours after Mrs. Bolton had given this vital piece of information to the police, John Purford at last got in touch with them. It wasn't that he was afraid or stalling, but simply that he didn't know the Childon bank robbery had ever taken place. The event had almost slipped his mother's mind. After all, it had been more than three weeks ago, the manager and the girl were sure to be dead, it was a tragedy, God knows, but life has to go on. This was what she said in defence when John saw a little paragraph in the paper about the car being found. He told his partner the whole thing, including the business in the back of the car with Jillian Groombridge. He said it must all be in his head, mustn't it? He had been at school with Marty Foster.

"That's no argument," said the partner. "There were folks must have been at school with Hitler, come to that."

"You think I ought to tell the police?"

"Sure you ought. What have you got to lose? I'll come

with you if you want. They won't eat you. They'll be all over
you, nice as pie."

In fact, the police were not particularly nice to John Purford. They thanked him for coming to them, they appreciated that he was able precisely to point out on a street plan
the cafe where he had met Marty Foster and Nigel Something, but they scolded him soundly for giving away information of that kind and asked him, to his horror, if he knew
the age of Jillian Groombridge.

They seized upon the fairly unusual Christian name of
Nigel. A couple on Dr. Bolton's list had a son called Nigel.
The police went to Elstree. Dr. and Mrs. Thaxby said their
son was in Newcastle. They gave the police the address of
the Kensington commune, and there Samantha's mother was
interviewed. She also said Nigel was in Newcastle. Marty
Foster's father didn't know where his son was, hadn't set
eyes on him for two years and didn't want to. The police
found Mrs. Foster, who was living with her lover and her
lover's three children in a council house in Hemel Hemp-
stead. She hadn't seen Marty for several months, but when
she had last seen him he had been on the dole. Immediately
the police set about tracing Marty Foster's address through
the files of the Ministry of Social Security.

Nigel got his passport out of the rucksack and read it. Mr.
N. L. Thaxby; born 15.1.58; occupation, student; height, six
feet; eyes, blue. The passport had only been used twice,
Nigel not being one of those enterprising and adventurous
young people who hitchhike across Europe or drive vans to
India. He thought he'd take a flight to Bolivia or Paraguay
or somewhere they couldn't extradite you. He'd have about
fifteen hundred pounds left, and once he was there he'd contact some newspaper, *The News of the World* or *The Sunday
People*, and sell them his story—for what? Five grand? Ten?

Twice more he had asked Joyce to take two thousand as the price of silence, and twice more she had refused. This time he went up to her with the gun levelled and watched her flinch and begin to put up her hands to her face. He wondered vaguely if she felt like he did as the result of their long fast, drugged as if with one of those substances that don't stupefy but make the head light and dizzy and change the vision and bend the mind. Certainly, she looked at him as if he were a ghost or a monster. He thought of shooting her there and then and keeping all the money for himself, but it was broad daylight and he could hear Bridey in the next room and, beyond the other wall, old Green's whistling kettle.

"What did you say it for if you didn't mean it? Why did you say you wouldn't talk?" Nigel pushed one of the bundles of money into her face. He rubbed it against her tears. "That's more than you could earn in a year. Would you rather lie here bleeding to death than have two grand for yourself? Would you?"

She pushed the money away and covered her face, but she didn't speak. Nigel sat down. Standing made him feel a bit faint. He was acutely aware that he was doing it all wrong. He shouldn't be pleading for favours but compelling by force, yet he began to plead and to cajole.

"Look, it doesn't have to be for two weeks, just long enough to let me get out of the country. You can go to a big hotel in the West End. And they'll never find out you've had the money because you can spend it. Don't you realise you can go to a jeweller's and spend the whole lot on a watch or a ring?"

Joyce got up and went to the door. She stood at the door, waiting wordlessly, until Nigel came over and listened and unlocked it. Joyce went into the lavatory. Behind her door Bridey was playing a transistor. Nigel waited tensely, won-

dering what was the point of a deaf man having a whistling
kettle. It was whistling again now. Nigel heard it stop and
thought about Mr. Green until a clear plan began to form in
his mind, and he wondered why he had never considered
Mr. Green from this aspect before. Nobody ever spoke to
him because they couldn't make themselves understood, no
matter how loud they shouted, and he hardly ever spoke because he knew the answers he might receive would be
meaningless to him. Of course the plan was only a tempo-
rary measure and it might not, in any case, work. But it was
the only one he could think of in which, if it didn't work,
there would be no harm done.

The idea of at last getting something to eat made him
hungry again. The saliva rushed, warm and faintly salty,
into his mouth. He could revive and perhaps bribe Joyce
with food. She came out of the lavatory and he hustled her
back into the room. Then he hunted in there and in the
kitchen for an envelope, but he had no more luck than Joyce
had had when she wanted to write her note, and he had to
settle as she had done for a paper bag or, in this case, for
part of the wrapping off Marty's cigarette carton. Nigel
wrote, "In bed with flu. Could you get me large white loaf?"
Of all the comestibles he could have had, he chose without
thinking man's traditional staff of life. He folded the paper
round a pound note. Joyce was lying on the sofa face-downwards, but only let him be out of sight for more than a couple of minutes, he thought, let him start down those stairs,
and she'd be off there raring to go as if she'd just got a plate-
ful of roast beef inside her. The saliva washed round the
cavities and pockets of his mouth. He went out onto the
landing and pushed the note under Mr. Green's door, having
remembered to sign it: M. Foster.

Mr. Green went out most days. He had lived for years in
one room, so he went out even if he had nothing to buy and

although climbing back again up those stairs nearly killed him every time. The note, which suddenly appeared under his door when he was making himself his fifteenth cup of tea of the day, worried him intensely. This wasn't because he even considered not complying with the request in it. He was afraid of young people, especially young males, and he would have done far more than make a special journey to buy a loaf in order to avoid offending the tall fair one or the small dark one, whichever this Foster was. What worried him was not knowing whether his neighbour meant a cut or uncut loaf, and also being entrusted with a pound note, which still seemed to Mr. Green a large sum of money. But when he had drunk his tea he took his string bag and put on his overcoat and set off.

A young man in a blue jacket caught him up a little way down the road. Asking the way to somewhere, Mr. Green supposed. He did what he always did, shook his head and kept on walking, though the young man persisted and was quite hard to shake off. Because the cut loaf was more expensive than the uncut Mr. Green didn't buy it. He bought a large white loaf, crusty and warm, carefully wrapping it in tissue paper himself, and in the shop next door he bought *The Evening Standard*. This he paid for out of his own money. Then he went for a little walk in his own silence along the noisy Broadway, returning home by a different route and not taking too long about it because it would be wrong and inconsiderate to keep a sick man waiting.

Halfway up the stairs he had to stop and rest. Bridey Flynn, coming home from the Rose of Killarney, caught up with him and passed him, not speaking to him but reading out of curiosity the note which lay spread out on the flat top of the newel post. She disappeared round a bend in the stairs. Mr. Green placed the change from the pound note, a fifty-pence piece and two tens and a one, on the note and carefully wrapped the coins up in it. Then he laboriously climbed the rest of the stairs. At the top he put the folded newspaper on the floor outside Marty Foster's door, the loaf on top of the newspaper, and the little parcel of coins on top of the loaf. He tapped on the door, but he didn't wait.

Nigel didn't at once go to the door. He thought it was probably old Green who had knocked but he couldn't be positive and he had cause to be nervous. Between the time he had put the note under old Green's door and now, the doorbell had rung several times, in fact half a dozen times. The second time it rang Nigel pushed Joyce up into the corner of the sofa and stuck the barrel of the gun, safety catch off, hard into her chest. She went grey in the face, she didn't make a sound. But Nigel hardly knew how he had borne it, listening to that bell ringing, ringing, down there. He gritted his teeth and tensed all his muscles.

It was about half an hour after that that there was a tap at the door. Nigel was still, though less concentratedly, covering Joyce with the gun. At the knock he jammed it against her neck. When he heard the sound of Mr. Green's whistling kettle he went cautiously to the door. He opened it a crack with his left hand, keeping Joyce covered with the gun in his right. There was no one on the landing. Bridey was in the bathroom, he could see the shape of her through the frosted glass in the bathroom door.

The sight of the bread, and the smell of it through its flimsy wrapping, made him feel dizzy. He snatched it up with the newspaper and the package of change and kicked the door shut.

Joyce saw and smelt the bread and gave a sort of cry and came towards him with her hands out. He was still pointing the gun at her. She hardly seemed to notice it.

"Sit down," said Nigel. "You'll get your share."

He didn't bother to cut the loaf, he tore it. It was soft and very light and not quite cold. He gave a hunk to Joyce and sank his teeth into his own hunk. Funny, he had often read about people eating dry bread, people in ancient times mostly or at least a good while ago, and he had wondered how they could. Now he knew. It was starvation which made it palatable. He devoured nearly half the loaf, washing it down with a cup of water with whisky in it. Now his hunger was allayed, the next best thing to bread Mr. Green could have bought him was a newspaper. Before he had even finished eating, he was going through that paper page by page.

They had found the Escort in Dr. Bolton's garage. Not that they put it that way—"a shed in Epping Forest." They'd be onto him now, he thought, via the commune, via that furniture guy, that school friend of Marty's. He turned savagely to Joyce.

"Look, all I ask is you lie low for two goddamned days. That's a thousand quid a day. Just two days and then you can talk all you want." Inspiration came to Nigel. "You don't even need to keep the money. If you're that crazy, you can give it back to the bank."

Joyce didn't answer him. She hunched forward, then doubled up with pain. The new bread was having its effect on a stomach empty for five days. As bad as Marty, as bad as that little brain, thought Nigel, until he too was seized with pains like iron fingers gripping his intestines.

At least it stopped him wanting to eat up all the remaining bread. The worst of the pain passed off after about half an hour. Joyce was lying face-downwards on the mattress, apparently asleep. Nigel looked at her with hatred in which there was something of despair. He thought he would have to give her an ultimatum, she either took the money and promised to keep quiet for a day or he shot her. It was the only way. He couldn't remember, but still he was sure his fingerprints must be somewhere on that Ford Escort, and they'd match them with his prints in the commune, his parents' home, every surface of it, being wiped clean daily, he thought. John Something, the furniture guy, would link him with Marty Foster and then . . . How long had he got? Maybe they were already in Notting Hill now, matching prints. Had Marty ever been to the commune? That was another thing he couldn't remember.

If he was going to South America it wouldn't make much difference whether he shot Joyce or not. He would try to do it when the house was empty but for old Green. And he would like to do it, it would be a positive pleasure. Although he knew the view from the window by heart, could have drawn it accurately or made a plan of it, he nevertheless went to the window and looked out to check on certain aspects of the lie of the land. This house was joined to only one of its neighbours. Nigel eased the window up—the first time it had been opened since Marty's occupancy—and craned his neck out. Joyce didn't stir. He was seeking to confirm that, as he remembered from the time before all this happened and he was free to come and go and roam the streets, no curtains hung at the windows of the second-floor flat next door. This was in the adjoining house. It was as he had thought, the flat was empty and there would be no one on the other side of the kitchen wall to hear a shot. Very likely the people in the lower flats were out at work all day.

He had withdrawn his head and was closing the window when he noticed a man standing on the opposite pavement. Nigel closed the window and fastened the catch. There was something familiar about the man on the pavement, though Nigel couldn't recall where he had seen him before. The man was wearing jeans and a dark pullover and a kind of zipper jacket or anorak, and he had thickish fair-brown hair that wasn't very short but wasn't long either. He looked about thirty-five.

Nigel decided he had never seen him before, but that didn't make him feel any better. The man might have been waiting for someone, but if so it was a strange place to choose, outside a church in a turning off Chichele Road. He could be a policeman, a detective. It could be he who had kept on ringing the bell. Nigel told himself that the man's clothes looked new and his get-up somehow contrived, as if he wasn't used to wearing clothes like that and wasn't quite at ease in them. He made himself turn away and sit down and go through the paper once more.

Ten minutes later when he went back to the window, the man had gone. He heard Bridey's door close and her feet on the stairs as she went off to work.

22

Alan was almost sure he had got the wrong room. The young man with the fair hair, who just now had opened the window and leant out as if he meant to call to his watcher, must be the Green whose name was on the third bell. After the window had closed and the angry-looking face vanished, Alan had crossed the road and pressed that third bell several times, stood there for seconds with his thumb pressed against the push, but no one had come down to answer it.

He walked away and was in the corner shop buying a paper when he saw the girl called Flynn go by. He would talk to her just once more, he thought. The Rose of Killarney was due to open in ten minutes.

This was the second time since Monday that he had come to Cricklewood. He would have come on Wednesday and made it three times, only he couldn't do that to Una, couldn't keep on lying to her. Besides, he thought he had exhausted his powers of invention with Tuesday's inspiration, which was that he had to see his solicitor about Alison. Una accepted that without comment. She was busying herself with preparations for their departure on Friday, writing letters, taking Ambrose's best dinner jacket to the cleaners, ordering a newspaper delivery to begin again on Saturday. But Tuesday's sortie did him no good, he was no forrarder. Although he had spent most of the afternoon watching the house and walking the adjacent streets, he had seen no one, not even the Irish girl, come in or go out.

When he got back he had to tell Una he had been with the solicitor and what the man had said. It was easy for him to say that he would be giving up his share of his house to Alison because there was a good deal of truth in this, and he was rather surprised as well as moved when Una said this was right and generous of him, but how he must feel it, having worked for so many years to acquire it!

"You must think me very weak," he said.

"No, why? Because you're giving up your home to your wife without a struggle?"

Of course he hadn't meant that, but how could she know? He longed to tell her who he really was. But if he told her he would lose her. He had done too many things for which no one, not even Una, could forgive him: the theft, the betrayal of Joyce, the lies, the deceitfully contrived fabric of his past.

That evening they had gone out with Caesar and Annie, but on the Wednesday they spent the whole day and the evening alone together. They found a cinema which was showing *Dr. Zhivago* because Alan had never seen it, and then, appropriately, they had dinner in a Russian restaurant off the Old Brompton Road because Alan had never tasted Russian food. When they got home Ambrose phoned from Singapore, where it was nine o'clock in the morning.

"He was sweet," said Una. "He said of course he understands and he wants me to be happy, but we must promise to come back and see him for a weekend soon and I said we would."

Alan thought he would feel better about Joyce once he was in Devon and couldn't sneak out up to Cricklewood in the afternoons, for he knew he was going to sneak out again on Thursday. It was Una who put the idea into his head, who made it seem the only thing to do, when she said she'd buy their tickets and make reservations and then go on to the hairdresser. He could go out after she had gone and get back before she returned. He would definitely get hold of the Irish girl or of Green if Foster didn't answer his bell. It ought to be simple to find out what time Foster came home from work, and then catch him and, on some pretext, speak to him. With pretexts in mind, Alan picked up from the hall table in Montcalm Gardens a brown envelope with *The Occupier* written on it, and which contained electioneering literature for the County Council election in May. He put it into his pocket. After all, it would hardly matter if Foster opened it in his presence and saw that it was totally inappropriate for someone who lived in Brent rather than Kensington and Chelsea, for by then Alan would have heard his voice.

It was a cool grey day, of which there are more in England than any other kind, days when the sky is overcast with unbroken, unruffled vapour, and there is no gleam of sun or spot of rain. Alan was glad of his windcheater, though there was no wind to cheat, only a sharp nip in the air that lived up to its name and seemed actually to pinch his face.

He began by pressing Foster's bell several times. Then he walked a little before trying again. It was rather a shock to see an old man come out of the house, because he had somehow got it into his head by then that, in spite of the names on the bells, only the Irish girl and the fair-haired young man inhabited the place. The old man was deaf. Alan caught him up a little way down the road and tried to ask him about Foster, but it seemed cruel to persist, a kind of torment, and he felt embarrassed too, though there was no one else about to hear his shouts.

He tried the bell marked Flynn, and because there was no answer to that one either, went back to the Broadway and had a cup of tea in a cafe. He supposed he must have missed seeing the girl come home because he had been back to the

house and tried Green's bell in vain and was now buying his
paper when he caught sight of her turning into Chichele
Road, plainly on her way out, not her way home. There was
a paragraph on an inside page of the *Evening Standard* to
the effect that the car stolen in Capel St. Paul had been
found in Epping Forest. *Kidnap Car in Forest Hideaway*.
But the paper contained nothing else about the robbery, its
leads being *Man Shot in Casino* and *77 Dead in Iran Earth-
quake*. He walked along the wide pavement, which had
trees growing out of it, until he came to the Rose of Killarney. When it got to five, the Flynn girl herself came out to
open the doors.

Bridey had been frightened of the man in the windcheater only for a very short space of time. This was in the
seconds which elapsed between her opening the front door
to him and her return of the five-pound note. She was no
longer afraid, but she wasn't very pleased to see him either.
She felt sure he was a policeman. He said good afternoon to
her which made her feel it was even earlier than it was and
reminded her of the great stretch of time between now and
eleven when they would close. Bridey made no answer beyond a nod and walked dispiritedly back behind the bar
where she asked him in neutral tones what he would have.

Alan didn't want anything but he asked for a half of bitter
just the same. Bridey accepted his offer of a drink and had a
gin and tonic. An idea was forming in her mind that, although she would never dream of calling the police or going
out of her way to shop anyone to the police, in this case the
police had come to her, which was a different matter. And
she would like to have revenge on Marty Foster for insulting
her and showing her up in front of the whole saloon bar. She
had never really believed that story of the five-pound note
being dropped by Marty as he left the Rose of Killarney.

More probably the man in the windcheater was after him
for theft or even some kind of violence. Bridey wasn't going
to ask what he was wanted for. She listened while the policeman or whatever talked about ringing bells and not get-
ing answers, and about old Green and someone else he
seemed to think was called Green—she couldn't follow half
of it—and when he had finished she said:

"Marty Foster's got flu."

Alan said, half to himself, "That's why he doesn't answer
the door," and to Bridey, "I suppose he's in bed." She made
no answer. She lit a cigarette and looked at him, gently
rocking the liquid in her glass up and down.

"If I come to see him tomorrow," he said, "would you let
me in?"

"I don't want any trouble now."

"You've only to let me into the house. I don't mean into
his place, I know you can't do that."

"Well, if I open the door and a fella pushes past me," said
Bridey with a sigh, "and makes his way up the stairs, it's no
blame to me, is it, and me standing no more than five foot
two?"

Alan said, "I'll come in the afternoon. Around four?"

Bridey didn't tell him it was her day off, so she would be
home all day and he could have come at ten or noon or in
the evening if he'd wanted. She only nodded, thinking that
that gave her a long time in which to change her mind, and
got off her stool and went round the back out of his sight.
Alan was sure she would only come back when more customers came in. He drank up his beer and went to catch the
thirty-two bus.

Una was still out when he came back to Montcalm Gardens. It was nearly six. She walked in at five past with a bottle of wine, Monbazillac, which he and she both liked, for
their supper. It was quite a long time, while they were eat-

ing that supper, in fact, before he realised that she must
have been home in his absence. The skirt and jumper she had
on were different from what she had worn to go to the station and the hairdresser. But she didn't ask him where he
had been, and he volunteered no information. They went
downstairs to say good-bye to Caesar, for they would be
gone on the five-thirty out of Paddington before he came
home on the following day.

"Send me a card," said Caesar. "I'll have one with Dartmoor Prison on it. I went and had a look at it once, poor
devils working in the fields. D'you know what it says over
the doors? *Parcere Subjectis.* Spare the captives."

That made Alan feel they were really going, that and the
tickets Una had got. He wished now that he had arranged
with the Irish girl to be let into the house in the morning instead of the afternoon, but it was too late to alter it now.
And in a way the arrangement was the best possible he
could have made, for it meant that he could make his phone
call and immediately afterwards leave London. The police
would trace the call to a London call box, but by then he
would be on his way to Devon. That is, of course, if he made
the call at all, if it didn't turn out to be a false trail and
Marty Foster quite innocent.

Sitting in his room that night, he told Una that he didn't
intend to divorce his wife. He told her because it was true.
A dead man cannot divorce. He wanted no more lies, no
more leading her into false beliefs.

"I'm still married to Stewart," she said.

"I shall never be able to divorce her, Una."

She didn't ask him why not. She said quaintly and very
practically, as if she were talking of the relative merits of
travelling, say, train or air, first-class or second-class, "It's
just that if we had children, I should like to be married."

"You'd like to have children?" he said wonderingly, and

then at last, in so many words, she told him about Lucy. In doing so she gave him the ultimate of herself while he, he thought, had given her nothing.

The dream was the first he had had for several nights. He was in a train with two men and each of his hands was manacled to one of theirs. They were Dick Heysham and Ambrose Engstrand. Neither of them spoke to him and he didn't know where they were taking him, but the train dissolved and they were on a bleak and desolate moorland before stone pillars which supported gates, and over the gates was the inscription *Parcere Subjectis*. The gates opened and they led him in, and a woman came out to receive him. At first he couldn't see her face, but he sensed who she was as one does sense such things in dreams. She was Pam and Jillian and in a way she was Annie too. Until he saw her face. And when he did he saw that she was none of them. She was Joyce, and blood flowed down her body from an open wound in her head.

He struggled out of the dream to find Una gone from his side. He put out his hands, speaking her name, and woke fully to see her standing at the tallboy, opening and emptying the drawers.

It was a reflex to shout. He shouted at her without thinking.

"What are you doing? Why are you going through my things?"

The colour left her face.

"You mustn't touch those things. What are you doing?"

"I was packing for you," she faltered.

She hadn't reached the drawer where the money was. He sighed, closing his eyes, wondering how long he could keep the money concealed from her when they were living together and had all things in common. She had let the clothes fall from her hands and stood, lost and suffering. He went up to her, held her face, lifting it to his.

"I'm sorry. I was dreaming and I didn't know what I said."

She clung to him. "You've never been angry with me before."

"I'm not angry with you."

She came back into bed with him and he held her in his arms, knowing that she expected him to make love to her. But he felt restless and rather excited, though not sexually excited, more as if the deed he was set on accomplishing that day would set him free to love Una fully and on every level. And now he saw clearly that if he could show the two men to be the same and act on it, he would undo all the wrong he had done Joyce and himself on the day of the robbery. Ahead of him, once this hurdle was surmounted, seemed to stretch a life of total peace and joy with Una, in which such apparent obstacles as namelessness, joblessness, and fast decreasing capital were insignificant pinpricks.

Nigel and Joyce finished the loaf up on Friday morning. It was another grey day, but this time made gloomy by fog. Nigel wondered if he could get old Green to do more shopping for them—not more bread, certainly. Even a deaf old cretin like him would begin to have his doubts about a sick man on his own, a man with flu, eating a whole large white loaf in a day. He heard Mr. Green's kettle and then his footsteps crossing to the lavatory, but he didn't go to the door.

The first thing he had done on getting up was look out of the window for the watcher of the day before. But there was no one there. And Nigel told himself he was getting crazy, hysterical, imagining the police would act like that. The police wouldn't hang about outside, they'd come in. They would have firearms issued. They would evacuate the sur-

rounding houses and call out to him on a loud hailer to
throw down his gun and send Joyce out.

The street looked as if it could never be the backdrop to
such a drama. Respectable, shabby, London-suburban, it
was deserted but for a woman pushing a pram past the
church. The man he had seen outside yesterday, Nigel decided, was no more likely to be the police than that woman.
As for whoever kept ringing the bell, that could be the elec-
tricity meter man. The meter was probably due to be read.
But, for all these reassurances, he knew he had to get out.
There was no explaining away the evidence of the newspaper. Nigel thought how helpful his parents would be to
the police once they'd been located via the Boltons. They'd
shop him without thinking of anything but being what they
called good citizens, rack their brains to think where he
might be, sift their memories for the names of any friends he
had ever had.

"Just keep quiet for twelve hours," he said to Joyce, "then
you can phone the bank's head office and tell them all you
want about me and this place, and hand over the money."
He added, appalled at the thought of it, the waste, "Jesus!"

Joyce said nothing. She was thinking, as she had been
thinking for most of the night, if she could do that with
honour. Nigel thought she was being defiant again. Get
some food inside her and all the old obstinacy came back.

"I can kill you, you know," he said. "Might be simpler
when all's said and done. That way I get to like keep all the
bread myself." He showed her the gun, holding it out on his
left palm.

Joyce said wearily, "If I say yes, can we get out of here
today?"

The hue and cry for Marty Foster had awakened memories in the mind of a policeman whose beat included Chi-

chele Road. One foggy morning he had found a sick young man crouched on a wall and had helped him into Dr. Miskin's where, as he let go of his arm, the young man had whispered to the receptionist, "Name of Foster, M. Foster." All this came back to him on Friday and he passed it on to his superiors. Dr. Miskin directed them to the hospital in Willesden where Marty was in a ward along with a dozen or so other men.

Marty had been feeling a lot better. Apart from being confined within four walls, he rather liked it in hospital. The nurses were very good-looking jolly girls and Marty spent a good part of every day chatting them up. He missed his cigarettes, though, and he dreadfully missed his alcohol. They had told him he mustn't touch a drop for at least six months.

That he would have a choice about what he did in the next six months Marty was growing confident. He was glad Nigel hadn't come in. He didn't want to see Nigel or Joyce or, come to that, the money ever again. He felt he was well rid of it, and he felt cleansed of it too by removing himself in this way and voluntarily forgoing his share. Marty really felt he had done that, had done it all off his own bat to put the clock back, alter the past, and stay the moving finger.

So it was with sick dismay that after lunch on Friday, when they were all back in their beds for the afternoon rest, he raised his head from the pillow to see two undoubted policemen, though in plainclothes, come marching down the ward, preceded by pretty Sister, at whom only five minutes before he had been making sheeps' eyes. She now looked stern and aghast. Marty thought, though not in those words, how the days of wine and roses were over and the chatting up of the girls, and then they were beside his bed and drawing the screens round it.

The first thing he said to them was a lie. He gave them as his address the first one he had had in London, the squat in

Kilburn Park. Then he said he had been with his mother on 4 March, hadn't seen Nigel Thaxby for two months, and had never been to Childon in his life. After a while he recanted in part, gave another false address, and said that he had lent his flat to Nigel Thaxby, who he believed to have perpetrated the robbery and kidnapping in league with the missing bank manager.

Outside the screens the ward was agog, humming with speculation. Marty was put into a dressing gown and taken to a side room where the interrogation began afresh. He told so many lies then and later that neither the police nor his own counsel were ever quite to believe a word he said, and for this reason his counsel dissuaded him from going into the witness box at his trial.

That Friday afternoon he finally disclosed his true address but by then it had also been given to them by the Ministry of Social Security.

The few clothes Alan possessed went into the suitcase, but he didn't put the money in there. Suppose Una were to ask him at the last moment if he had room in his case for something of hers? Besides, how could he be sure of being alone when he unpacked it? What he should have done was buy a briefcase with a zip-up compartment. He could put the money in the compartment and books and writing paper, that sort of thing, in the main body of the case. For the time being he stuffed the bundles of notes into the pockets of his trousers and his windcheater. It bulged and crackled rather, and when Una, off up the road to fetch Ambrose's dinner jacket from the cleaners, came up to kiss him—they always kissed on meeting and parting—he didn't dare hold her close against him as he would have liked to do.

Her going out solved the problem of how to get out him-

self. It was almost three. He wrote a note: "Una, Something
has come up which I must see to. Meet you at Paddington at
5. Love, Paul." This he left on the hall table with the house
keys Una had given him three weeks before.

23

Joyce had given him the answer he wanted, but now that he had it Nigel couldn't believe it. He couldn't trust her. He saw himself at the airport going through the place where they checked you for bombs, reaching the gate itself that led you to the aircraft—and a man stepping out in front of him, another laying a hand on his shoulder. If Joyce was merely going to surrender the money to the bank, there would be no compulsion for her to respect her promise to him. She would break it, he thought, as soon as he was out of sight.

He would kill her when the house was empty.

Nigel didn't know who lived on the ground floor, certainly people who were out all day. The red-haired girl and her "fella" were out a lot. Bridey didn't work every day, but she always went out for some part of the day. Nigel thought it possible that Joyce's body might lie there undiscovered for weeks, but there was a good chance the police would arrive that weekend and break the door down. By then he would be far away, it hardly mattered, and it was good to think of Marty getting the blame and taking the rap, if not for the killing, then for a great deal else.

He listened for Bridey, who hadn't gone to work for the eleven o'clock opening. At three she was still moving about in her room, playing a transistor. Nigel packed his clothes into Samantha's mother's rucksack. He put on his cleanest jeans, the pair Marty had taken to the launderette, and his jacket, into the pocket of which went his passport. In the

kitchen, over the sink, he removed with Marty's blunt razor
the half inch of fuzzy yellow down which had sprouted on
his chin and upper lip. Shaven and with his hair combed, he
looked quite respectable, the doctor's son, a nice responsible
young man, down from his university for the Easter holiday.

Joyce too had dressed herself for going out in as many
warm clothes as she could muster, two tee-shirts and a
blouse and skirt and pullover. She had put the two thousand
pounds along with her knitting into the bag in which Marty
had bought the wool for that knitting. She said to Nigel, in a
voice and a manner nearer her old voice and manner than
he had heard from her for weeks, that she didn't know what
a hotel would think of her, arriving without a coat and with
rubber flip-flops on her feet. Nigel didn't bother to reply. He
knew she wasn't going to get near any hotel. He just wished
Bridey would go out.

At three-thirty she did. Nigel heard her go downstairs,
and from the window he watched her walk away towards
Chichele Road. What about the red-haired girl? He was wondering if he dared take the risk without knowing for sure if
the red-haired girl was out of the house, when the phone
began to ring. Nigel hated to hear the phone ringing. He always thought it would be the police or his father or Marty
to say he was coming home, by ambulance and borne up the
stairs on a stretcher by two men.

The phone rang for a long time. No one came up from
downstairs to answer it. Nigel felt relieved and free and private. The last peal of the phone bell died away, and as he
listened, gratified, to the silence, it was broken by the ringing of the front doorbell.

At Marble Arch Alan had bought a briefcase into which
he put the money, having deposited his suitcase in a left-
luggage locker at Paddington Station. In the shop-window

glass he looked with a certain amusement at his own reflec-
tion. He had put on his suit because it was easier to wear it
than carry it, and his raincoat because it had begun to rain.
With the briefcase in his hand, he looked exactly like a bank
manager. For a second he felt apprehensive. It would be a
fine thing to be recognised now at the eleventh hour. But he
knew no one would recognise him. He looked so much
younger, happier, more confident. I could be bounded in a
nutshell, he quoted to himself, and think myself a king of
infinite space, were it not that I have bad dreams. . . .

He was a little late getting to Cricklewood, and it was ten
past four when he walked up to the house and rang the bell.
He rang Marty Foster's bell first because there was a chance
he might answer and he didn't want to bother the Flynn girl
unnecessarily. However, there was no answer. He tried
again and again and then he rang the Flynn girl's bell.
Somehow it hadn't crossed his mind there might be no reply
to that either, that she could have forgotten her promise or
simply be indifferent to her promise and go out. She hadn't
exactly promised, he thought with a sinking of the heart.

Of course a taxi could get him from here to Paddington in
a quarter of an hour, there was nothing to worry about from
that point of view. He stepped back and down and looked
up at the windows, which looked back at him like so many
wall eyes. Maybe the bells weren't working. He couldn't hear
any sound of ringing from outside. But the Flynn bell had
been working on Monday. . . .

Along the street the old deaf man was coming, a string
bag in his hand containing some cans and a packet of tea.
Alan nodded to him and smiled, and the old man nodded
and smiled back in a way that was suspicious and ingratiat-
ing at the same time. Slowly he fumbled through layers of
clothing to retrieve a key from a waistcoat pocket. He put

the string bag down on the step and unlocked the front door.

Knowing it was useless to speak to him but feeling he must say something to excuse his behaviour, Alan muttered vaguely about people who didn't answer bells. He edged past the old man into the passage and, leaving him on the doorstep wiping his feet, began to climb the stairs.

Immediately when he heard the bell, the first time it rang, Nigel pointed the gun at Joyce and made her go into the kitchen. She understood this was because there was someone at the door he feared might be the police, but she didn't reason that therefore he wouldn't dare shoot her. There was something in his face, an animal panic, but the animal was a tiger rather than a rabbit, which made her think he would shoot her before he did anything else. He had taken off the safety catch.

He forced her into a chair and got behind her. Joyce slumped forward, the gun pressing against the nape of her neck. With his left hand Nigel felt about all over the draining board and the top of the bookcase and the drawer under the draining board for the rope. He found it in the drawer and wound it round Joyce as best he could, tying her arms to the back of the chair. When he had got the black stocking off his own bundle of notes, he put the gun down and managed to gag her. By then the doorbell had rung again and was now ringing in Bridey's room. Nigel shut the kitchen door on Joyce and went back into the living room to listen. From downstairs he heard the sound of the front door being softly closed. No more ringing, silence.

Then footsteps sounded on the stairs. Nigel told himself they must belong to old Green. He told himself that for about two seconds because after that he knew that they weren't the footsteps of a stout seventy-five-year-old but of a

man in the prime of life. They came on, on, up to the bathroom landing and then up the last flight to the top. There
they flagged and seemed to hesitate. Nigel went very softly
to the door and put his ear against it, listening to the silence
outside and wondering why the man didn't knock at his
door.

Alan hadn't knocked because he didn't know which was
the right door. There were three to choose from. He
knocked first at the door to the room on the side of the
house, the detached side. Then he tried the door that faced
it because the remaining door must be the one to the front
room, which was evidently occupied by Green. The old man
was coming slowly and heavily up the stairs. Alan stepped
aside and attempted some sort of dumb show to indicate
whom he wanted, but how do you indicate Foster in sign
language? The old man shook his head and unlocked the
door at which Alan had last knocked and went inside, closing the door behind him. Alan tried the door to the front
room. He waited, sure that he could hear on the other side
of it the sound of someone breathing very close by.

Nigel put the gun in its holster underneath his jacket, and
then he unlocked the mortice with the big iron key. There
was only one man out there. Very probably he knew the
room was occupied, so it might be less dangerous to let him
in than keep him out. Nigel opened the door.

The man outside was in a suit and raincoat and carrying a
briefcase, which Nigel somehow hadn't expected. The face
was vaguely familiar, but he immediately dismissed the idea
that this might be the man he had seen watching the house.
This was—he was convinced of it even before the brown envelope was produced—some canvasser or market researcher.

Alan said, "I'm looking for a Mr. Foster."

"He's not here."

"You mean he lives here? In there?"

A nod answered him. "I understood he was ill . . ." Alan
was almost deterred by the look on the handsome young
face. It expressed amazement initially, then a growing suspi-
ciousness. But he went on firmly. "I understood he was at
home with the flu."

At that the face cleared and the shoulders shrugged. Alan
felt sure Marty Foster was somewhere in there. He hadn't
come so far to give up now, on the threshold of Foster's
home. The door was moving slowly, it was about to be shut
in his face. Daring, amazed at himself, he set his foot in it
like an importunate salesman, said, "I'd like to come in a
minute, if you don't mind," and entered the room, pushing
the other aside, though he was taller and younger than he.

The door closed after him. They looked at each other,
Alan Groombridge and Nigel Thaxby, without recognition.
Nigel thought, he's not a convasser, he's not from the hospital—who is he? Alan looked round the room at the tumbled
mattress, the scattering of bread crumbs on the seat of a
chair, a plastic bag with knitting needles sticking out of it.
Foster might be in whatever room was on the other side of
that door.

"I have to see him," he said. "It's very important."

"He's in hospital."

From behind the door there came a thumping sound, then
a whole series of such sounds as of the legs of a chair or
table bumping the floor. Alan looked at the door, said
coldly:

"Which hospital?"

"I don't know, I can't tell you any more." Joyce was working herself free of the rope which tied her to the chair, as
Nigel had guessed she would. He put himself between Alan
and the kitchen door, his hand feeling the holster round the
gun. "You'd better go now. I can't help you."

It was twenty minutes to five. He was meeting Una at

five, he was leaving London—hadn't he done enough? "I'm going," Alan said. "Who's behind that door, then? Your girl friend?"

"That's right."

Alan shrugged. He began to walk back to the door by which he had entered as Nigel, striding to open it, called back over his shoulder:

"O.K., doll, one moment and you can come out."

Alan froze. He had been pursuing one voice and had found the other—"Let's see what's in the tills, doll. . . ." He turned round slowly, the blood pounding in his head. Nigel was opening the door to the landing. Alan was a yard away from that door, perhaps only a hundred yards away from a phone box. He stopped thinking, speculating, wondering. He took half a dozen paces across that room and flung open the other door.

Joyce had got her arms free and was taking the gag off her mouth. He would hardly have known her, she was so thin and haggard and hollow-eyed. But she knew him. She had recognised the voice of the man she had supposed dead from the moment he first spoke to Nigel. She threw the black stocking onto the floor and came up to him, not speaking, her face all silent supplication.

"Where's the other one, Joyce?" said Alan.

She whispered, "He went away," and laid her hands on his arms, her head on his chest.

"Let's go," he said, and put his arm round her, holding her close, and walked her out the way he had come. Nigel was waiting for them at the door with the gun in his hand.

"Leave go of her," he said. "Let go of her and get out, she's nothing to do with you."

It was the way he said it and, more than that, the words he used that made Alan laugh. Nothing to do with him, Joyce whom his conscience had brought into a bond with him closer than he had ever had with Pam, closer than he had with Una. . . . He gave a little dry laugh, looking incredulously at Nigel. Then he took a step forward, pulling Joyce even more tightly against him, sheltering her in the crook of his right arm, and as he heard the roar and her cry out, he flung up his left arm to shield her face and threw her to the ground.

The second bullet and the third struck him high up in the body with no more pain than from two blows of a fist.

24

Nigel grabbed the bundle of notes he had given to Joyce and stuffed it into the carrier with the other one. He had a last swift look round the room and saw the briefcase lying on the floor a little way from Joyce's right foot. He unzipped it a few inches, saw the wads of notes, and put the briefcase into his rucksack. Then he opened the door and stepped out.

The noise of the shooting had been tremendous, so loud as to fetch forth Mr. Green. Bridey, coming in when she thought the coast would be clear, heard it as she mounted the second flight. Neither of them made any attempt to hinder Nigel, who slammed the door behind him and swung down the stairs. In his progress through the vertical tunnel of the house, he passed the red-haired girl, who cried out to him:

"What's going on? What's happening?"

He didn't answer her. He ran down the last dozen steps, along the passage, and out into the street where, though only five, it was already growing dark from massed rain clouds.

The red-haired girl went upstairs. Bridey and Mr. Green looked at her without speaking.

"My God," said the red-haired girl, "what was all that carry-on like shots? That fella what's-his-name, that fair one, he's just gone down like a bat out of hell."

"Don't ask me," said Bridey. "Better ask that pig. He's his pal."

Mr. Green shuffled over to Marty's door. He banged on it with his fist, and then the red-haired girl banged too.

"I don't know what to do. I'd ask my fella only he's not back from work. I reckon I'd better give the fuzz a phone. Can't let it just go on, can we?"

"That's a very serious step to take, a very serious step," Bridey was saying, when Mr. Green looked down at the floor. From under the door, across the wood-grained linoleum, between his slippers, came a thin trickle of blood.

"My godfathers," said Mr. Green. "Oh, my godfathers."

The red-haired girl put her hand over her mouth and bolted down to the phone. Bridey shook her head and went off downstairs again. She had decided that discretion, or a busman's holiday in the Rose of Killarney, was the better part of social conscience.

In the room, on the other side of the door, Alan lay holding Joyce in his arms. He felt rather cold and tired and he wasn't finding breathing easy because Joyce's cheek was pressed against his mouth and nose. Nothing would have induced him to make any movement to disturb Joyce, who felt so comfortable and relaxed in her sleep. He was quite relaxed himself and very happy, though not sure exactly where he was. It seemed to him that they must be on a beach because he could taste saltiness on his lips and feel wetness with his hands. Yet the place, wherever it was, also had the feeling of being high up and lofty, a vaulted hall. His memory was very clear. He repeated to himself, Alas, said Queen Guinevere, now are we mischieved both. Madam, said Sir Lancelot, is there here any armour within your chamber that I might cover my poor body withal? And if there be any give it me, and I shall soon stint their malice, by the grace of God. Truly, said the queen, I have none armour, shield, sword, nor spear. . . .

He couldn't remember the rest. There was a lot of it but perhaps it wasn't very appropriate, anyway. Something about the queen wanting to be taken and killed in his stead, and Lancelot saying, God defend me from such shame. Alan smiled at the indignation in that, which he quite understood, and as he smiled his mouth seemed to fill with the saltiness and to overflow, and the pressure on his face and chest became so great that he knew he must try to shift Joyce. She was too heavy for him to move. He was too tired to lift his arms or move his head, too tired to think or remember or breathe. He whispered, "Let's go to sleep now, Una. . . ."

They started breaking the door down, but he didn't hear them. A sergeant and a constable had come over from Willesden Green, supposing at first they had been called out to a domestic disturbance because the red-haired girl had been inarticulate on the phone. The sight of the blood, flowing in three narrow separate streams now, altered that. One of the panels in the door had given way when up the stairs appeared two very top-brass-looking policemen in plainclothes and an officer in uniform. These last knew nothing of the events in the room and on the landing. They were there because Scotland Yard had discovered Marty Foster's address.

The door went down at the next heave. The couple from the ground floor had come up, and the red-haired girl was there, and when they saw what was inside, the women screamed. The sergeant from Willesden Green told them to go away and he jammed the door shut.

The two on the floor lay embraced in their own blood. Joyce's face and hair were covered in blood from a wound in her head, and at first it seemed as if all the blood had come from her and none from the man. The detective superintendent fell on his knees beside them. He was a perceptive

person whose job had not blunted his sensitivity, and he
looked in wonder at the contentment in the man's face, the
mouth that almost smiled. The next time I do fight I'll make
death love me, for I'll contend even with his pestilent
scythe. . . . He felt for a pulse in the girl's wrist. Gently he
lifted the man's arm and saw the wound in the upper chest
and the wound under the heart, and saw too that of the
streams of blood which had pumped out to meet them, two
had ceased.

But the pulse under his fingers was strong. Eyelids trembled, a muscle flickered.

"Thank God," he said, "for one of them."

There was no blood on Nigel. His heart was beating
roughly and his whole body was shaking, but that was only
because he had killed someone. He was glad he had killed
Joyce, and reflected that he should have done so before.
Bridey wouldn't take any notice, old Green didn't count,
and the red-haired girl would do no more than ask silly
questions of her neighbours. Now he must put all that behind him and get to the airport. By cab? He was quite safe,
he thought, but still he didn't want to expose himself to too
much scrutiny in Cricklewood Broadway.

On the other hand, it was to his advantage that this was
rush hour and there were lots of people about. Nigel felt
very nearly invisible among so many. He began to walk
south, keeping as far as he could to the streets which ran
parallel to Shoot-up Hill rather than to the main road itself.
But there was even less chance of getting a cab there. Once
in Kilburn, he emerged into the High Road. All the street-
lights were on now, it was half-past five, and a thin drizzle
had begun. Nigel felt in the carrier for the bunch of Ford
Escort keys. If that Marty, that little brain, could rip off a
car, so could he. He began to hunt along the side streets.

Nearly half an hour had gone by before he found a Ford Escort that one of his keys would fit. It was a coppery-bronze-coloured car, parked halfway down Brondesbury Villas. Now he had only to get himself on the Harrow Road or the Uxbridge Road for the airport signs to start coming up. The rain was falling steadily, clearing the people off the streets. At first he followed a bus route which he knew quite well, down Kilburn High Road and off to the right past Kilburn Park Station. It was getting on for six-thirty but it might have been midnight for all the people there were about. The traffic was light too. Nigel thought he would get the first flight available. It wouldn't matter where it was going—Amsterdam, Paris, Rome, from any of those places he could get another to South America. His only worry was the gun. They weren't going to let him on any aircraft with a gun, not with all these hi-jackings. Did they have left-luggage places at Heathrow? If they did he'd put it in one, and then, sometime, when it was safe and he was rich and had all the guns he wanted, he'd come back and get it and keep it as a souvenir, a memento of his first crime. But he wouldn't go after Marty Foster with it, he wasn't worth the hassle. Besides, thanks to his skiving off, hadn't he, Nigel, pulled off the whole coup on his own and got all the loot for himself?

When he got to the end of Cambridge Road, he wasn't sure whether to go more or less straight on down Walterton Road or to turn left into Shirland Road. Straight on, he thought. So he turned right for the little bit preparatory to taking Walterton and pulled up sharply behind a car stopped suddenly on the amber light. Nigel had been sure the driver was going to go on over and not stop, and the front bumper of the Ford Escort was no more than an inch or two from the rear bumper of the other car. Suppose he rolled back when the lights went green?

There was nothing behind him. Nigel shoved the gear into reverse and stamped on the accelerator. The car shot forward with a surprisingly loud crash into the rear of the one in front, and Nigel gave a roar of rage. Once again he had got into the wrong gear by mistake.

In the other car, a lightweight Citroën Diane, were four people, all male and all staring at him out of the rear window and all mouthing things and shaking fists. The driver got out. He was a large heavily built black man of about Nigel's own age. This time Nigel got the gear successfully into reverse and backed fast. The man caught up with him and banged on the window, but Nigel started forward, nearly running him down, and screamed off in bottom gear across lights that had just turned red again, and straight off along Shirland Road into the hinterland of nowhere.

The Diane was following him. Nigel cursed and turned right and then left into a street of houses waiting to be demolished, their windows boarded up and their doors enclosed by sheets of corrugated iron. Why had he come down here? He must get back fast and try to find Kilburn Lane. The Diane was no longer behind him. He turned left again, and it was waiting for him, slung broadside across the narrow empty street where no one lived and only one lamp was lighted. The driver and the other three stood, making a kind of cordon across the street. Nigel stopped.

The driver came over to him, a white boy with him. Nigel wound down his window, there was nothing else for it.

"Look, man, you've caved my trunk in. How about that?"

"Yeah, how about that?" said the other. "What's with you, anyway, getting the hell out? You've dropped him right in it, you have. That's his old man's vehicle."

Nigel didn't say a word. He took the gun out of its holster and levelled it at them.

"Jesus," said the white man.

Nigel burst the car door open and came out at them, stalking them as they retreated. The other two were standing behind the Diane. One of them shouted something and began to run. Nigel panicked. He thought of the money and of help coming and his car trapped by that other car, and he raised the gun and squeezed the trigger. The shot missed the running man and struck the side of the Diane. He fired again, this time into one of the Diane's rear tyres, but now the trigger wouldn't move anymore. The jacket had gone back, leaving the barrel exposed, and the gun looked empty, must be empty. He stood, his arms spread, a choking feeling in his throat, and then he dropped the gun in the road and wheeled round back to the car.

The four men had all frozen at the sound of the shot and the splintering metal, even the running man. Now he came slowly back, looking at the useless weapon on the wet tarmac, while the others seemed to drop forward, their arms pendulous, like apes. Nigel pulled open the door of the Ford, but they were on him before he could get into it. The driver's white companion was the first to touch him. He swung his fist and got Nigel under the jaw. Nigel reeled back and slid down the dewed metal of the car, and two of them caught him by the arms.

They dragged him across the pavement and through a cavity in a broken wall where there had once been a gate. There they threw him against the brickwork front of the house and punched his face, and Nigel screamed, "Please!" and "Help me!" and lurched sideways across broken glass and corrugated iron. One of them had a heavy piece of metal in his fist, and Nigel felt it hammering his head as he sagged onto the wet grass and the others kicked his ribs. How long they went on he didn't know. Perhaps only until he stopped shouting and cursing them, twisting over and over and trying to protect his bruised body in his hugging arms. Perhaps only until he lost consciousness.

When he regained it he was lying up against the wall, and he was one pain from head to foot. But there was another and more dreadful all-conquering pain that made his head and his neck red-hot. He moved a bruised cut hand to his neck and felt there, embedded in his flesh, a long stiletto of glass. He gave a whimper of horror.

By some gargantuan effort, he staggered to his feet. He had been lying on a mass of splintered glass. His fingers scrabbled at his neck and pulled out the long bloody sliver. It was the sight of the blood all over him, seeping down his jacket and through into his shirt, that felled him again. He felt the blood pumping from the wound where the glass had been, and he tried to cry out, but the sound came in a thin strangled pipe.

Nigel had forgotten the car and the money and escape and South America. He had forgotten the gun. Everything had gone from his mind except the desire to live. He must find the street and lights and help and someone to stop the red stream leaking life out of his neck.

Round and round in feeble circles he crawled, ploughing the earth with his hands. He found himself saying, mumbling, as Marty had said to him, "You wouldn't let me die, you wouldn't let me die," and then, as Joyce had said, "Please, please. . . ."

His progress, half on his hands and knees, half on his belly, brought him onto concrete. The street. He was on the pavement, he was going to make it. So he crawled on, looking for lights, on, on along the hard wet stone as the rain came down.

The stone ended in grass. He tried to avoid the grass, which shouldn't be in the street, which was wrong, a delusion or a mirage of touch. His head blundered into a wooden

fence, at the foot of which soft cold things clustered. He lay
there. The rain poured on him in cataracts, washing him
clean.

Much later, in the small hours, a policeman on the beat
found the abandoned car and the gun. Everything was still
in the car as Nigel had left it, his rucksack and his carrier,
his passport and the stolen money—six thousand, seven hundred and seventy-two pounds. The search for Nigel himself
didn't last long, but he was dead before they reached him.
He was lying in a back garden, and during that long wet
night snails had crept along the strands of his wet golden
hair.

25

When the train had gone and Paul hadn't come, Una went back to Montcalm Gardens. Whatever it was that had "come up" had detained him. They could go by a later train, though they would have no seat reservations. Una decided not to indulge in wild speculations. Ambrose said these were among the most destructive of fantasies, and that one should repeat to oneself when inclined to indulge in them, that most of the things one has worried about have never happened. Besides (he said) it was always fruitless to imagine things outside our own experience. One thing to visualise a car crash or some kind of assault if we have ourselves experienced such a thing, or if one of our friends has, quite another if such imaginings are drawn, as they usually are, from fictional accounts. Una had never known anyone who had been killed in a car crash or mugged or fallen under a train. Her experience of accidents was that her child had been burnt to death.

She made a cup of tea and washed the teacup and tidied the kitchen again. The phone rang, but it was a wrong number. At seven she read the note again. Paul's handwriting wasn't very clear and that five could be an eight. Suppose he had thought the train went at eight-thirty, not five-thirty? He had been so preoccupied and strange these past few days that he might have thought that. Una combed her hair and put on her raincoat, and this time she took a taxi, not a bus, to Paddington. Paul wasn't there.

Although there was a later train, she took her case out of the left-luggage locker where she had left it at five-thirty, because she felt that to do so was to yield to, not tempt, Providence. The curious ways of Providence were such that if you bought an umbrella you got a heat wave for a month, and if you lugged a load of luggage from a station to your home, you were bound to have to take it back again. This thought cheered her, and by the time the taxi was taking her back through the stair-rod rain in the Bayswater Road she had convinced herself that Paul would be waiting for her in Montcalm Gardens with a long story of some tiresome happening that had held him up.

Her first real fear came when she got in and he wasn't there. She went down into the basement and found the bottles he had left outside Caesar's door with a note to Caesar to have them. Caesar hadn't come home, he had gone straight to Annie's. Una poured herself some brandy. It nearly knocked her over because she hadn't eaten since one. They had planned to eat dinner on the train. She tried to obey Ambrose's injunction not to think of imaginary disasters, and told herself that no one gets mugged in the afternoon or falls under trains unless they want to or has a car crash if they don't have a car.

But then her own experience of life showed her what could have happened. Neo-Empiricism, applied by her, showed her what men sometimes did and where men sometimes went after they had left notes and gone out alone. She pushed the thought away. He would phone, and then he would come. She took a piece of cheese out of the fridge and cut a slice off the new loaf she had bought for Ambrose. She tried to eat and she succeeded, but it was like chewing sawdust and then chewing the cud.

At ten she was in his empty room, looking at the tallboy in which there had been papers or letters or photographs he hadn't wanted her to see. It frightened her now that he had left his keys, though what more natural than that he should leave them?

While she had been out that afternoon he must have had a phone call. She knew who would have phoned, perhaps the only person to whom he had given this number. Hadn't she phoned once before to make an appointment? Since that appointment, that visit, Paul had been a changed man. Una went upstairs and sat in the immaculate exquisite drawing room. She picked up the phone to see if it was out of order, but the dialling tone grated at her. Stewart's letter was up on the mantelpiece. She had left it there for Ambrose to read. Now she read it again herself, the bit about hoping she would be happy with her new man.

For a while she sat there, listening to the rain that beat steadily against the windows and thinking that it was a long time since it had rained like that, a month surely. A month ago she hadn't even known Paul. She got out the phone directory. His name on the page made her shiver. Browning, Paul R., 15 Exmoor Gardens, N.W.2. She looked hard at his name on the page and touched the phone and paced the length of the room and back again. Then, quickly, she dialled the number. It rang, three times, four times. Just as she thought no one was going to answer, the ringing stopped and a woman's voice said:

"Hallo. Alison Browning."

"Is Mr. Paul Browning there, please?"

"Who is that speaking?"

She had been told, hadn't she? It wouldn't be a revelation. And yet . . . "I'm a friend of his. Is he there?"

"My husband is in bed, asleep. Do you know what time it is?"

Una put the receiver back. For a while she lay on the floor. Then she went upstairs and got into bed in the room where she hadn't slept for three weeks. Three weeks was no time, nothing, a nice period for an adventure or an interlude. It is anxiety, not sorrow, which banishes sleep, and at last Una slept.

She had never had a newspaper delivered since Ambrose went. Not since Christmas had she heard the sound the thick wad of newsprint made, flopping through the letter box onto the mat. Any sound from the front door would last night have made hope spring, but no longer.

Una went downstairs and picked up the paper. The headlines said, *Joyce Alive* and *Bank Girl Recovers in Hospital*, and there was a big photograph of a girl on a stretcher. But it was the other photograph, of a man in a garden with a woman and an older man, which caught Una's eye because the man looked a little like Paul. But any man, she thought, with wistful eyes and a gentle mouth would remind her of Paul. It was bound to happen. She went into the drawing room and read the paper to pass the time.

. . . The nature of Alan Groombridge's wounds have made police believe he died protecting Joyce. She regained consciousness soon after being admitted to hospital. Her head injury is only superficial, says the doctor attending her, and her loss of memory is due to shock. She has no memory of the shooting or of events of the past month in which she and Mr. Groombridge were held prisoners in a second-floor rented room in North London. . . .

Una read the rest of it, turned the page, waiting for Ambrose to come.

M   73331
REN   Rendell, Ruth
               Make Death
           Love Me.

           <u>Mystery</u>

Texarkana Public Library Association
RULES

1. Six books may be borrowed on the card at one time.

2. All books may be kept two weeks.

3. A fine ~~of five cents~~ will be charged for each day a book is overdue.

4. All injuries to books beyond reasonable wear and all losses shall be made good to the satisfaction of the Librarian.

5. Each borrower is held responsible for all books drawn on the card and for all fines accruing on it.